MW01486884

THE LADY'S MISSION

THE QUILTING
CIRCLE SERIES

THE
LADY'S MISSION

The Quilting Circle Series

By Mary Davis

The Lady's Mission
Published by Mountain Brook Ink
White Salmon, WA U.S.A.

The website addresses shown in this book are not intended in any way to be or imply an endorsement on the part of Mountain Brook Ink, nor do we vouch for their content.

This story is a work of fiction. All characters and events are the product of the author's imagination other than those stated in the author notes as based on historical characters. Any other resemblance to any person, living or dead, is coincidental.

The author is represented by and this book is published in association with the literary agency of WordServe Literary Group, Ltd., www.wordserveliterary.com

Scripture quotations are taken from the King James Version of the Bible. Public domain.

The Team: Miralee Ferrell, Tim Pietz, Kristen Johnson, Cindy Jackson
Cover Design: Indie Cover Design, Lynnette Bonner Designer

Mountain Brook Ink is an inspirational publisher offering fiction you can believe in.

Printed in the United States of America

Dedication

Dedicated to my nephew Thomas who begged and pleaded with me to put him in one of my novels. This is for you. Sorry, I couldn't make you a "world-expert, buffalo-wing quilter." I hope this will suffice. It's definitely a speaking part, so your role in the "movie version" should have dialogue. I also dedicate this book to his sisters, Laura and Anna, for having to put up with him.

"Two are better than one; because they have a good reward for their labour."-Ecclesiastes 4:9

One

LAMAR KESNER STOOD IN THE LARGE, barn-style double-doorway opening of his workshop in a pair of lightweight trousers from last year, with his shirt sleeves rolled to his elbows. Grandmama had retired both articles of clothing from social use as they were "old" and "out of date," but they were suited for tasks in his shop.

He lifted a narrow copper tube from the heating apparatus of his hot air balloon and peered through it. No blockage. Then the issue must be with some other part.

He favored spending his time in Kamola to any of the family's properties back East, with the fewer social obligations. He had reliable, loyal people managing Grandmama's holdings and reporting to him. Staying here allowed him to partake in his hobby. Grandmama indulged him, because she knew it kept him here rather than elsewhere.

Grandmama could move back East, but she preferred to oversee the Washington State Normal School his grandfather had a hand in bringing to fruition before he passed two years ago. Grandpapa had also encouraged Lamar's interests and had the outbuilding constructed for him. Together they had started this current endeavor, hot air ballooning. This was his third such balloon. High in the air, he felt as though he could get away from all the demands and expectations. It was a place no one could bother him.

One of the footmen approached. Mr. Derby cleared his throat before he spoke. "Your grandmother wishes an audience with you."

"Thank you. I'll come right in." He set the tubing on his work counter and headed toward the manor house.

The distraction would give him a chance to contemplate what aspect of the device to address next.

As he entered, Rogers stood waiting. The valet scrutinized Lamar. Though the man's expression didn't change, Lamar knew the servant would have something to say about what he wore.

Lamar lifted a hand. "She'll have to take me as I am. I plan to return to my workshop posthaste."

"Very well. She's in the parlor."

Lamar strolled along the hallway and into the room.

Grandmama sat in her usual place, a high wing-backed, stuffed chair with claw feet. The size and stature of it almost resembled a throne. Well, she was queen of her castle. "Lamar! Gracious, your attire. Hurry and change." She glanced toward the doorway. "Rogers?"

The valet appeared. He must have been around the corner out of sight. "Yes, ma'am?"

"See to it my grandson has something proper to wear."

"I have his suit out and ready." Rogers obviously knew something Lamar didn't.

Grandmama wiggled her fingers toward Lamar in a shooing fashion. "Go on. You can't greet our guests looking like that."

Guests? Guests his grandmother had conveniently forgotten to tell him about. "Grandmama, you didn't invite another marriage candidate, did you?"

She beamed a sweet smile. "Be nice. She could be the one."

That was doubtful. Another vapid socialite to contend with.

"When are you going to give up on this?"

"I'm not. Now go make yourself presentable." Grandmama's quest to locate him a suitable wife had grown tiresome.

She meant well, but he didn't need help in finding a wife. The Lord would bring the right woman into his life in His time.

Rogers led the way upstairs.

Lamar washed and dressed in the chosen suit before returning to the parlor. He joined his grandmother and stood by the fireplace mantel, too nettled with the prospect of another boring débutante to sit. He would rather be in his workshop. "Who is it this time?"

"A young lady from Connecticut with impeccable breeding." Grandmama would choose nothing less. "I think you'll like this one."

Doubtful if she was anything like so many of the others. "Does she have a name?"

"Miss Cordelia Armstrong, and I hear she is a rare beauty."

Of course. Rare beauty or not, it would be rarer still if she was an interesting conversationalist or had the tiniest bit of intellect. Fashion and beauty were what most of them cared about. Like those things mattered to men. Maybe he was being unfair by setting his expectations too high.

Rogers poked his head into the parlor. "Carriage approaching, milady."

Every nerve in Lamar's body tightened. Time to be companionable.

Soon enough the front door opened, and a scurry of low voices filtered into the room.

Grandmama pinned him with a stern look and spoke softly so her words wouldn't carry outside the room. "Smile, Lamar. How can you ever catch a lady with a scowl? You don't want to scare her off."

Maybe he did, but he hadn't realized he'd been scowling. He flashed his best smile. "I will be ever the gentleman."

"That's better."

An impeccably dressed middle-aged man and woman entered with a younger lady lingering behind them.

Rogers announced them. "Mr. and Mrs. Armstrong and their daughter."

Lamar crossed the room and greeted them. "Welcome. I'm Lamar Kesner." Then he indicated his grandmother. "May I present Mrs. Henry Kesner?"

Mr. Armstrong dipped his head. "We are honored to be welcomed into your home."

Behind them stood their daughter with dark locks cascading over her shoulder. She appeared older than he'd anticipated. He'd assumed she would be around eighteen to twenty. This young woman was likely in her early to mid-twenties, only four or five years younger than himself. Why wasn't she married yet?

Lamar tried to assess what kind of person she was but wouldn't be able to tell until he interacted with her. Grandmama hadn't exaggerated her physical appeal. But was there anything more to her? Or did she hope to catch a husband by looks alone? "Who is this raven-haired beauty?" This was how the game was played.

"Our daughter Cordelia Armstrong."

The young lady gave a coquettish smile and lifted her hand to him.

He took her offered hand and bowed over it. "It is a pleasure to make your acquaintance."

She giggled.

He flinched inside. *Please, not a giggler.* It grated on him when young ladies giggled for no apparent reason. Nerves he supposed.

She gazed up at him with that same starry-eyed expression he'd seen so many times before and fended off. Of course, she came from money, had the right breeding, and had no doubt been trained in the finest finishing schools money could buy. And she had the quality Grandmama thought he valued most—beauty—like the previous dozen proper young ladies she'd tried to foist on him.

Was there anything intriguing in Miss Armstrong's pretty little head with which he could hold even the briefest of conversations? All that social convention required of the woman he married was to behave appropriately for *his* station and to give him children, but he wanted more than a mother to his heirs. A woman with whom he could have decent conversations about things of the world. Someone who could form her own opinions.

He had met a few captivating ladies of breeding. He'd shown a passing fascination with Isabelle Atwood—now Dawson. She rode a bicycle and didn't let convention tell her how to behave. Then there was Nicole Waterby—now Keegan—who came to town in buckskins and could shoot as well as any man. Talk about unconventional. Last but not least, Geneviève Marseille—soon to be Gladwell. A French socialite who traveled halfway around the globe and discovered her American roots.

Three unique ladies who could have held his attention, but each of their hearts belonged to another. Three fortunate men. To have a woman like one of them give him their love would be wonderful, but maybe he wasn't destined to have love. If he couldn't have love, did he even want to bother with a wife?

Keeping her hand in his, he guided her to the settee in the parlor. "Please have a seat."

She did and continued to stare up at him.

Then giggled.

This was destined to be a long visit. Lamar resumed his stance at the fireplace. If he removed himself from the center of the people, maybe they would forget to include him in the conversation.

After an exchange of a few pleasantries, Grandmama directed a question to Miss Armstrong. "How do you like Kamola so far?"

"You have a quaint little town here, but I haven't seen much of it. Only from the train station to the Atwood Hotel and then here. I would love to see more of it."

"That's a wonderful idea." Grandmama smiled and shifted her attention to him. "Lamar, show Miss Armstrong Kamola. Drive her all around."

Mr. and Mrs. Armstrong nodded their approval, and Mr. Armstrong answered for his daughter. "Cordelia would be honored to have you escort her."

"Oh, I would." Miss Armstrong gazed at him expectantly, blinking.

Lamar was outnumbered. Apparently, the young woman's parents were as eager to make a match as Grandmama. *Trapped alone with the giggling girl in a buggy?* He would rather stay here where there were others to help carry a conversation. With no acceptable excuse to offer, he had to concede. "It would be my pleasure."

Grandmama addressed Rogers. "Have the stable hitch a conveyance. Preferably an open-air one. It's a pleasant summer day."

Perhaps Miss Armstrong was, in some way,

unmarriageable. A simpleminded person?

All too soon, Lamar sat in the buggy next to the young lady. Hopefully, this wouldn't be as bad as he anticipated. How short could he make this little excursion without raising Grandmama's ire—and eyebrow.

Miss Armstrong twirled her parasol over her shoulder. "Mr. Kesner, tell me *all* about your town."

He would rather not. "Please call me Lamar."

Her eyes widened. "Are you sure? That's not proper."

"I'm quite sure." If she conceded, it would give him a better idea of the kind of person she was.

She bit her bottom lip. "If you insist...*Lamar.*" She giggled.

Mercy. Time spent with this young woman was going to be tedious. At least she had agreed to use his first name.

She gave him a sly smile and spoke in a small, almost childlike voice. "I don't think my parents would approve, so I can only use your Christian name when no one else is around. It will be our little secret."

Very tedious. How could he convince Grandmama that Miss Armstrong was not a suitable candidate?

"Does that mean you will call me Cordelia?"

"If you'll allow me the privilege."

"I think I might like that."

That was a positive in her favor. "I am honored, Cordelia."

She giggled. "I've never had a gentleman use my first name before."

A part of Lamar inwardly cringed at her tittering, while another suddenly felt bad for thinking poorly of this lady. She did seem sweet even while being insipid. There were much worse socialites to have to spend the rest of his life with. She wouldn't be near the equal partner he hoped for, but she did seem to need someone to look after her. He would hate for some cad to take advantage of her. Was concern for her well-being enough to build a relationship on? Enough to entertain the idea of courting? No. He could easily see she would not make a suitable lifelong match for him. The question was, how to convince Grandmama of that and not end up on her bad side.

Cordelia batted her eyelashes at him. "What do you

like to do in your free time?"

Grandmama had cautioned him against discussing his hot air balloon hobby to potential marriage candidates. How could Lamar skirt her question? In his experience, women didn't like men to have frivolous vices. If this one became too much of a nuisance, he would show her exactly how frivolous he could be.

She whipped her head to the side. "Is that a college?"

That was a fast change in subjects and spared him from answering her previous question. "Washington State Normal School. They train teachers. Did you attend a college or university?" He could guess at her answer.

"Me? Oh, no. I did go to Mrs. Patterson's School for Girls and learned about proper behavior for a lady. Or at least they tried to teach me all of it. There was so much, I couldn't remember everything."

No interesting conversations happening on this buggy ride. "Have you ever wanted to go to college?"

She tilted her head toward him and hesitated a moment before answering. "Oh, I'm not smart enough for anything like that."

Apparently, nothing but silly lady musings going on in her head. Yet something danced in her green eyes that said, if given the chance she could do more.

She glanced away almost shyly then pointed. "Is that a dressmaker's establishment?"

He shifted his attention to *Mademoiselle* Dumont's shop. "It is."

"May I go?"

"Wouldn't you rather explore it with your mother and my grandmother?"

She widened her bright green eyes on him and batted her lashes. "Please. You don't have to come in. You can go wherever you want and return later."

Grandmama would skin him alive if he abandoned their guest on an outing, but it would give him a break from this vapid débutante. "It would have to be another one of our little secrets."

"Oh, yes." She put her index finger to her rosy lips. "*Shhh*, our secret."

He redirected the carriage and parked in front of the

establishment. He got out, rounded the vehicle, and offered his hand.

She closed her parasol as she accepted his help. Her voluminous dress or foot caught on something, causing her to wobble, and she tumbled into him. He clasped her in his arms. She fit nicely. Their gazes locked for a long moment. He was surprised to find he liked having her in his arms.

"Oops. I guess I'm clumsy today. Thank you for rescuing me."

He'd hardly rescued her, but he had kept her from a nasty spill. "Shall I escort you inside?"

She stepped from his embrace and placed a gloved hand on the front of his jacket. "You don't need to do that."

He resisted the urge to take hold of her hand. "How long do you think you'll be? Would an hour be enough? Or two?" He hoped two.

"I could look at clothes all day."

Of course, she could. What woman couldn't?

"Would three be all right?"

That would be wonderful. "I'll return in three hours." He spoke before she could change her mind.

She gave him an impish smile, spun with a flourish, and entered the dressmaker's.

He stared after her but caught himself. "Stop it, man. She's nothing but another silly socialite."

Though holding any kind of meaningful intelligent conversation with this woman would be out of the question, he found her mildly intriguing. Something in her twinkly green gaze said there was more to this lady than what met the eye.

Or was that merely wishful hoping on his part?

A bell over the door of the dressmaker's shop jingled as Cordelia Armstrong entered. She had hoped for a silent arrival so she could depart in the same manner, unnoticed. That would not be the case.

A stylish woman of about thirty descended upon her position.

Cordelia glanced over her shoulder and wiggled her fingers at Lamar Kesner. She hoped he didn't plan to stand there for long, or worse, decide to come inside.

The woman stopped in front of her and spoke with a French accent. "Good afternoon. I am *Mademoiselle* Celeste Dumont. What may I help you with? I see by your dress that you have very good taste in fashion."

Cordelia's parents had seen to that. Nothing but the best. "I simply wanted to pop in and take a look around." She glanced out the window.

Though still watching her, Mr. Kesner—or rather Lamar—rounded his carriage and climbed aboard. He touched the brim of his hat and put the horse into motion.

Cordelia heaved a sigh of relief. She hadn't known how much longer she could keep up the feeble, meaningless conversation. It wasn't easy talking about worthless nonsense. She'd almost put her foot in it by mentioning the college. Fashion was always a good option, as it was expected of ladies and men shunned the topic. It also served as an effective suitor deterrent.

She retrained her attention on *Mademoiselle* Dumont and continued her witless act. "I'm not planning to purchase anything today. I merely wanted to peruse your offerings. Is that all right?"

"Of course. I have books with my original designs in the sitting area if you are interested in viewing them."

No, that would take too much time. "Thank you. I'll start here. You have so many beautiful things." She pointed to the rack of trims. "I just love lace. I don't think a gown can have too much."

"Any piece of fashion adornment can be overdone, but there are ways to manage it without it being tasteless."

Lamar Kesner had driven out of sight.

"Thank you for letting me look around. I'll bring my mother to help me choose something." Cordelia opened the door. *"Au revoir."* She dashed out before the proprietress could delay her.

A glance both directions along the street assured her Mr. Kesner had indeed left.

Two

CORDELIA HURRIED DOWN THE STREET. MR. Lamar Kesner wasn't going to be so hard to escape from as some of the others. If she didn't know better, she might think it had been him to divest himself of her. It mattered not, as long as she was free to go about her business.

So tiresome keeping up a conversation with no substance. Hopefully it wouldn't be more than a few days before he tired of her vapid topics and begged his grandmother to put an end to this.

She headed toward the White Hotel. How much longer could she evade her parents' matchmaking attempts? Eventually, they would find a suitor who didn't mind if she had a thought in her head or not. One who only cared if she could bear him heirs. Though she longed for children of her own, she also desired more from a marriage. She needed freedom to follow God's calling on her life.

Master Kesner was no doubt nothing more than another shallow, overindulged dandy who had the skills and personality of a bump on a log, like all the rest. Handsome—yes. She had to give her parents that. But did he have any abilities beyond appropriate conversation at dinner parties and soirées? Oh, that he would realize there could be more to life—so much more.

Come out of your palace walls, oh privileged prince, and see the needs around you of the underprivileged.

Instead of going to the Atwood Hotel where she and her parents had rooms, she darted into the White Hotel lobby, retrieved a key from the desk clerk, and hurried up to her secret room.

She unlocked the door to find her confidant and friend inside. "Nan, you made it. You didn't have any trouble, did you?"

Nan tucked the clothes in her hands inside the bureau drawer. "None whatsoever."

"Is Dutch here?" Cordelia leaned her parasol against the wall by the door.

"He has the room across the hall. That man can pack in thirty seconds and unpack in half that time."

"You *are* packing and unpacking for the both of us." Cordelia appreciated all Nan did to help her. "Shall we let him know I'm here?"

Nan waved off the suggestion. "He's out getting the lay of the land."

"Good. Hopefully, he will have found something by the time I've changed." Cordelia took off her wide-brimmed hat and tossed it onto the bed. Why she needed a parasol, too, was a mystery. One generally interfered with the other, but Mother always insisted upon both.

Her friend removed a brown flower-print dress from a carpetbag and shook it. "This hasn't had time to air and let the wrinkles relax."

"There isn't time to be fussy. I managed to wrangle three hours." Cordelia much preferred the simpler calico dress Nan had brought for her. Far more practical. "Can you help me out of this gown?"

After laying the brown dress on the bed, Nan stepped behind Cordelia to unfasten the back of her teal bodice. "What is this one like?"

"Master Kesner? I suppose he's like all the other self-indulgent high-society bachelors of privilege." But there *was* something about him that was different. She couldn't tell yet if it was in a good way or not.

"Did he talk about himself the whole time?" Nan laid the fancy linen bodice on the bed.

Cordelia unfastened the matching skirt. "No." And she'd given him the perfect opportunity by asking how he filled his free time. He'd avoided it by offering her the use of his first name.

Nan lowered the brown calico skirt to the floor. "Did he ply you with over-exaggerated, empty compliments?"

He'd called her a raven-haired beauty but hadn't gone on and on to impress as most would. Cordelia stepped into the garment. "No." He'd almost avoided complimenting her.

Nan scrunched her eyebrows. "He didn't try to press his advantage and kiss you, did he?"

"No." He almost seemed disinterested in her. Fascinating. She hadn't experienced that before. It would make getting rid of him easier.

However, something about him intrigued her. What was it? He behaved much like all the others with impeccable manners and was equally as handsome.

Yes, Cordelia was rapidly approaching old-maid age. Hopefully, her parents would soon give up on finding her a husband. It wasn't that Cordelia despised men or marriage but rather the restrictions both would place on her as a woman. If she could be free to do as she pleased *and* have a family, she would. She prayed the Lord had a husband and children in her future.

Maybe Mr. Kesner's allure was that he didn't look at her as an object to be owned. Also, he treated his grandmother with tenderness and affection. "I think he might be the one."

"The one?" Nan cocked her head.

"To break my parents' determination to see me wed. If I can turn him away, they might deem me beyond hope, having grown weary of this battle. I even overheard them say they think I might be unmarriageable." Then she could do as she pleased.

"What if they force you into a marriage?" Nan held out the matching shirtwaist.

Cordelia slipped it on and fussed with the buttons. "They have tried before, but they have to find a willing groom, and so far, I have thwarted their champions. I have figured out the key to repelling unwanted suitors."

"What's that?"

"Give them everything they *think* they want—to a point, mind you. Attention, compliments, dote on them, and let them know you will be at their side *every* moment of *every* day."

Nan grinned. "In other words, smother them?"

"Exactly. They can't get away fast enough. Most want a wife as well as their freedom. I show them they won't have both with me." So far, her tactics had worked.

"Say you succeed with this one and your parents do

give up on their quest to marry you off. What's to stop them from sending you to a nunnery or something? I've heard of parents doing that."

That was a risk. "They have never mentioned doing such a thing. If they do, I might need to resort to my alternative plan."

"You have an alternative plan? What is it?"

"Marriage."

Nan shook her head. "Isn't that what you're trying to avoid?"

"No, I'm trying to avoid having my every action controlled." Cordelia stood in front of the mirror atop the bureau to refashion her hair into something a little less elaborate to suit with this attire and not seem out of place. "Marriage to a very old man who either won't live very long or whom will be so happy to have a young bride, he will allow me to do pretty much anything I want."

"You are crafty."

"Determined. I have a calling from the Lord to help others. If He directs me to marry a gentleman a *bit* older than myself to fulfill that calling, I will make the sacrifice."

"That's dedication."

Either that or folly.

She pinned a large straw hat onto her head. She shouldn't be recognized.

Three soft raps on the door, a pause, and then two more.

Nan crossed to the door and opened it.

A whispered voice from the hall said, "Is she here?"

"Yes. Hurry inside."

The barrel-chested man slipped through the opening. "You made it. We were not sure how easy it would be for you to get away."

"Easier than I had imagined. Mention dress shopping and most men will take any opportunity you offer up." Lamar Kesner had almost seemed relieved for her to set him free for three hours. He wouldn't be too difficult to manipulate.

Dutch scrunched up his face. "A smart man will take the opportunity to be doing anything else but shopping for lady things."

This conversation could continue, but Cordelia didn't have time for that. She may have three hours, but that would be gone before she knew it. "What have you learned?"

The European man's Dutch accent was distinct but not heavy. "It is not as good as we normally hope for with this not being a big city, but I think we can do good here."

Kamola was quite a bit smaller than most of the places they visited, but it had a college so there was promise. "Did you find out the information we need?"

"I located a pastor. I could not see him right away, but we have an appointment in about an hour. We did not expect you to be able to meet up with us so soon."

"It was easier than usual. An hour will be cutting my time allotment close." She only had three hours total and some of that had been spent dressing. More time would be used changing back.

Nan lifted her shoulders. "Since the minister isn't expecting us for a bit yet, shall we stay put?"

"I can't simply wait around. Perhaps his previous appointment will end early." Cordelia sent a silent prayer heavenward that such would be the case.

Dutch escorted them to the lobby and opened the hotel door. "This way, ladies."

Cordelia glanced up and down the street to make sure Master Kesner wasn't about. With the coast clear, she strolled along with her friends until they reached the minister's home.

A woman answered the door. "May I help you?"

"We have an appointment with the minister in twenty minutes. I'm Delia Strong"—merely shortened versions of both her names—"and these are my friends, Nannette Barwick and Dutch Mulder."

She tipped her head toward Dutch. "I remember you. Please come in. You'll have to wait in here. My husband, Pastor Woodman, is with someone at the moment."

"Thank you." Cordelia nodded. "We realize we're early. We don't mind waiting." By being here, not one minute would be wasted in between his current appointment and hers. She sat on a bench in the alcove.

The minister's wife slipped through a doorway at the

end of the hall.

Nan sat beside Cordelia, and Dutch leaned against the door jam.

About five minutes later, the pocket doors to a parlor room slid open. A man—Cordelia assumed was the minister—exited with a middle-aged woman. "I'll help you in any way I can."

"Thank you, Matthew." The woman turned, smiled with a nod to Cordelia and her friends, then left.

Cordelia and Nan stood. Dutch pushed away from the doorframe. Cordelia stepped forward. "Minister Woodman, I'm Delia Strong. My friends, Nannette Barwick and Dutch Mulder."

The minister smiled. "Please come into the parlor."

Mrs. Woodman said, "I'll bring tea in straightaway."

Cordelia and Nan entered then sat on the settee. Dutch stood.

The minister motioned to a chair for Dutch. "Please have a seat."

Dutch hesitated, preferring to stand, but he lowered his large frame into the chair, nearly dwarfing it.

Mrs. Woodman entered from another door with a tray. She set it on the serving table in the middle of the sitting area then poured a cup for Cordelia and her friends. She added some fresh tea to her husband's cup.

"Thank you, love."

Mrs. Woodman smiled at her husband and left.

The minister shifted his attention to his guests. "Make yourself welcome to the sugar and cream."

Cordelia and Nan added sugar to their tea, Dutch declined both. He preferred coffee.

The minister added a splash of cream to his own. "Where are you folks from?"

Cordelia didn't want to talk about herself or where she was from, but conversation was part of being polite. "Connecticut."

Then he asked how long they would be staying and other pleasantries. Cordelia tapped her foot under the hem of her dress where it couldn't be seen. She had limited time. "Minister Woodman, we have a favor to ask."

"Please call me Matthew, especially if I'm to grant you a favor."

Did everyone in this town insist upon first names? Not that she minded. The relaxed atmosphere was refreshing. "Matthew, as I said, I don't know exactly how long we'll be in town. While we're here, I'd like to help some of the less fortunate people in the area. A man of God, such as yourself, usually knows who in town is in the most need."

The minister raised his eyebrows. "I've never heard of strangers wanting to help downtrodden locals before."

Her mission was unusual, but with her parents' quest to wed her, she had to fulfill God's calling wherever He led. This time He had brought her to Kamola. There must be a reason. "The Lord has blessed me, and I want to bless others." She had seen the pitiful circumstances of the less fortunate.

She would never forget the time she'd joined their ranks at age six. She had become lost in the city and ended up in a seedy part of town. A woman with seven children had taken her in, consoled her, and fed her dry bread with a scant layer of jam. The last from the small pot. She'd played for over an hour with the other children until she'd been found by the police.

The woman had been arrested for kidnapping Cordelia. After pleading and crying, Cordelia finally convinced her father to see to it the woman was released. With Cordelia's insisting, her father procured better jobs for the woman and her husband. After that, Cordelia wanted to do things for the less fortunate, but her parents soon curtailed her actions, not out of malice but for her protection.

Two years later, a matronly aunt advised her that her intelligence would get her married and settled faster than anything else. No one wanted a clever lady running loose. Once married, her husband would control her, so helping those whom no one else was inclined to offer assistance to would be out of the question. Her aunt had schooled her in how to behave to keep from being tied down in a restrictive marriage. Hence, the vapid débutante emerged. She missed Aunt Tempy.

Cordelia returned her focus to the minister's parlor. "In every city I've visited, there are those in need who are overlooked. No one sees them. But I do."

"I commend you." He sipped his tea. "Most people—even those who want to help—ignore certain undesirable segments of the population. Who is it you consider unseen and neglected?"

"Those others pretend don't exist and want to wish them away or think it's best if they remain invisible. That's not best."

"The individuals you're talking about are generally proud people who don't readily accept charity."

"I know, but we want to try. If we can make life a little less hard for some of them, we want to. If we can fill one child's belly, or give a mother the means to clothe her children, or aid a young man to get a worthwhile job, we will count our time here successful."

Both Nan and Dutch nodded. Nan spoke up. "She has helped countless others."

"Who are the people, more specifically, you want to help? Are you thinking like the child who goes to school without a lunch?"

"No doubt that child has needs, but in my experience, there are organizations who already try to aid them. I'm more interested in the ones no one thinks to help. Those individuals people don't know are even there and in need." She indicated her friend. "For example, Miss Barwick was living in an abandoned building along with other vagrants. With food and better clothing, she was able to obtain a job because she looked respectable. Mr. Mulder was ostracized simply because he's an immigrant. I convinced a sympathetic business owner to employ him. They chose to join me in helping others like themselves."

"What do you want from me?"

"Only to tell me who these people are and where to find them."

"I must say your request is unusual, but so very welcome. There's a woman you should speak with. She was just here. You saw her leaving. Her name is Aunt Henny. Our town has had a recent influx of immigrants and the kind of so-called undesirable people you're talking about. They have formed a sort of loose-knit community near the edge of town. Aunt Henny is organizing an effort to collect items to take to them. We fear for their survival once winter sets in. As long as they go unseen, the townsfolk pretend they aren't there."

"Your aunt often helps those in need?"

"She's not my aunt. She not anyone's aunt, but she's welcoming to all. If you're genuine in your desire, she could use extra hands in gathering and preparing things to take out to their encampment."

Cordelia smiled. "Sounds like exactly the kind of people we want to serve. I will seek out Miss Henny."

The minister gave them directions to the woman's home which also served as a boarding house.

This had been a profitable day.

Lamar headed over to Thomas Spencer's ramshackle cabin. Why did his friend choose to live this way when he didn't have to?

The front door hung open as it often did during the summer so the heat didn't get trapped within. It was doubtful Thomas was inside, but Lamar took a peek anyway. Though the outside of the shack—and the owner himself—appeared disheveled, the orderly interior was welcoming.

As he suspected, no sign of his friend, so Lamar wandered along the path toward the creek. At Thomas's favorite fishing spot, an abandoned pole wedged in some rocks angled over the meandering water. Where was he?

A twig snapped.

"I got a gun," a gruff voice said behind Lamar. "Turn around slowly."

Lamar held his hands out from his side and pivoted. "You don't want to shoot me. Too much trouble to bury my body."

Still sporting his six-inch wooly beard, Thomas offered his infectious smile as he lowered his shotgun. "Nah. I wouldn't bury you. I'd toss you in the creek and let you float downstream. Wash that fancy cologne right off you."

Lamar chuckled. "Good to know."

"What brings you out my way?" His friend leaned his shotgun against a tree.

Evading a wife candidate. "Picking up a package, but it hasn't come in yet. Should be on the afternoon train." Lamar had stopped by the post office before venturing out to Thomas's place.

His friend squinted. "Something is up. You could easily go home to your workshop and tinker with your hot air balloon then return this afternoon. Or, better yet, send a servant to retrieve it. Why are you avoiding your grandmother? She hasn't invited another socialite she hopes you'll marry, has she?"

"You always were astute."

Thomas rolled his eyes. "What's this one like?"

No sense denying it. "Miss Armstrong's very pretty."

"That doesn't matter as much as her personality and how she talks. She doesn't have one of those screechy voices, does she?"

"No." Lamar shook his head. "She's a giggler."

Thomas pinched a sour face. "That's just as bad. Tell me you aren't considering this match."

He wasn't. "To appease my grandmother, I have to at least pretend—for a little while, anyway. I feel bad for her."

"How so?"

"Not to be unkind, but she's a bit simpleminded."

"I know that look." Thomas gripped Lamar's shoulder. "You *are* considering her. Run away from this one."

That was Lamar's plan, but... "There's something about her I want to figure out. You should have seen the way her face lit up when we passed by the Washington State Normal School."

Thomas removed his hand from Lamar. "You're hopeless. Always have been a sucker for a lost cause."

Lamar didn't want her to be taken advantage of by some unscrupulous rogue. "I'm sure she'll tire of me in a few days."

His friend shook his head. "By then, it'll be too late for you."

"I promise not to fall for a simpleminded giggler."

"We'll see about that."

Thomas didn't have to worry. Lamar was well schooled in socializing without becoming entangled.

Three

HENNY STOOD BESIDE THE UNMADE BED in one of her boarders' room and shook out a sheet. As it fluttered to the mattress, she breathed in the peace and quiet. At the moment, everyone was off elsewhere. Rare these days, with a new husband, her two grown children, a lady's maid, and two long-time boarders under her roof. She loved having a full house but missed quiet moments like these.

After finishing making the bed, she gathered up the dirty bedding and headed downstairs.

A light rapping sounded on her front door.

She set the sheets on the bottom step and turned the knob. Two ladies and a tall gentleman stood on her porch. "May I help you?"

"Are you Henny?"

"I am. Are you seeking a room to rent?" She only had one vacancy.

"No. Minister Woodman sent us."

"Yes, I remember seeing the three of you as I was leaving. Come in." Henny guided them to the parlor.

The two ladies sat in the stuffed, wing-backed chairs. The large blond gentleman stood.

Henny sat on the settee. She addressed the man. "Won't you have a seat?"

When he hesitated, one of the ladies spoke for him. "He prefers to stand if that's all right with you."

Why hadn't the man answered for himself? Was he a mute?

"Of course. I didn't want to seem inhospitable. Why don't you start by introducing yourselves?"

"I'm Delia Strong. This is Nannette Barwick and Dutch Mulder."

Apparently, Miss Strong was the leader of this little group. "I'm pleased to meet you all. Why has Matthew sent you to me if you aren't seeking lodging?"

"He said you're collecting items for a community of outsiders to your town. We wish to help you in your efforts."

Henny's glee spiked. "That's wonderful. Do you live in Kamola? I don't think I've seen you about."

"We are merely visiting and want to do some good while here."

That sounded fishy. Something was off about this little band of self-professed good Samaritans. She sensed they were hiding something. Were they truly here to help the outsiders? Or would they aid those in town who wanted to discover the location and run the unfortunates off?

Lord, I don't trust these people. What should I do?

The truth shall set you free.

Yes, the truth. Henny had recently experienced such a freedom of truth when her estranged children arrived in Kamola a few months ago. She had hidden from her troubled past by traveling across the country, going so far as using a nickname, of sorts. She didn't want to see the outcasts run off as she had been over two decades ago. "Though your offer is generous, I sense you're hiding something. I don't want to see those downtrodden people harmed or sent away. They simply require a little assistance. I must decline your offer." The best help she could give those in need was to not invite additional trouble on them.

Miss Barwick gave Miss Strong a worried glance, which confirmed Henny's suspicions.

Henny stood. "Thank you for stopping by." She hoped the beefy gentleman didn't decide to cause trouble because of Henny's refusal of their help.

Miss Strong slowly lifted her chin to focus on Henny. An action and expression Henny recognized from someone who was high-born and bred at the finest finishing schools. Why was she dressed to contradict that?

Miss Strong motioned toward the settee. "Please, be seated, and I'll explain."

Miss Barwick darted her gaze to Miss Strong. "C— Delia?"

The leader of this group lifted a hand. "It will be fine.

I have a sense about this woman." With her attention still on Henny, she waited.

Henny should turn them away, but being the curious sort, she sat. It couldn't hurt to listen.

Miss Tibbins padded on her four furry paws and strolled about the room, rubbing against each of Henny's guests, first Miss Strong, then Miss Barwick, who both petted the cat's head, and finally Mr. Mulder. The calico stretched up the man's leg with her arms and pawed at his knee. He bent and lifted the cat in a very natural motion. Miss Tibbins's instant purr could be heard across the room.

That was a good sign. Though Henny didn't rely on a cat's opinion about the character of a person, the fact the large man didn't shoo Miss Tibbins away and treated her kindly, spoke to his moral qualities.

Miss Strong proceeded. "I appreciate your dedication to protect these individuals. Your caution makes me want to help you all the more. I am hiding something."

"Only you?" Henny glanced at the other two.

"They are innocent and precisely who I introduced them as."

Henny focused her attention on the authority figure in this little troop. "But not yourself?"

The young woman straightened her shoulders. "My name is Cordelia Armstrong."

"Delia Strong? So, you merely shorted your names? Is that all?" Even Henny didn't go by her given name. She knew there must be more, for starters, why this young woman was attempting to disguise her society breeding. Would she admit it? There were many legitimate reasons to dress beneath one's station. What was this lady's motive?

"Yes, I shortened my names, and no, that isn't all."

Henny glanced at the big man wearing her cat. Miss Tibbins had climbed onto his shoulders and made herself comfortable, by wrapping her tail around his neck. That her cat had made herself at home with the man who didn't seem to mind did afford Henny a small amount of assurance. "What else are you hiding?"

"I come from a prominent family back East."

As Henny had suspected.

"My parents don't exactly encourage me to help the sort of people we are talking about. Which means, if I wish to make a difference, I must do so by unconventional means."

"Why not volunteer with a charitable organization from where you hail?"

"I do, but those organizations only aid certain subsets of those in need. I'm more interested in assisting those whom official organizations choose to ignore."

Miss Barwick cleared her throat. "I'm a perfect example. I was living in an abandoned building. No charitable organization would give me aid even when I asked because I lived in a building where several men also resided. They claimed I was a woman of loose morals and refused to offer aid. I am *not* such a woman." She dipped her head. "I am ashamed to say I was so hungry I considered it. Fortunately, Cordelia found me and gave me food. She gave all the people in the abandoned building food. She provided me with nice clothes so I could get a respectable job. I worked as a salesgirl in a department store. I waited on those very same women who had refused me assistance and none of them recognized me. In the right clothes, I was good enough to wait on them, but in the wrong clothes, they wouldn't even feed me."

Henny felt the girl's pain. She knew what it was like to be rejected by the *good* people of polite society, and Henny had possessed money and nice clothes.

Mr. Mulder thumped his chest with his fingertips and spoke with a slight foreign accent. "She helped me too. I got a job because she convinced someone to take a chance on me."

So, he could speak.

Miss Armstrong leaned forward. "Will you allow us to assist you? I think we could get so much more accomplished together than separately."

Henny agreed and now had a peace about this little trio of philanthropists. "I believe we can work together. If you must keep your actions a secret from your parents, allow me to invite you and Miss Barwick to join my quilting circle. We meet on Fridays to sew, quilt, or work on other projects, such as helping this community of outcasts. The quilting circle will give you a legitimate excuse for coming here."

The young woman's eyes brightened. "That sounds perfect."

"Where are you staying? In case I need to reach you."

Cordelia's countenance returned to slightly guarded. "I'm staying with my parents at the Atwood Hotel. Nan and Dutch are staying at the White Hotel."

Miss Barwick piped up. "In separate rooms."

Henny fixed her gaze on Cordelia. "Does that mean your parents don't even know about your friends?"

"It's best if they can move about freely for me. They scout cities and towns to determine where we can help people."

This was definitely an intriguing trio, and, despite her earlier reservations, Henny felt the Lord prompting her to include them in her ministry to those in need, as an answer to her prayers. "I would offer to rent you rooms here, but I'm pretty full at the moment. I only have one available. It would be more convenient for at least one of you." She pointed to Miss Barwick and Mr. Mulder.

Cordelia glanced at her friends. "What would you like to do?"

Mr. Mulder frowned. "We will stay at the hotel."

Miss Barwick gave the big man a sideways glance that said she could speak for herself. "Though this would be nicer, I think I'll also remain at the hotel. At least for now."

Cordelia inclined her head. "Thank you for the offer."

Henny hadn't expected them to uproot themselves but knew it was right to at least offer. "If any of you change your mind, let me know." She gave a nod to Miss Barwick and then one to Mr. Mulder.

He reached around and petted Miss Tibbins on his shoulders.

Henny guessed that the young man might consider changing locations, if a certain calico had anything to do with it.

Cordelia and Miss Barwick stood. "We must be going. Thank you." The trio left.

Saul, Henny's most recent resident and her new

husband, entered from the kitchen. "Who were they?"

"Some people who have volunteered to help with the outcasts."

"They aren't going to stay here, are they? We almost have a full house."

"No. They have rooms at the White Hotel."

"I'm pleased that big brute won't be staying here."

"Saul Hammond! That isn't a very nice thing to say."

Saul shrugged. "He's a very big man. I don't know if I could protect you from him."

Henny loved her new husband, but sometimes he grated on her nerves with his overprotectiveness. "He hasn't done one thing to raise suspicions. Besides, Miss Tibbins was quite taken with him."

"It's not good practice to judge people by your cat's mood. I don't know why you are taking any boarders. With your inheritance, you don't need the money anymore."

"The Lord blessed me with this house so I could bless others. I wouldn't know what to do with all my time."

Saul wrapped his arms around her waist. "I could think of a thing or two."

Cordelia and her cohorts hustled down the street. "I need to be quick. Master Kesner will be returning to the dress shop soon."

Nan scurried up beside her. "What will you tell him if he arrives there first?"

"I'll say I finished at the shop and decided to walk about town."

"Will he believe you?"

With most men she would say yes, but Mr. Kesner had already proven different than other gentlemen. He'd ask questions most wouldn't. Would his grandmother approve of him asking Cordelia to use his first name? Her parents certainly wouldn't approve. "He will have little choice but to believe me."

The White Hotel was on the next boardwalk. She stopped short.

Nan plowed into her shoulder. "What is wrong?"

Cordelia spun around and pulled one side of her wide brimmed straw hat close to her face. "That's him. Standing in front of the hotel." Why was he lingering there? Was he waiting for someone? For her?

Nan narrowed her eyes then widened them. "My, he's a handsome one."

That was beside the point. "He's not supposed to be here."

"Are you sure you don't want to keep this one?"

Cordelia gave her friend a withering glance. "I'm sure. What am I going to do?" She hadn't run into this situation with any of the other suitors. But she sensed Lamar wasn't like the others.

Dutch stepped forward and spoke in a little bit of a menacing voice. "I will take care of him."

Cordelia put her hand on his arm. "We don't want trouble."

"I will not draw any blood." He gave her a cheeky grin.

"Are you a court jester now?" Cordelia shifted her attention to Nan. "Do you think you could distract him long enough for me to slip inside the hotel?"

Nan pulled her golden locks over her shoulder. "This is going to be fun."

Oh, dear. "What are you planning to do?"

Nan wiggled her eyebrows. "A little distraction, a little flirting, and he wouldn't even notice if his hair caught on fire."

"I don't know if flirting is a good idea."

"Let's see what kind of man he is." She walked away.

Cordelia peeked over her shoulder around the brim of her hat. Her friend sashayed along the boardwalk with quite a swing to her hips.

With her head dipped and hidden behind her hat, Cordelia inched along the boardwalk, knowing she might not have more than a moment or two if Nan was successful.

Nan scurried past Lamar with a bright smile to him and trotted down the three steps to the street level. She masterfully stumbled and landed on her backside in the street.

Lamar rushed to her aid and extended a hand. Nan looked up at it in what appeared to be awe and placed one of her hands in his. "My, I've never had such a handsome gentleman offer to help before."

He pulled Nan to her feet.

She held on to his hand. "Who do I have to thank for my speedy rescue?"

Cordelia couldn't take her eyes off the scene.

Dutch tugged on her elbow and whispered. "You best get inside while you can."

"Lamar Kesner, miss."

Cordelia slipped into the hotel lobby. She turned and gazed through the window to let her friend know she was safely inside.

Lamar still had Nan's hand. Or was it Nan who had his captive?

"Come on, miss." Dutch shuffled his feet beside her. "You need to get upstairs."

"What about Nan?"

"I'll see to it she comes in straight away and meets you in her room."

Cordelia couldn't believe the bold flirting Nan was practicing with the man who was supposed to be courting Cordelia. She hastened to the second floor. The sooner she was out of sight the sooner Nan could cease her outlandish behavior.

Lamar freed his hand from the young lady's grasp. As he'd suspected, she hadn't fallen by accident but on purpose. Why? She must know his family had money and wanted to garner his attention. "You aren't hurt, are you?"

"No. I'm fine." She gave him that endearing smile he'd seen so many times from young ladies who wanted nothing more than for him to make them his wife. If ladies such as this one were all he would have to choose from, maybe he wouldn't marry. He could remain a bachelor, an eccentric one who floated around the world in a colorful balloon. Appealing, yet lonely even thinking about it.

"I'm glad to hear that." He touched the brim of his hat. "Good day." He walked away before she could engage him in more conversation.

He needed to return to the post office anyway. The valve he'd ordered for his heating apparatus for his hot air balloon was due to arrive today on the afternoon train. He pulled his watch from his pocket and pressed the catch button on the top. The lid flipped open, and he grimaced. If he went to the post office, he would be late in picking up Miss Cordelia Armstrong. A breech in etiquette. What should he do? He wouldn't be more than a few minutes late, and Cordelia likely wouldn't notice anyway. She had said she could look at clothes all day.

He entered the joint post office and telegraph office.

A young mother with a baby on her hip stood at the window. Good, only one customer ahead of him.

Morton South, the postmaster and telegraph operator, riffled through a small crate of letters. "The mail arrived a few minutes ago, so I haven't had a chance to sort these, Beatrice."

She rubbed the child's back. "That's all right. I can wait."

But could Lamar? He glanced toward the window in the direction of the dressmaker shop but couldn't see it from his vantage point. He was here and needed that valve, so he would wait. At least for a minute or two.

The child peered over his mother's shoulder at Lamar. The boy had pools of unshed tears in his big brown eyes.

Lamar puffed out his cheeks, making a silly face.

The tyke smiled, so Lamar made another face.

Finally, the postmaster turned, made eye contact with Lamar, and raised his eyebrows.

Lamar ceased his antics and gave Mort a stiff smile.

Mort handed a small parcel and a couple of letters to Beatrice who thanked the man and left.

Lamar stepped to the counter. "Did my package arrive on the afternoon train?"

"I haven't had a chance to check. Give me a minute." He left through a door to the back room.

Lamar consulted his watch again. A few more minutes late at this point probably wouldn't make much difference in the scolding glare she would likely bestow upon him.

Finally, Mort returned with a package in his hand.

"Here it is." He set it on his side of the counter, retrieved a ledger, and wrote in it, consulting the package. He then turned the ledger. "Sign here."

"Thank you." Lamar signed, but Mort held on to the bread-loaf sized parcel. "Are you going to give that to me?"

The postmaster leaned on the counter but held the package beyond Lamar's reach. "I saw you with the little Drummond boy. You like children. When are you going to get married and have children of your own?"

Obviously, Lamar had been in often enough and become too friendly with the man for him to be bold enough to ask such a personal question. Lamar leaned forward and whispered, "When the Good Lord sees fit to bring the right woman into my life. May I have my package now?"

Mort harrumphed and handed it over.

Lamar accepted it and left. He walked to the livery where he'd left his carriage and paid the young man who had taken charge of it. "Thank you, Bean." The gangly youth was a good kid.

"Welcome, Mr. Kesner."

Lamar climbed aboard and drove to the dressmaker shop.

Cordelia Armstrong stood on the boardwalk in front of *Mademoiselle* Dumont's establishment. She held her opened shade parasol above her head.

Now, he felt bad for inconveniencing her. He climbed down and approached her. "Pardon my ill manners. I hope you weren't standing here long." On the bright side, he didn't have to go inside the ladies' shop.

She giggled. "Oh, I wasn't waiting. I just stepped out here."

Then why did she appear flushed?

She gazed toward the sky. "It's such a beautiful day." She closed her parasol.

Wasn't she refreshing? Most women of her station would be irate with a withering glare and prattle on endlessly about his poor conduct. It seemed as though keeping a high-born lady waiting was about the worst travesty a man could commit. He proffered his hand. "Shall we go?"

She giggled as she took it and ascended into the carriage.

Lamar had not missed that tittering but rather enjoyed his day of freedom. He would have relished it more if he'd been able to slip back home to his workshop, but that would have been too risky of Grandmama discovering he had abandoned Miss Armstrong for hours.

At his residence, a stable hand took hold of the horse's halter, allowing Lamar to descend from the carriage and then assist Cordelia. She didn't hold on to him one second longer than she needed. Unlike the brazen young lady outside the White Hotel.

She extended her index finger and spoke to him as though he were an errant child. "Remember, we can't use each other's first name."

Rather adorable. "I remember." He didn't want to receive one of Grandmama's admonishing glances.

Inside, he escorted Cordelia into the parlor where Grandmama and the Armstrongs still sat.

All eyes turned to Lamar and Cordelia, no doubt waiting for some glowing report of how wonderful their time together was and how suited they were for each other. Neither of which were true, even if Miss Cordelia had an air of inexplicable intrigue about her. She seemed a bit simpleminded but in some complex way. An enigma.

Grandmama addressed a question to Cordelia. "Miss Armstrong, did you like Kamola?"

"Oh, yes. Very much. You have the nicest dressmaker shop."

With a smile, Grandmama replied. "We are most fortunate to have *Mademoiselle* Dumont in Kamola." She shifted her focus and narrowed her eyes at Lamar. "Tell me you didn't abandon our guest at the dressmaker shop."

He had but didn't know how to phrase it to keep himself and Miss Cordelia from a scolding.

Cordelia spared him by speaking first. "He was a perfect gentleman. Very attentive but gave me the space I needed. Patient too. We had a very nice carriage ride, and he drove me around. You have a charming little town here. Imagine, a teachers' college. I never would have guessed." She had artfully shifted two—maybe three—subjects away from the question.

Had that been on purpose? Or did her mind just meander like that?

Even though he looked elsewhere, most of his attention remained on Cordelia. She was worse than all the other débutantes combined. Was she truly that simpleminded? Was anyone? Or was she putting on a front? Could she merely be an excellent actress?

Lamar was determined to discover the truth. The quest to unravel the mystery of her made her a touch more interesting. At least for a little while. Not interesting enough to spend the rest of his life in her company. She deserved someone who could truly love her. With his connections, perhaps, he could find her someone suitable.

Four

HENNY STOOD IN HER KITCHEN ROLLING out crust for a cherry pie to be served after supper. Her visit with the three newcomers in town drifted through her thoughts. Unusual for outsiders to wish to do charity work, but they were welcome to help ease the burden. More hands made light work.

The front screen door banged shut on its spring, causing her to jump. *Mercy! Who was that?*

Rapid footsteps rushed up the staircase, and another door slammed overhead.

Must be Geneviève. She was more high-strung than her level-headed brother, Pierre, and struggled to find her way in a new kind of life. What on earth had upset her grown daughter this time?

Henny wiped her hands, went up to the second floor, and stopped at her daughter's room. Crying came from within. She knocked. "Geneviève? Are you all right?"

The sobs on the other side abated. "No."

What had grieved the girl? "May I come in?"

"Oui."

Henny turned the knob and entered. She'd never had the opportunity to raise the young woman stretched across the bed, sobbing into her pillow. Her daughter was in pain, and she longed to kiss her hurt away and make her better, but her little girl wasn't a child anymore.

Henny sat on the edge of the bed and placed a gentle hand on her daughter's trembling shoulder. "What's wrong?"

Mumbles issued up from the pillow.

Whether the words were in English or French, Henny couldn't tell. "What?"

Geneviève turned her head sideways but remained prone. "My wedding is not to be."

What? "That can't be. Plans are being made for the event in two weeks. All couples have arguments. You'll patch things up, just like an old quilt."

"I am afraid this is too big to patch."

Henny couldn't imagine Deputy Montana not wanting to reconcile. "What happened?"

Geneviève rolled to her side and sat up. "I bought a house, and Monte has forbidden me to keep it." Monte was the name Geneviève had settled upon calling Deputy Montana.

"He what? You what? When did you buy a house? What house?" Had Henny misheard?

Geneviève shifted to the edge of the bed to let her legs dangle off. "It is on Pearl Avenue. It is blue like my eyes with cerulean trim."

Henny knew which one she spoke of, and if memory served, it was roughly twice the size of Henny's boarding house. "Let me see if I understand. You *want* to buy this house, but Montana doesn't want you to, correct?"

"No, I buy it. When I told Monte, he says it is too big and I cannot keep it. It is not too big. It is small. I want to keep it. I have never had a home that was mine. This house belongs to me."

True, that particular house, though large by a lot of people's standards, was vastly smaller than any house her daughter had resided in. It was also larger than any home Montana had likely ever lived in or dreamed of living in. So, the Pearl Avenue dwelling sounded as though it was right in the middle of what they each grew up in. "I'm sure he didn't mean you must sell it."

"That is what he means. He said he wants to add on a room or two to his cabin." Geneviève held her hands out, palms up. "It is not big enough. Felicity already lives there and where would Silvie fit." Her daughter's lady's maid. "It is not big enough for two let alone four people. We would be stepping on each other every time we turned around. The Pearl house could hold us all."

Henny agreed that her daughter and Montana needed a different place than his cabin. "Don't you think Montana would have liked to have been consulted on where he is going to live?"

Geneviève remained silent for a moment, then her mouth formed a pout. "I did not think of that. I did not like it when my grandparents told me everything I could do and where I was to live. I should have asked Monte first."

"A house is a big decision. One that should be made together."

Geneviève heaved a heavy sigh. "I have made a mess of everything. When will I learn to make the right decisions?"

Henny patted her daughter's arm. "I'm sure you and Montana will work this out."

"Do you think so?"

"I do. You two need to talk these things over first. May I ask a question about your house?"

Her daughter nodded.

"If you have your own house now, why haven't you made plans to move into it?"

The girl glanced away and drew in a deep breath.

"You aren't having second thoughts about marrying the deputy, are you?"

Geneviève jerked her gaze back. "No. I love him. Truly I do. It is just..."

"What? I'm sure whatever it is, you and he can work it out."

She glanced away. "I do not know enough to run a household. I am only beginning to learn to cook with your help. Monte will starve."

Henny mentally shook her head. "Deputy Montana isn't going to starve. You have Silvie to help you, and you can hire someone to cook and keep house."

"If Monte does not want the house, he certainly would not be agreeable to servants."

Her daughter had a point. The deputy had never lived in a home with servants.

Henny patted her daughter's hand. "It's all in how you present it. By having others to take care of things around your home, you will be free to lavish him with all your attention."

Geneviève smiled. "That is wonderful."

However, Henny sensed there was more to her daughter's hesitation. "Is there anything else?"

She nodded. "I find I want to stay here in your boarding house. I have only just met you. I want to get to know you better."

That warmed Henny's heart and tears sprang to her eyes. "I will always be here for you. You and Montana are welcome to eat supper here every Sunday." Henny wouldn't mind every night, but the new couple needed to find their own way together without her as an onlooker. She stood. "Come with me."

Geneviève followed her downstairs and into the kitchen. Henny retrieved a battered cookbook from her pantry and handed it to her daughter. "I learned to prepare meals from this. I have every confidence you will be able to follow the recipes within it."

"You would give this to me? But how will you cook?"

"I have others, but I found that one particularly helpful when I didn't know what I was doing. The recipes are tasty and not difficult. Deputy Montana isn't expecting anything fancy when he sits down to eat."

"You truly believe I will be able to cook for my husband?"

"I do. You are smart and have been doing fine here in my kitchen. Pick a recipe you think you can make and follow the directions. Every meal you prepare might not be perfect, but your husband will appreciate your effort." Henny would make sure of it by encouraging Montana to be patient with his new wife's limited abilities in the kitchen and encouraging her.

Geneviève hugged the cookbook. "*Merci Beaucoup.* I will treasure this." She took the book up to her room.

Henny never realized how challenging it would be to have her daughter and son around. With them being adults and Henny missing out on raising them, she assumed they would have their lives figured out. Why she assumed that, she didn't know. Henny had done a lot of her own growing up after being abandoned and on her own.

Her daughter had made her realize one thing—how unfair Henny had been to Saul. She needed to speak with him. She had been on her own for so long, she didn't know how to be a good wife. That would need to change fast. She had avoided Proverbs 31 because she had been cast off as a wife. Therefore, if she wasn't anyone's wife, she didn't need to consider that particular chapter. How wrong her thinking had been all these years. Regardless of any circumstances on earth, she was the Bride of Christ. She would read it now and pray to figure out what she should do about the future of running her boarding house—no—the future of her and Saul's boarding house.

Henny pinned on her hat and walked the few blocks to the sheriff's office where she hoped Montana was on duty. When she entered, the deputy stood at the filing cabinet, sifting through folders. Thankfully, he was alone. "Deputy Montana?"

He turned. "Aunt Henny. What can I do for you?" Though he smiled, it appeared strained.

Henny had to give him credit for trying to act happy to see her. He probably suspected she had spoken to his distressed fiancée and wished he'd escaped before Henny had arrived. "May we talk?"

He rubbed the nape of his neck. "I'm kind of busy."

An excuse.

"Doing what, exactly?"

He glanced inside the file cabinet drawer, then at the desk, and rested his gaze on his boots. "Nothing." He slid the drawer closed. "Before you go and tell me I'm wrong, we don't need a house that large. It has *three* floors *and* a cellar. No one needs that much space. Frankly, it terrifies me."

Henny imagined it did. "I understand. Where one resides is a big decision. However, living in a place the size of your cabin—even with adding on to it—is terrifying to her. You must understand how much of a sacrifice a home like the one on Pearl Street is for her. She chose something—in her estimation—that she thought would meet with your approval, but one that wouldn't make her feel too closed in. She grew up in houses the size of the Kesners'."

He held his hands out from the sides. "I can't afford a place that large."

"You don't have to. Geneviève can. Let her do this for the two of you."

"I'm supposed to be the provider."

"It's not the size nor who paid for it that matters, but the love you both fill it with. By rejecting the house she bought, she feels rejected by you, that you don't accept who she is. Do you want her to be a different person than the one you fell in love with?"

"Of course not." He rubbed the nape of his neck again. "I never considered what she was giving up. I just assumed we would live in my cabin. I suppose I felt a little rejected that my home wasn't good enough for her."

He did understand.

"You and Geneviève need to tell each other how you feel. Then decide together to keep this house or not. By both of you having a say, wherever you choose will feel more like home."

He nodded. "Thank you for coming. I'll have to think about what to do."

"And pray to see how the Lord will direct you?"

Montana frowned. "What if I don't like His answer?"

"Do you really want to go up against the Lord's will?"

The deputy shook his head. "I'll pray."

"I will too. For both of you. All couples have rough patches, especially at the beginning as they are trying to figure out their life together. Don't be discouraged by this. You and my daughter have enough love for each other to work through this."

"You think so?"

"I do."

"Thank you."

"You're welcome. May I give you one more small piece of advice?"

He nodded.

"Be patient with her cooking. She's just learning."

He seemed to brighten. "I can do that. I've eaten some pretty terrible grub I've fixed myself. She can't possibly do worse."

Her daughter and the deputy were going to be fine. Smiling, Henny left and hoped she hadn't meddled too much.

That evening after the supper dishes were cleaned up, Henny cut a slice of cherry pie and headed to the barn where Saul worked on...whatever it was he worked on out there.

He stood beside a saddle on a wooden A-frame, oiling it to keep the leather from cracking.

Henny extended her arms. "Peace offering?"

He looked up and eyed the plate with the cherry syrup oozing onto it. "Were we fighting? If so, I'm too dull to know what it was about. You'll need to fill me in."

Henny tilted her head. "Would you just take the pie?"

He took it but didn't make a move to eat it. "You plan to tell me what this is about?"

"I must apologize. I've been unfair to you. I'm not used to having someone I'm so accountable to."

Saul furrowed his eyebrows. "I can't think of one way you have been unfair to me. You agreed to marry me."

"Which makes me your wife."

"That was the idea."

"Yes, but I've been treating you like a boarder for the past month and a half. I didn't mean to. The Lord brought my oversight to my attention earlier today."

"Well, this has been your home for a long time. It takes time for people to get used to things when circumstances have changed."

"You are too sweet, Saul Hammond. I don't deserve you."

He set the plate on the seat of the saddle and took her hands. "I never expected you to turn your life upside down for me. We've both been around long enough to be set in our ways."

That she was, but her attitude needed to change. "I'm married now, and that means we should do things together, make decisions together."

"Like what? You want to help me decide if I should repair that buckboard myself or have someone else do it?" He tipped his head toward the wagon.

She was glad he could make light of this. "No, that's not what I'm talking about. Wait, that is what I'm talking about. We aren't simply two individuals anymore. We're a couple. You left your home to live in mine. I think of this as *my* house, but it's *ours* now."

"I know that."

"But do *I*? I never even considered asking you if I—*we* should continue running it as a business."

He furrowed his eyebrows. "Where would your boarders go?"

She pointed at him. "See? You called them *my* boarders. That's how I think of them too, but they are *our* boarders. We should decide together. I know you worry about me working so hard. If you ask me to close our home to boarders, I will." She hoped he didn't.

He pulled her closer and slipped his arms around her waist. "Thank you for considering me and my feelings. I'm not going to ask you to shut down your business. It's a part of who you are. The boarders are almost like family. Especially professors Lumbard and Tunstall who have been here for several years."

"Two of our residents literally are family." A part of her wanted to keep her adult children close, but another part knew they needed to leave her little nest and make lives of their own. She would cherish this time she had with them.

"I enjoy having the professors at the supper table. And I'm pleased your children have come and are living here, at least for a time. You are a very caring and giving person. Without the boarding house, that part of you would be stifled. Besides, I believe the Lord is prompting me to talk with Professor Job Lumbard. The man needs a friend, a true friend. I'm ashamed to say I haven't considered him much before now."

"I think a *true friend* would do him so much good. I have tried to get him to attend church and to speak to him about his drinking so heavily on the weekends, but my words have fallen on deaf ears. Does this mean we have decided to continue the boarding house together then?"

"I believe we have. I love you just the way you are, but perhaps, you—we could consider hiring someone to help you with things. That would give you more time to spend with your children."

And her husband. Wasn't that the same advice she'd given her daughter? Henny's eyes teared at his understanding and kindness. "Saul Hammond, you are the sweetest."

He cocked one shoulder in a shrug. "Does this mean I should fix the buckboard or do you want to?"

"Funny." She sent up a silent prayer of thanksgiving to be blessed with Saul.

"Besides, you aren't the only one having to get used to new things. Living in a house with people who aren't family is an adjustment for me—the reason I spend so much time out here—but I knew full well they came as part of the deal. And just so you know, I've made a few decisions myself without consulting you."

"You have?" Henny couldn't think what they could possibly be. He was always very considerate.

He released her and tipped his head toward a corner. "See those shovels, the hoe, and the rake?"

Henny nodded. What did they have to do with anything?

He indicated toward the rear of the barn. "They were over there, but I decided they would be more accessible there." He pointed to the corner again.

Henny was grateful he found humor in this serious topic and planted her hands on her hips. "Saul Hammond, how dare you move those without consulting me. You put them right back."

Saul grinned and studied her mouth. "You're about to smile. I can see it right there at the corners of your pretty little lips."

Henny struggled to keep a straight face. "I am not." With that, she failed.

"That's the look I like." Saul took her into his arms again. "You are most beautiful when you smile."

With his simple, endearing gaze, she felt twenty years younger. She couldn't imagine anyone else she'd rather share her life with.

Five

LAMAR SAT AT THE DINING TABLE with his empty breakfast plate before him. He should go out to his workshop and tinker with his hot air balloon.

Grandmama set her tea cup into its saucer. "I'm sorry Miss Armstrong won't be coming over today."

The Armstrongs had sent word that Cordelia was under the weather, so none of them would be visiting as originally planned.

"Miss Armstrong is different from the others." Grandmama's expression turned mischievous. "I can tell you like her."

Lamar rolled his eyes. "I do not. She seems like a sweet lady, but I doubt there is any chance of a future with her." Best to set Grandmama straight early on in this matchmaking attempt. "Men in my generation want wives with whom they can hold a halfway intelligent conversation." However, he did wonder how Cordelia was doing.

"I think Miss Armstrong might surprise you if you give her a chance. Your problem is you dismiss people too quickly." Grandmama set her napkin aside. "I have a meeting with the president of the normal school. I will see you later."

Lamar stood and went to his grandmother, gripping the back of her chair. "I'll go with you." Why had he said that?

"I thought you were going to fuss about in your workshop." She wiggled her hand in the air.

He pulled the chair out and assisted her to her feet. "I can do that later."

Turning to face him, she eyed him suspiciously. "You have never shown any interest in these meetings at the school."

She was right, of course, and it would be dangerous to set a precedent he would regret later.

"Correct as usual. An institution housing dozens of young ladies with matrimony on their minds is a place I choose to steer clear of. Drop me off at the Atwood Hotel. I want to inquire after Miss Armstrong's health."

Grandmama smiled. "That would be lovely."

This too could set a dangerous precedent. "Don't read anything into my visit. I just want to make sure it's nothing serious."

"Yes, dear." She gave him an impish smile and turned with a flourish. "We'll leave in fifteen minutes."

Lamar groaned. He had probably made a big mistake. He should have kept silent, saddled a horse, and rode there surreptitiously. Too late for that now.

Yesterday, Lamar had spent a pleasant day by himself. Not exactly by himself, but absent of the Armstrongs. He'd made sure his duties overseeing Grandmama's holdings and accounts kept him out most of the day. No need for the Armstrongs to pay them a visit. Plus, he was free of Cordelia's giggling.

Strangely, Cordelia had occupied many of his thoughts. First, at the bank speaking with Oliver Mallory, then over to the attorney's office and the land office. Each place, the beautiful socialite popped into his head. Wondering what she was doing. Would he run into her? He hadn't—even though he kept his eye out for her— which made him think about her even more. Shouldn't the absence of a person drive them farther from one's thoughts?

Lamar, get a hold of yourself.

When he'd gotten up this morning, he'd actually had fond anticipation of her coming for luncheon. Even though he'd been planning to spend the majority of the day in his workshop.

So, why wasn't he?

Later, Grandmama's driver pulled the carriage up to the Atwood Hotel.

Lamar climbed out. "I'll find my own way back home."

Grandmama gave him another impish smile. "Give the Armstrongs my regards and extend an invitation to supper tomorrow. I meant to invite them the other day but forgot. My mind must be slipping."

Lamar doubted that. Grandmama was as sharp as ever.

The carriage drove off, and he faced the entrance. Since the hotel wasn't technically open for business yet, no doorman stood at the ready to open the large etched-glass doors.

He pulled on the ornate gold handle, entered the posh lobby, and hesitated at the sight of staff and workers rushing around preparing things.

Two movers carried a round settee across the lobby while others transported small end tables and plants to various areas. All of it in preparation for the grand opening of the hotel next week. Likely, staff scurried about in the unseen areas, such as the kitchen and on each of the floors preparing for the big day. The Armstrongs were the only guests for the time being.

They planned to stay through the end of the summer and into the fall. With their large investment in the hotel, they had come for the final preparations and the scheduled celebration. Lamar and Grandmama would also be there as she had invested as well. Lamar had been both disappointed and elated. The Armstrongs' extended visit meant he would have many opportunities to endure the giggly socialite, but strangely anticipated learning more about her.

This high-class hotel was going to be a good addition to Kamola.

He strolled up to the carved front desk, where he saw a familiar face. Grant Dawson appeared to be instructing the clerk. Dawson used to work at the White Hotel's front desk until his father-in-law built this one. Nicer than the White. He had moved up from desk clerk to assistant hotel manager.

Mr. Dawson finished speaking to the young gentleman and turned to Lamar. "Mr. Kesner, what can I do for you?"

"I'm here to see the Armstrongs."

"Your timing is impeccable. They're coming down as we speak." Mr. Dawson nodded toward the staircase.

Lamar turned. Mr. and Mrs. Armstrong had just reached the bottom, but no Cordelia. "Thank you." He tapped the desk before strolling across the lobby. "Good morning, Mr. and Mrs. Armstrong. It's good to see you." He stretched out his hand toward Mr. Armstrong.

The man hesitantly shook it. "Mr. Kesner. Uh... We weren't expecting you."

That was apparent by the older man's tentative greeting and his wife's wide-eyed expression.

"I came to inquire after Miss Armstrong's health. Is she feeling any better?"

Mrs. Armstrong's eyes widened farther—if that were possible. "She'll be fine. Nothing a little uninterrupted rest won't solve."

Lamar got the distinct impression these people were hiding something. They certainly didn't want him to see Cordelia. For the life of him, he couldn't figure out why *he* wanted to see her. "Perhaps I could bring her something to help her recover more quickly."

Mr. Armstrong put a hand on Lamar's shoulder and leaned a little closer. "Son, once you're married, you'll learn that ladies are delicate creatures. There are certain times it's best to not press a woman. I'm sure our little Cordelia will be in blooming health tomorrow." He patted Lamar on the shoulder.

Lamar found himself at the entrance to the hotel on the opposite side of the lobby where he'd just been. The man had expertly maneuvered there without Lamar realizing it. Now, he knew they were trying to keep him away from Cordelia. But why? Did she often have bouts of ill health? "My grandmother wished for me to extend a supper invitation to the three of you for tomorrow night."

"We look forward to it. Thank you for stopping by. I'll give Cordelia your best wishes. If you'll excuse me, I need to attend to several things for the opening. Until tomorrow."

Now, Lamar knew where Cordelia learned to change subjects without notice. With a nod, he exited. It was for the best. He didn't want to see Cordelia anyway. She held no interest for him. Definitely not the right woman to take for a wife. If the three Armstrongs were hiding some secret about Cordelia, it was best he cut all ties with them sooner rather than later.

Out on the street, he glanced around. Where should he go? He could stop by the attorney's office and ascertain if the man had learned anything since yesterday. Or he could go to Davenport's Hardware Store to find out if his order had come in. It would be a bit of a walk, but he looked forward to stretching his legs.

As he approached the main part of town, still some distance from his destination, a stylish lady in pink with a large brimmed hat caught his attention as she exited Waldon's Mercantile across the street.

He returned his thoughts to his task at hand, the hardware store, but the woman pulled his attention back to her. Did he know her? He scrutinized her for a moment. Miss Armstrong? Couldn't be. She was in her hotel room, resting.

As she turned and headed quickly down the boardwalk, he caught a better glimpse of her. Definitely Cordelia Armstrong. She didn't appear sickly at all. What was she doing about town? Did her parents know? Probably. It could be the reason for their odd behavior. What was this family hiding?

He followed on the opposite side of the street to determine where she was off to in such a hurry.

Unexpectedly, she darted into the White Hotel. Why would she go there?

Lamar waited outside to discover if she would exit soon. When she didn't, he decided to go inside. Not finding her in the lobby, he wandered the ground floor and peered into the dining room. No Miss Armstrong. Where had she gone? He crossed to the front desk. "Excuse me. Did you notice a young woman enter a few minutes ago? Miss Armstrong? Dark hair, pink dress."

"She went up to her room."

Her room? What did she need a room at this hotel for? Lamar tapped the desk. "Thank you." He left quickly to give him time to think.

How odd for Miss Armstrong to have a room *here*. Did she have a clandestine meeting with someone? A man? Or was it something else? She didn't seem the type to plot big scheming plans. Why have a room when she had accommodations at the new Atwood Hotel? Certainly, she and her parents couldn't be unhappy there. They were part owners.

He would have to see how long she would remain inside. Soon enough, she exited, wearing drab brown clothes of a common design. She almost looked like a different person. If he hadn't been waiting for her, he wouldn't have realized it was her under the large straw hat. Another woman accompanied her.

He studied the second young lady. Something registered as familiar about her. She flashed a smile, and he instantly placed her. Two days ago, she had pretended to fall to garner his attention.

As the pair stepped off the boardwalk, he shifted into the shadows of the alleyway between the buildings. *What are you up to, Miss Armstrong?*

They crossed the street, and he followed on foot. They ended up at Waldon's Mercantile. Instead of going inside, she spoke with a large blond man next to a buckboard with a few crates in the tail end. He assisted the ladies up to the seat, climbed aboard, and drove off.

What was going on?

Lamar hustled to the livery. "I would like to rent a horse. How quickly can you have one ready for me?"

"I can saddle Petunia."

"I'll pay double if you can have her ready posthaste."

The kid twisted his mouth and squinted one eye. "What?"

"Quickly. Quickly."

"Of course." The boy hurried as Lamar kept a vigilant watch on which way Cordelia had gone. When she turned a corner, Lamar rushed back inside. "Is the horse ready?"

"Almost. Just need to cinch the strap and lower the stirrups."

"I'll get the one on this side." Lamar lowered it and swung up as the boy adjusted the other.

"You shouldn't be riding her until you get outside. It could spook her."

Lamar would have to risk it. He walked the horse until he was beyond the doorway, then prodded her into a trot.

When he turned the corner Cordelia had gone down, she and the wagon were nowhere in sight. He'd lost her. He rode along at a slower pace. How far could she have gone?

Cordelia swayed on the wagon seat next to her friends. Dutch had hold of the reins and followed behind Miss Henny and her husband, Saul, in their wagon.

How was Master Lamar Kesner occupying his time today? She wished she had allowed him to answer her question about what he did in his spare time on that first day so she could picture what he might be doing. The best she could do was conjure up the image of him standing near the fireplace with one elbow resting upon the mantel. So handsome.

She would need to be available tomorrow for any plans her parents had in store for her. Even once she'd convinced them she had gone for a walk today and gotten lost, they would keep an eye on her for a few days. So went this game she played, which would be much harder if she were married.

After having traveled a mile or so out of town, the road—if it could be called that—opened up to a meadow with a cluster of smaller groups huddled by nationality around what appeared to be a stream.

As they drove closer to the water source and the middle of the encampment, face after leery face eyed them. Cordelia identified at least five different races, Indians, Blacks, Chinese, Irish, and a group from a Scandinavian country. Most appeared thin, downtrodden, and hungry. They wouldn't make it through a winter if they didn't accept help. A black mother corralled her two young children behind the safety of her skirt. Their dwellings were patched tents and lean-tos constructed from branches. One fortunate group had a small wagon with a mule tied up near it.

Odd to have so varied a collection of nationalities in close proximity. How had all these outcasts ended up clumped together? They did have two things in common.

The townsfolks didn't want them sullying their town, and they each needed water.

As the lead wagon slowed, Dutch pulled the reins to stop the rig he drove. After he helped Cordelia down, she went to the back of Henny's wagon to help unload. "Not knowing what they might need, we brought food staples and some clothes. We can get more for the next time."

"By the looks of it, everything." Aunt Henny gave a wan smile. "Anything will help. The church donated many items for these people. Things they will need this winter. Blankets, clothes, food, cooking pots. We even have a few laying hens and two dear friends of mine, Lily Hammond and Nicole Keegan pledged to donate a milking cow. They will all eat better this winter if we can get everyone here to cooperate. That won't be easy with all the different races."

Cordelia nodded. "We'll have to make them understand the importance of working together." It was unusual to have so many nationalities living in close proximity, but because everyone needed water, they seemed willing to tolerate each other. In total, she guessed around twenty-five to thirty people lived here.

A red-haired man barked in an Irish accent. "We don't want no handouts." His clothing harbored fewer tattered edges than others.

Was he the self-appointed spokesman for the loose band of outcasts?

Cordelia smiled to ease the tension and to show these people they had nothing to fear. "We are only trying to help."

He narrowed his eyes. "We know what whites did to the Indians with their *generous* gifts of blankets. Infected with disease." He spat on the ground.

Whites? This man was as white as she was, but he had reason to be leery of outsiders bearing gifts.

Aunt Henny spoke up. "I understand your caution. I promise these items are safe."

People of various races trickled closer.

Cordelia held up her hand. "Who here speaks English?"

Only a few raised their hands. Some because they didn't understand, and others likely because of stubbornness.

"Please tell the others that we have brought these things for everyone to share."

A man called out, "We do not share with the Chinese."

"Nor do we. Or your kind." This man directed his second comment to the previous man who spoke.

"You are all in need. Help each other, and you will all do better."

Several men spoke in their own languages, shook their heads, and walked away.

After the men had left and taken their families with them, a few women with their children approached. Though they spoke in their own language, their pleas were clear. They wanted things for their children but were reluctant to take anything for themselves.

Cordelia outfitted the first brave woman's children with shoes and coats then gave her the first two hens. Cordelia pointed to the other mothers and children who watched longingly from afar. "Share with the others." She doubted the lady could understand her words but hoped her meaning came across.

Once the first woman had gotten treasures of clothes and food for her children, it emboldened others to approach. Both wagons still held many unclaimed items.

Cordelia had hoped these people would have taken all of their gifts.

Aunt Henny sighed. "I thought they might be more eager for the supplies. Half the children still need shoes and coats. And they all could use more blankets. We can store the rest of this in my barn and come back. As winter draws closer, their pride will weaken and they'll be more receptive."

That wasn't good enough for Cordelia. These people had needs now. She spoke to Dutch and Nan. "Unload the rest."

"Where?"

"To the side. If we leave it here, someone will take it even if they slip out during the cover of night to do so." Hopefully, several someones. She pitched in to unload the wagons then spoke to Henny. "I will bring you funds to purchase more supplies. Thank you for helping me."

"I'm just sorry you can't assist people openly."

"If my parents found out, my father would lock me in my room. He doesn't mind my doing charity work as long as it reflects well on him. He prefers it if I focus my efforts on the more fortunate of the less fortunate. People who look clean and don't have patched clothes. Granted, they need help too but not as badly as these folks. And he prefers to give aid to Americans, people who were born here, but not the true natives, the Indians. He's actually quite generous but is just careful to whom he gives assistance." How did Lamar feel about helping the less fortunate?

Henny nodded. "I understand that better than you realize. We should be going now. It looks as though Dutch has made a new friend. That could further our cause here."

Cordelia turned her attention to her friend. He stood with another blond man, and they seemed to be getting on well with smiles and nods as they spoke in their own language. How long had it been since he had heard someone else speak his native tongue? She hated to pull him away, but it was time. "Dutch?"

Her companion glanced her way then bid his new friend farewell before assisting her and Nan onto the wagon seat. "Hans knows of a group of Dutch over the mountains."

The excitement in his voice told her he wanted to find them and see if they were the relatives he suspected had traveled west all those years ago. As much as she would miss him, she wouldn't prevent him from going. He deserved to have the chance to locate them and be with them. She would talk to him about it later.

He snapped the reins, and the horse plodded into motion.

Would Dutch leave her and Nan behind as easily as they all were leaving this little community behind?

Six

AFTER AN HOUR OF RIDING UP and down the streets of Kamola, Lamar had failed to locate Miss Armstrong. How could she have disappeared? Being closer to his home than the livery, he rode there. He would have one of their grooms return the rented horse.

At their stable, Hank approached and grasped the halter. "Did you purchase a new horse, sir?"

Lamar dismounted. "I rented this one. Could you...? Never mind." He couldn't shake Cordelia Armstrong and her disappearance from his thoughts. Another perusal around town couldn't hurt. "Please saddle Edelweiss for me."

Soon his beautiful white thoroughbred was ready. He rode back to the livery to return the rented horse. Another trip around the streets of Kamola still didn't produce Miss Armstrong's whereabouts, so he headed to Thomas's place.

His friend sat on a stool which rested on the planks that served as his porch. As Lamar approached, Thomas halted the movement of a large knife on a sharpening stone and shook his head. "If you're coming out here again so soon, must be that lady who's gotten tangled up in your thoughts. My best advice is to run as fast as you can away from her. She's twisted you around her little finger. You'll suffocate and die."

Lamar chuckled as he dismounted. "Rest assured, I have not capitulated to her wiles." Not that he thought Miss Armstrong capable of subterfuge, though something was going on, and he intended to get to the bottom of it.

Thomas harrumphed. "You just can't see it." He had become jaded after being jilted by a woman he'd given his whole heart to. Sad thing was, his friend would probably take her back if she asked him to, even after four years.

She had pushed Thomas to his life in the wild. Her, and disagreements with his father. "If you didn't come because of this woman, what induced you my way instead of your workshop?"

Lamar couldn't very well denounce the impetus for his presence. "You're right, but it's not what you think."

Thomas rolled his eyes. "What could this woman have possibly done to have you so taken with her?"

"I'm not taken with her. I merely need to ascertain what she's up to."

"Well, let's see." Thomas held up one hand with his index finger extended. "She's a woman." He straightened his next finger. "She's of marrying age." Another finger. "She's looking for some sap to marry her." Fourth finger raised. "And she's got you on her hook. That's what she's up to."

Lamar shook his head. His friend didn't understand. "Being part owners, she and her parents are, of course, staying at the Atwood Hotel for the opening next week. They were supposed to have luncheon with Grandmama and me today. They cancelled due to Cordelia not feeling well."

Thomas's eyes widened. "Cordelia, is it? Sounds like you're getting cozy."

Lamar would ignore that comment and skip telling him about seeking her out at the hotel. "While I was in town, I saw *Miss Armstrong* strolling about. She didn't appear the least bit ill."

"Ladies feign illness all the time. It means she's typical."

"She entered the White Hotel. Why? She and her parents have rooms at the Atwood."

With a shrug, Thomas resumed sharpening the blade. "The White Hotel *does* have a dining room."

The swishing of the metal against stone, both soothed and irritated Lamar's frustration. "She wasn't in the dining room. When I inquired, the desk clerk said she had gone to her room—*her* room."

"A clandestine rendezvous?" Thomas leveled his gaze at Lamar. "There's your proof. I stand by my earlier decree. Run from her as fast as you can."

This wasn't helpful. "She exited a short time later dressed entirely different. Like a common farmer's daughter in a drab, brown dress. All vestiges of her social class erased. She climbed into a wagon—a *wagon*, mind you—with a big brute of a man and a woman who had distracted me two days earlier. Why was she secreting around town, and why did she deem it necessary to disguise herself?"

Thomas pointed the tip of the blade in Lamar's direction. "I can see why she intrigues you."

"I tried following her today, but I lost her. That's why I came to your place. What should I do? Confront her? Or attempt to follow her again?"

"I know exactly what to do." Thomas gave Lamar his full attention now. "We should take a trip to Europe. That will get your mind off Miss Cordelia Armstrong. By the time we return, she'll be gone."

Lamar wasn't so sure about that. "Her parents are investors in the new Atwood Hotel. They plan to stay in town for a while."

"Ah, but by then some other poor sap will be dangling from her hook."

Lamar waggled a finger at him. "I see that mischievous twinkle in your eyes. You're as curious to know what she's up to as I am."

Thomas relaxed his shoulders and raised an eyebrow. "Do you think it's something illegal?"

"She's a bit too simpleminded for nefarious endeavors."

"Or is she?" Thomas squinted one eye.

Lamar did suspect there was more to her than what fluttered at the surface, but her tedious giggling and vacuous conversation said otherwise. "I plan to discover what she's been off doing today."

"I'm in."

She would never know if Thomas were tailing her. He could be a great help.

Edelweiss nickered.

Lamar patted the horse's withers. "If she slips away again, I wouldn't be able to let you know without losing her."

"Don't worry about that. You say she's staying at the Atwood? I'll determine who she is and keep an eye on her."

"How about I wait for her to return to the Atwood, and you can see her when I talk to her?"

"Phenomenal idea. Would certainly save time. Let's go."

A little while later, Lamar sat on the railing of the veranda that stretched along the front of the Atwood Hotel. He'd inquired within and learned Miss Armstrong hadn't returned yet, but she would eventually. He couldn't believe that after nearly two hours of searching the streets, he hadn't been able to locate her. Not even a glimpse of the wagon.

Until now. At the sight of the vehicle, he straightened. The wagon stopped a short distance away from the hotel, and the large man assisted her down. She had donned her fancy clothes again.

Lamar motioned to Thomas waiting on the street. His friend understood, looked in Cordelia's direction, then gave him a nod.

Cordelia hurried along the street toward the Atwood Hotel. She had been gone far longer than she had anticipated. Her parents were going to be furious with her. However, it was worth it to have given some aid to those unfortunate people, misery etched on their faces.

A hunched beggar lumbered toward her. He held out a gnarled hand with bent fingers. "Can you spare a penny for a wandering soul?"

"What happened to you?" She tried to peer at him under his floppy hat, but shadows and a lengthy beard cloaked his features.

His whiskers held a twig and a small leaf. "I was a cobbler for many years until my hands decided to quit working. I'm sorry to have bothered you." He raked twisted fingers through his beard.

"You poor man. I don't have any money with me." It was safer if she didn't carry any when she visited the underprivileged.

Suddenly, a well-dressed man appeared at her side. He dropped a coin in the bedraggled man's hand. "Be gone. Don't bother the guests of the hotel."

Cordelia was capable of taking care of herself. She squared her shoulders and turned on the interloper. Then froze. "Mr. Kesner?" Oh, dear. She dipped her head and giggled. "What are you doing here?"

"I came to see you. How are you fairing?"

The beggar shuffled sideways a step. "I'll leave you be, miss. I meant no harm. Don't want no trouble."

She extended her hand to the poor man. "No, wait." She needed to be careful how she spoke with Mr. Kesner present. She raised her voice to a slightly higher pitch. "This is the Atwood Hotel. You go around back to the kitchen. Tell them Miss Armstrong sent you. They won't likely have anything hot, but they'll give you some food."

The man choked up. "Thank you, miss. May the Lord bless you." He scurried off.

"You shouldn't have done that. He'll only return and pester you further."

Cordelia so much wanted to tell this self-indulgent, spoiled dandy a thing or two, but that would ruin her ruse. Instead, she smiled insipidly and giggled. "Oh, I don't think he's hurting anything. You were pretty harsh to him."

"I'm sorry for that. I didn't want him bothering you again."

She didn't want to discuss the underprivileged with this overprivileged society gentleman. "It was kind of you to stop by. As you can see, I'm fine."

"You recovered from your earlier illness quickly."

Evidently that was what her parents had told him, so that meant he'd likely been here this morning. "Much better. My walk-around helped too." She giggled for good measure. She wanted to gag, but the ploy was necessary.

"I'll escort you inside."

"You don't have to do that."

"I would hate for that vagabond to return."

"I'm sure he won't." She slipped her hand around his arm. "But it's awful kind of you to be concerned for my wellbeing. You'll make a fine husband." She tilted her head against his upper arm and felt his muscles under the fabric stiffen. Good. He was tiring of her already.

At the entrance, she tightened her hold. "You will come in, won't you? I'm sure Father and Mother will want to speak with you. You could stay for supper." She gazed up at him with her enamored expression and batted her eyelashes.

He pulled from her grasp. "I'm sorry. I'll have to decline." He bowed over her hand. "My grandmother has invited you and your parents to supper tomorrow night."

"All right. Until tomorrow." She bit her bottom lip and slipped into the hotel. That was a close one. Good thing he hadn't followed her earlier. He could have ruined everything.

Glancing around the lobby revealed a clear path to the elevator without detection from either of her parents. If she could steal up to her room on the fifth floor, she could claim to have been there longer than they realized.

Reaching her door without notice, she took a deep breath. A successful outing completed. Upon entering, she stopped short at the sight of her parents in the sitting area.

"Where have you been, young lady?" Father snapped the paper he'd been reading.

She forced a smile and added the light, singsong lilt to her voice. "I took a walk. What are you doing in my room?"

"Being part owner has its benefits."

She always knew it was a possibility, but they had rarely exercised that option before.

"You have been gone all day. Where were you?" He folded the newspaper, veins pulsing in his neck.

Oh, dear. "I took a walk and got lost. You can't believe how..." She retrieved her fan and waved it in front of her face. "...how harrowing that was."

"You expect me to believe there wasn't one person you could have asked to direct you back to this hotel?"

Time to employ a different tactic. She willed tears to her eyes and plopped down on the settee. "I didn't think of that." She sniffled.

"You better not ruin this match with Kesner. I won't

live forever. Then who will take care of you?" He marched from the room.

She knew her father worried about her, but he didn't need to.

Her mother sat next to her and patted her forearm. "There, there, dear. It's nothing to cry over."

She blinked away the tears and straightened her shoulders. "What if I don't want to marry Mr. Kesner?"

"You could do a lot worse. He's a very nice gentleman. You have to marry someone."

"Why?"

"You need someone to take care of you."

Cordelia stood and crossed to the credenza. "I can take care of myself."

"That's what we all think until we try to navigate a society ruled by men. If you succeed at not marrying, your father will put your inheritance in a trust with a man in charge of it. One way or another, a man *will* control your life."

How awful. "Why can't I simply have access to my own money and do what I like with it?"

"That's not how the world works."

Well, it should. Women were every bit as capable.

If Father was determined to marry her off or give her inheritance to another to hold sway over her, she may need to resort to some other more drastic measure. What? She didn't know. At least, a nunnery hadn't been brought up. Marrying Master Kesner would be preferable to that.

Lamar waited across the street with his horse for Thomas to return from his trip to the Atwood Hotel kitchen. Edelweiss tossed her head, so he rubbed her nose. "He'll be along soon."

Sure enough, Thomas hobbled away from the building, still in vagabond character. When he reached Lamar, he straightened to his normal stature, a brown-paper wrapped item in one hand and a small cloth bag in the other. He held them up. "Look at what I got."

Lamar shook his head. "I can't believe you actually

took food from the hotel."

"I didn't *take* it. They gave it to me." Thomas raised the brown paper closer to Lamar's face. "Take a whiff of that. Roast beef sandwich. Smells divine."

Lamar had to admit it did smell good. "What possessed you to pretend to be a beggar?"

"I wanted to see how she would treat a dirty bedraggled person." Thomas ripped off a bite of his sandwich.

When his friend didn't continue his thoughts on Miss Armstrong, Lamar prodded him. "And how did she treat you?" From Lamar's viewpoint, she seemed to have been kind.

Thomas swallowed. "Sweet as taffy. Real concern in her honeyed voice."

That spoke well of her.

"However, I agree that something is up with her. When she was talking to me alone, there was a strength to her words. As soon as you arrived, she became a different person. Like her intelligence dropped. And then there was her giggle." Thomas gave a dramatic shiver. "My original assessment stands. Run."

No, Lamar couldn't do that now. Interesting that she had behaved different around just Thomas, but it thrilled him a little to know she wasn't so vapid. He needed to figure her out first and confront her on her ruse. "I plan to ascertain what she's really up to."

Thomas swallowed another bite of roast beef. "I suspected you would say that. I'll keep an eye on her for you. If I discover anything, I'll let you know."

"I would appreciate that." Lamar would keep a closer eye on her as well. He bid his friend good-bye, mounted Edelweiss, and rode to the dressmaking shop.

Upon entering, a bell over the door jingled, and he cringed at the bold pronouncement of his arrival. The scents of various garden flowers accosted him with a hint of something sugary. The interior teemed with women clustered in small groups around the room, and all eyes focused on him, the solitary man in the room. He recognized several from around town, mothers with eligible daughters. He swallowed hard at all the attention from so many ladies at once. Had he just stepped into a lioness den? He merely needed to identify someone who worked here.

No one spoke for several seconds. It was as though they weren't believing their eyes at seeing a gentleman in this normally female establishment.

He took a deep breath and trained his gaze on a lady at a cutting table with a pair of shears hovering over shiny yellow fabric, a pattern lying atop it. "Excuse me. Are you employed here?"

Her mouth turned upward as she set the shears down and crossed to him. "How may I assist you?"

Lamar spoke in a low voice to keep his words from reaching everyone in the establishment. "I'm interested in some information about a lady."

Her smile stretched wider. "This shop is full of ladies." She seemed to be enjoying his discomfort.

He resisted the urge to pull at his collar. "I'm interested in a particular lady. She came in two days ago."

Mademoiselle Celeste Dumont approached with her hands clasped together in front of her torso. "*Merci*, Ruth. I will see to *Monsieur* Kesner."

Ruth nodded and returned to her work at the cutting table.

Mademoiselle Dumont gazed up at him. "What can I do for you, *monsieur?*"

He breathed a little easier and kept his voice low. "A lady came in here on Monday. She had dark hair and wore a purple dress."

"*Oui*. I remember her. Her dress was orchid and exquisite."

Now, he was getting somewhere. However, he needed to word his inquiry carefully to not raise suspicions. "I wish to purchase a gift for her. Was there anything in particular she was interested in while here?"

The proprietress tilted her head. "I am sorry. I do not know. She left a few moments after arriving."

Lamar wasn't surprised, with what he'd since learned. So, where had she been for three hours? He could still feel the gazes of all the ladies on him.

Mademoiselle Dumont motioned toward a glass

display case. "I think I have something she will like." Once behind the display case, she removed an ornate silver hair comb. "Any woman would be honored to be given such a gift." She held it out to him.

He took it. If not mistaken, this was an expensive piece. One the proprietress knew he could afford. It would contrast exquisitely in Cordelia's dark hair with her wavy tresses hanging down dancing in the breeze. Were they as soft as they appeared? He shook the image from his head. "I'll take it."

Mademoiselle Dumont tucked the comb into a small red velvet bag.

Lamar paid then took the bag before leaving. Once outside, he drew in a deep breath. He'd almost felt like a caged animal in there but was now free.

Edelweiss nickered.

"Let's go girl, before Grandmama sends out a search party." He tucked the gift into his jacket pocket and climbed up into the saddle.

Without any encouragement, his horse headed for home.

Why had Cordelia asked him to leave her at the dressmaker shop for three hours if she had no intention to stay? In all probability, for the same reason she'd changed clothes and gone off today in a wagon.

What are you up to, Miss Armstrong?

Lamar eagerly anticipated the supper with Miss Cordelia Armstrong tomorrow evening. He would specifically be looking for a change in her demeanor. If he could see what Thomas had seen, just once, he would know how to proceed with her.

Seven

THE NEXT DAY, HENNY STOOD IN her entryway looking into the mirror to pin a modest hat on her head. Now that she better knew the needs of the outcasts, she planned to visit a few businesses in town to elicit donations, either provisions or money to purchase what the people needed. She collected her reticule and prepared to leave.

Before she could, Geneviève swept through the front door into the parlor and threw her hands into the air. "I do not understand men. They are as fickle as women. No—more."

Silvie, Geneviève's lady's maid, followed in her wake with a worried expression.

Henny studied her daughter a moment to ascertain what was going on. Unlike the other day when Geneviève came home in tears, today she seemed to lean toward frustrated. "Did you have another disagreement with your fiancé?"

"No. It is the same one." Geneviève stormed into the kitchen.

Henny glanced at Silvie.

Silvie gave a demure smile. "It is the house again. They cannot agree upon it."

Had her daughter decided to keep it in spite of what they'd talked about the other day?

Geneviève returned to the parlor like a flitting bumble bee and extended one hand palm up. "Before, he did not want me to keep the house." She held out the other. "Today, he wants me to keep it. I do not understand."

Obviously, when the two had talked per Henny's suggestion, they hadn't come to an agreement, and apparently, each had changed their position on where to live. They both needed a good chastising. However, it wouldn't likely make things better. By working through this themselves, they would have a stronger marriage. Henny resolved to be patient. She put her reticule on the tea table and sat on the settee. "Would you like to tell me what happened?"

Geneviève heaved a breath and sat in one of the chairs while her lady's maid hovered nearby. "I said I would sell the house so we could choose one together. He said no. Keep this house. Why? He did not like it."

It might come across that way. "It's not that he didn't like it. I think it might be a bigger house than he is used to. That can be intimidating."

Geneviève's expression turned worried. "It is already so small."

It would appear as such to her daughter. "It's all a matter of perspective." Henny stepped to the fireplace and snagged a candlestick with a half-burned candle in it from the mantel then set it on the tea table. "Is this big or small?"

"I would guess small."

Henny retrieved a little silver thimble from her sewing basket beside the settee and placed it near the candlestick. "What about the thimble?"

"It is definitely small."

"Compared to the thimble, the candlestick is big, right?"

"*Oui.*"

Miss Tibbins jumped up onto the settee and head-butted Henny's arm.

Henny petted her and scooped her onto her lap. "What about my cat?"

"Compared to the candlestick and thimble, she is big. I understand. The thimble represents the house Monte is used to, so the candlestick seems large to him. Your cat is the places I have lived." Geneviève grabbed a couple of books from a side table and a vase of daisies from the mantel. She set them on the table next to the candlestick, then indicated Miss Tibbins as well. "My grandparents have many homes. The candlestick is small."

"Yes."

"How do we find a house suitable for the thimble *and* the cat?"

"You both will need to make adjustments to living in a place different from what you are used to. If you explain it to Montana like this, he'll understand." At least Henny hoped as much.

"You think so?"

Henny had to give her privileged daughter credit for trying. "I do."

"I must speak to him right away." Geneviève stood and headed toward the front entry.

"Miss?" Silvie followed her. "Do you need me to come as well?"

"No. You may stay here. Would you mend those stockings that have a hole in them?" Her daughter swept out the door.

"Oui." Silvie heaved a sigh.

So did Henny. "I have some errands to complete. Do you need anything?"

"No, madam. I will be fine."

Henny retrieved her reticule from the tea table. "If you need any supplies for mending, my sewing basket is right there." She pointed to it. "Help yourself."

"Merci."

Henny left before anyone else delayed her.

Cordelia's stomach tightened that evening as she and her parents arrived at the Kesners' for supper. Yesterday had been a close call with Master Kesner almost catching her. She would need to tread carefully tonight.

A footman opened the carriage door. Cordelia alighted from the conveyance and went to the front of the manor with her parents. It opened to reveal Lamar lingering in the foyer to greet them. How strange.

Why wasn't he in the parlor where his grandmother presumably waited?

His expression transformed into a mostly authentic smile. "Good evening. We are so pleased you have come."

Cordelia kept one eye on Lamar as he escorted them into the parlor where she and her parents greeted their hostess. As Cordelia moved to sit in one of the chairs,

Lamar touched her elbow.

"It's a pleasant evening. Why don't we take some air in the garden until supper is ready?" He cocked his elbow toward her, eagerly awaiting her response.

She would rather sit where everyone else was so she could remain quiet and not have to put on her vacuous act. Why was he behaving strange?

Her father narrowed his eyes and gave her a negligible nod.

She pressed her mouth into a smile. "I would love to." She giggled for good measure as she hooked her fingers into the crook of his arm. Under normal circumstances, she would enjoy a walk rather than being cooped up inside. But nothing about Lamar Kesner seemed to be normal. Additionally, this little stroll would give her the opportunity to ask him about the tramp from yesterday.

He guided her to another room with French doors leading to a veranda.

The evening air seemed somehow fresher here than even in the front of the house when she'd arrived. Was it truly fresher? Or had the confines of the interior been a bigger contrast than the carriage?

He looked at her differently than before. Almost studying her. What was he thinking?

"Where did you go on your walk yesterday?"

"What?"

"When you left the hotel, which way did you go?"

She extended her left hand and flicked it back at the wrist. "To the right."

He studied her hand. "You're pointing left."

She glanced at her hand. "I always get those mixed up. I guess that's why I often get lost." She giggled to punctuate her inattentiveness.

He squinted a little to indicate his disbelief. "Did you turn left or right?" He indicated one direction then the other.

Was he actually more astute than all her previous suitors? As long as she didn't confirm his suspicions, he would never be quite sure. She pointed left. "That way."

"How far did you walk?"

"I don't know. Does it matter?"

"I suppose not. Perhaps the next time we go on a buggy ride, I could show you parts of Kamola you haven't seen yet."

He seemed *more* interested in her than the first day. He was supposed to be *losing* interest in her.

Lamar Kesner, are you going to be a problem for me?

Her turn to query him and change the subject. "It was awfully kind of you to give that beggar a coin. What made you decide to do that?"

"He obviously needed help, and I didn't want him bothering you."

"Oh, he wasn't bothering me, not really. He merely needed some assistance."

He studied her for a moment. "Some beggars aren't in as much need as one might think. They prey upon unsuspecting people who will too easily turn over money to get rid of them."

"Like you did?"

His mouth hitched up on one side, apparently realizing she had bested him in his own analogy. She probably shouldn't have done that, as it showed more astuteness than she should, but she couldn't help herself. Too bad she needed to discourage him from any kind of attraction toward her, because Mr. Kesner might be someone whom she could mentally spar with. In order to do that, she would have to drop her act. That was something she couldn't do. Even if she wanted to.

The following Monday evening, Lamar stood at the edge of the Atwood ballroom. The gala to celebrate the hotel's opening was in full swing. Everyone who was anyone in Kamola was in attendance as well as many who held no station in town. A refreshing mix.

He had been dreading this gathering all summer, feeling as though he would be on display for any eligible young lady seeking a husband. Now that this event had arrived, he was eager to be here. It gave him a chance to see how Miss Armstrong conducted herself around others. Though he'd seen glimpses of what Thomas was talking about, he had nothing tangible. The mystique surrounding her made him want to learn more—and he would. She couldn't be evasive forever.

While Grandmama circulated among the guests and prominent attendees, Lamar kept his attention on the most breathtaking lady here—Cordelia. Her hair was pulled up with curls cascading all around her head, exposing her long slender neck. She wore a stunning green gown covered in beads. The dress dropped off her slender shoulders with loops of beads dangling on her upper arms, and it hugged her form, fanning out toward the bottom. As she moved around the floor, it flowed like a rippling stream.

With every available man here wanting a dance with her, the poor girl would be exhausted before the night was half over. Everyone except him. He could gather more information from afar.

With the change in tunes by the string quartet, Ian O'Gillis stepped in to be her next partner. His flaming-red hair made him conspicuous in any crowd.

Lamar stiffened. On a good day, he didn't care for the man. Gritting his teeth, he strode onto the dance floor and tapped O'Gillis on the shoulder. When he turned, Lamar smiled. "May I cut in?" Before the man could refuse, Lamar waltzed Cordelia away. She fit nicely in his arms.

"Thank you."

"For what?" Lamar knew O'Gillis was questionable, but did Cordelia?

"I met him earlier." She shivered dramatically. "I felt uncomfortable around him. I don't know why."

Lamar knew. O'Gillis was one-part cunning, one-part scheming, and all cad. Even though his family had money, he was after more. Money he could control without his father lording over him.

"I'm probably being silly." Cordelia giggled.

This dance had been pleasant until that. He sensed she giggled for effect or was it a nervous titter? Was that all there was to her comportment? "Would you like to escape from here?" He knew he wanted to. Grandmama wouldn't be upset if he were with Cordelia. Even pleased he'd taken her away from the others who would want to steal her away from him.

She hesitated as though she might decline, then her green eyes brightened. "Oh, yes."

He escorted her off the dance floor, out of the ballroom, and into the English style gardens. Flowers, bushes, and trees dotted the landscape with a flowing fountain as the centerpiece.

The twilight sky was darker than usual because of the dense cloud cover. "It appears as though the rain that has threatened half the day might finally happen. Would you like to return inside?"

"Not really. I've had my fill of dancing for a while. I would like a respite." Thankfully, she didn't punctuate her words with a giggle.

Returning inside didn't appeal to him either. He guided her toward the fountain.

A small raindrop hit his arm then one on his cheek. Just a light sprinkle, but likely only the beginning.

She glanced skyward. "Oh, dear. The rain has started."

He cupped his palm around her elbow. "Come with me." He escorted her quickly along the stone path away from the building.

She followed, seemingly as anxious as him to not retreat to the hotel's interior. "Where are we going?"

"To the gazebo."

The sky freed its bounty before Lamar secured them cover under the pavilion. He guided her up the steps.

She shook water from her hands and wiped her face. Then she laughed. How unexpected. But not her normal irritating giggle, a normal laugh. A refreshing laugh. One he wouldn't mind hearing again.

The flowing bottom of her dress hung limp. "I'm sorry you got all wet."

"I'm not. When Mother sees me, I won't be permitted to return to the festivities." Though not cold outside, she shivered.

Lamar doffed his coat and wrapped it around her shoulders. As he faced her to make sure the covering sat well, he gazed into her green eyes.

She gazed up at him and whispered, "Thank you."

He brushed back a wet tendril clinging to her cheek. Her skin was soft under his touch.

For a moment, time stilled, and the rest of the world fell away. Only the two of them, nestled close. Neither one moving.

Aware of every breath from both of them and each beat of his heart, he felt rooted in place. He didn't want to leave her presence. How strange.

"Sir? I've brought umbrellas for you and the lady." Must be one of the hotel staff.

Cordelia took a deep breath but didn't shy away at someone being witness to their nearness.

Though disinclined to break the connection, Lamar knew he must and turned toward the man dressed in a black waitstaff suit, holding two open umbrellas. "Thank you, William." He took the first one and offered it to Cordelia. He waved off the second. "You keep that one so you don't get wet. We can both use this one."

Cordelia's eyes widened as though spooked by the prospect.

"Very well, sir." William nodded and strolled away.

He turned to her. "You don't mind us sharing, do you?"

"I don't mind at all." Her voice was soft and alluring.

Surprisingly, it pleased him that she would share an umbrella with him.

After a moment her countenance changed, and she giggled.

However, he didn't relish being outside with this Cordelia. He preferred the other one. The real Cordelia, the one Thomas had described. Could he lure her back out? Now probably wasn't the time. "Shall we head inside?"

Seemingly reluctant, she nodded.

A part of him, also, didn't wish for this moment to end.

Eight

ON FRIDAY, CORDELIA STOOD BEFORE HER parents in the sitting area in their rooms. Miss Henny was expecting her at the quilting circle, so she needed to convince Father to allow her to go. She was already going to be the last one to arrive, but that would be all right. She looked forward to meeting the ladies. And she had been good—very, very good—to give her parents no reason to suspect she was up to anything, which she wasn't today. She merely wanted to attend the quilting circle. If they spoke of how to help the outcasts, so be it.

Her father lowered his newspaper. "No. Unless you are with Mr. Kesner or your mother, you are not to leave your rooms. I can't have you roaming around town unattended." He was obviously afraid she would get "lost" again. "Since your mother has other duties today and Mr. Kesner hasn't called for you, you are stuck here. No pouting about it." He folded the newspaper on his lap.

Pouting often did the trick with her father, but since that was already declined, Cordelia tilted her head, which sometimes changed his mind. Never the giggle, unless she wanted her father to say no. "I thought it would be good to get to know some of the ladies in town. Isn't that what you want? For me to fit in here?"

Father glanced at Mother, presumably for support.

Mother lifted her shoulders slightly. "I don't think it would hurt. She'll get bored sitting in here all day. We don't want her wandering off."

Cordelia smiled inwardly at having Mother on her side. She could sense Father's resolve weakening, so she knelt in front of him and stacked her hands on top of his knee. "Please, Father."

He huffed out a breath. "*If* I allow you to go, I will handpick a driver to take you there, wait, and drive you back."

Cordelia would be there the rest of the day. That was a long time for the poor man to wait. Perhaps she could convince him to take some free time to do as he pleased. "Thank you, Father." She hopped to her feet, pecked him on the cheek, and pranced to her room. "I get to go."

Her lady's maid, Helena, stood at the vanity, tidying the contents there. "I'm so pleased for you."

"Would you help me finish dressing?"

A short time later, Father's handpicked driver stopped the carriage in front of Miss Henny's mint-green boarding house. He assisted her out.

She looped her bag of embroidery around one wrist and retrieved the decorated cake she'd had the kitchen make for her to bring. "Thank you, Bertram. I will be here the rest of the day. You are free to do as you please until I'm ready to leave around four."

The driver shook his head. "Thank you, miss, but I must decline. Mr. Armstrong gave me explicit instructions to remain here."

"I feel bad for you having to wait around idle." But there would likely be no convincing him. "I see the horses of the other visitors in the field. I'm sure it would be permissible to put this one there."

An elderly man approached. "I'm Mr. Hammond. I'll show you where you can park the rig and turn out the horse."

Bertram glanced at Cordelia before following the man.

A wagon pulled up to the house. Dutch and Nan. It halted and Nan hopped down. "We waited until your driver moved away. We didn't want him to know we were already acquainted."

From atop the wagon seat, Dutch spoke. "When do you want me to come get you?"

Nan turned to him. "This wasn't so far. I'll walk back to the hotel."

He gave a nod and drove off.

Cordelia motioned toward the gate. "Shall we go in?"

Nan held out her hands toward the cake. "Do you want me to take that?"

"I've got it. Thank you."

With a nod, Nan walked with her up to the door.

Before Nan could knock, Miss Henny opened the

screen door. "I was afraid you might not make it."

Cordelia had been afraid of that as well. "Please forgive our tardiness." She stepped inside.

"Nothing to forgive." Miss Henny took the cake and led the way to the parlor. "Ladies, I'd like to introduce Miss Cordelia Armstrong and Miss Nan Barwick." She lifted the cake higher. "They brought cake." Miss Henny set it on the dining table in the adjoining room.

Oohs rippled around the circle of visitors.

In a rush and a flurry, Cordelia was seated in a chair and the ladies greeted her and Nan, introducing themselves. They seemed to range from a little younger than herself to a bit older than Miss Henny, maybe as old as sixty. Some of the ladies held babies on their laps while others had various stages of quilt blocks sewn. "I'm very pleased to meet all of you. I'll do my best to remember as many of your names as possible."

Not wanting to appear as a layabout among these industrious ladies, Cordelia removed her project from her bag. Embroidery was an approved activity suitable for a lady of her station. She enjoyed it and liked the beauty it created.

One of the younger ladies across the circle gave a wave of her hand. "We'll help you remember who we are. I'm Franny."

"Thank you." Cordelia also remembered a few, Lily, Isabelle, Adelaide, Henny's daughter Geneviève, and a middle-aged woman named Dorthea. She was sure even those would flit from her memory soon enough.

Miss Henny cleared her throat. "I went out last week to see if I could garner a few more donations for the outcasts. Most of the individuals I spoke to weren't willing to donate. I secured precious little for those in need. There are far more people there than we realized. We need some way to raise money to help them."

Did these ladies not see the obvious in front of them? "What about making a quilt for people to bid on? This is a quilting circle."

"We thought of that, but we already make a quilt each year to auction off during the Founders' Day Festival in September."

Someone else said, "We also can't do a bake sale or a box social."

Miss Henny nodded then shook her head. "Basically, anything that might be seen as competing with the auction or sale of things which are normally part of Founders' Day. We still have some time, so if everyone can be thinking about this, we'll discuss it next week."

Nan held up her hand. "What about a female horse race?"

A dark-haired lady thrust her hand into the air. "I'll do that."

Miss Henny shook her head. "Nicole, you're expecting. You shouldn't be riding a horse and especially not racing one."

Nicole's bottom lip poked out a little.

Cordelia was going to like her.

Another lady, Isabelle, spoke up. "The problem is our ladies who would be most willing to participate are either pregnant, recently had a baby, or their husband or father wouldn't let them."

"Besides, if ladies announce they are going to race horses, the men will decide they need to race horses too. Then we wouldn't be able to."

Cordelia could see that happening. "Which means, we need to come up with something that isn't already being done and that men won't want to duplicate. What about a kissing booth?"

"The festival already has one of those. We have all the traditional booths and events."

This wasn't going to be easy. But there had to be something no one had thought of before that they could do to raise money. Perhaps Lamar might have some ideas.

Nine

ON WEDNESDAY THE FOLLOWING WEEK, LAMAR sat at the breakfast table with Grandmama.

She took a delicate sip of tea from a fine china cup. "Will you be seeing Miss Armstrong today?"

His initial gut reaction was *Do I have to?* However, he surprised himself by actually wanting to spend time with the giggling socialite. "I haven't decided." She hadn't disappeared in nearly two weeks. Thomas had given him daily updates. Perhaps she had finished whatever secret mission she had been on.

Grandmama gave a gentle smile, the one that said she knew something Lamar didn't. "I'll have cook prepare a basket for a picnic. Take her to the other side of our pond. You know the spot, under the big willow tree."

That sounded delightful. A peaceful location. *Wait. What am I thinking?* But he couldn't refuse Grandmama's suggestion, and Miss Cordelia might slip as to where she had gone. "A picnic would be lovely."

Rogers, their butler, entered, holding a small silver tray with an envelope on top. He stood next to Lamar. "Sir, a missive has arrived."

Lamar took it. "Thank you."

Grandmama inclined her head. "Rogers, would you tell Mrs. Blake to make up a picnic lunch for my grandson and Miss Armstrong?"

"Right away." The butler left.

Grandmama's eyes twinkled. "Maybe it's from Miss Armstrong requesting an opportunity to be in your company."

That might be pleasant. Lamar opened the letter. Not from Cordelia or any of the Armstrongs. Mr. Boswell Moseley. He had arrived in town last night with his two daughters and a niece, all of marriageable age.

"Grandmama, what have you done?"

His grandmother's expression turned solemn. "I have done a great many things." She held out her hand. "Let me see that." As she read, her eyes grew wider. "This wasn't my doing. I promise. You have already expressed your feelings about these young ladies. I must agree, none of them are right for you."

Relief swept through Lamar that Grandmama wasn't trying to position one of these young ladies to become a member of the family.

"I'm sorry about this, but your picnic with Miss Armstrong will have to be postponed. We will need to receive the Moseleys. I do hope they don't stay in town long." She picked up the small bell beside her plate and rang it.

Rogers entered a moment later. "Yes, ma'am."

"Call off the picnic basket."

Lamar found the cancellation unexpectedly disappointing. He had looked forward to getting another glimpse of the other Cordelia, the one she didn't allow to show. The one that intrigued him.

Grandmama waved her hand in the air. "Rogers, tell Mrs. Blake we'll be having five guests for lunch."

Had Lamar heard right? "Five?"

She nodded. "Mr. Moseley, his wife, and the three girls. Do you think the Armstrongs should be here for lunch?" Before Lamar could answer, she turned back to Rogers. "Make that eight guests. Have Mrs. Blake meet me in the parlor to discuss the menu."

Rogers bowed and left.

Now, Lamar wished for a solitary picnic with Cordelia, giggles and all. He sighed.

Grandmama tilted her head. "Don't be like that. We have to invite the Armstrongs. We don't want them to think we are attempting to supplant Miss Armstrong's position with you."

The young lady didn't have a position with him. He was biding his time until his grandmother, the

Armstrongs, or Cordelia decided he wasn't worth waiting for. But given the option of spending time with Cordelia or the three Moseley ladies, he would definitely choose Cordelia even if she tittered the whole time.

"I suppose I'll need to invite the Moseley ladies to my mother and daughter tea on Saturday."

Lamar cringed inwardly. "You think they are going to remain in Kamola?"

"If any one of them have designs on you, they will. Would you assist me up?"

If the Moseleys were in town, he was definitely a target. He pushed away from the table and rounded it to Grandmama's chair. Pulling it out, he offered her a hand up.

"While I tend to the menu, write a note inviting the Armstrongs to lunch." With her cane in hand, she glided toward the door.

He didn't really want to, but it was better than having only the Moseley girls here. "I'll do it right away and deliver it myself."

She turned back to him. "Oh, *not you*. Send one of the livery men. We can't have Mr. Moseley trapping you at the hotel with some excuse or lengthy conversation. It's best if you remain here."

Without question, Lamar didn't want to be waylaid.

Reading a book, Cordelia sat on the settee on her side of the adjoining suite with her parents. They had been watching her more closely, making it impossible to slip away. For today, she needed to be content to remain in the hotel or with her mother about town. If she didn't fuss, her parents would relax their attention toward her, then she could meet up with Nan and Dutch. Also, her father would be more inclined to allow her to attend the quilting circle again. She was anxious to know if the ladies had come up with a way to raise funds for the outcasts.

Mother swept into the room. "We have a problem. Get dressed for luncheon." She continued through the room and disappeared into Cordelia's dressing room. When she reentered, she held a flowing, pale-lavender gown draped across her outstretched arms. "Where is Helena?"

Cordelia had given her lady's maid some free time. "Since I wasn't going out today, I released her for the morning."

"This couldn't have happened at a worse time. This is dreadful. Simply dreadful." Mother laid the dress on the bed and strolled through the adjoining door as she continued to talk, mostly to herself.

What was Mother going on about? The opening of the hotel and gala had gone off without any trouble, and they all deserved a much-needed respite. Guests with reservations were arriving as well as ones without reservations. These were successful first days.

Mother reappeared with her own lady's maid. "Eva, my daughter needs to be dressed and her hair coiffed. The gown I've chosen is on the bed."

Cordelia stood, leaving her book on the settee. "Mother? What's going on?"

Mother stopped her fluttering about. "Now hurry and get ready." She whisked out of the room.

Eva took a step toward Cordelia.

Cordelia held up her hand. "I'll be right back." She traced her mother's path through the doorway. "What's going on? Why the urgency?"

Mother stared at her wide-eyed as she drank water. Almost guzzling it. She set the glass on the credenza. "Mr. Moseley checked in yesterday."

What concern was that to them?

Cordelia crossed to her. "What's wrong?"

Mother squared her shoulders. "We must curtail whatever damage has already been done." Her mother was obviously rattled. But why?

"What damage, and what does Mr. Moseley have to do with it?"

"He's brought his two daughters and his niece. He has his sights set on *your beau*. They will be at the Kesners' for luncheon. We have been invited. Hurry up. Get dressed. We want to make sure we arrive ahead of them."

Cordelia needed to stay far away from Lamar. Last week at the gala, something had happened between them in the pavilion. The way his gaze had reached areas deep inside her she didn't know existed. Her thinking had been muddled since.

"That reminds me." Mother picked up the inter-hotel telephone. "I need to call down to the front desk." She replaced the earpiece. "No, I should speak with Milton in person. He'll see to it our carriage is ready before theirs." Mother marched for the door. "Don't dawdle. We haven't time to waste. We don't want one of them taking your place at Mr. Kesner's side." The door clicked shut with finality.

Cordelia welcomed competition for Lamar. Having another lady—or three—stepping in to vie for his attention could solve her problem. Would any of the Moseley girls interest Lamar? Prunella? Colleen? Fancy? Who named their child *Fancy*? She pinched her face. She couldn't picture Lamar with any of those coquettish socialites. He deserved better.

"Miss Armstrong?" Eva spoke from the adjoining doorway. "I should get started on your hair." Her expression said, *We don't want to upset your mother any more than she already is.*

With a sigh, Cordelia returned to her room and plopped with a huff on the stool in front of the vanity.

Eva ran a brush through her hair. "Would you like me to pile it on top with curls or twist it into a chignon at the back?"

"I don't care." Cordelia didn't want to go but also eagerly anticipated seeing Lamar. *No, no, no. Get those kinds of thoughts right out of your head.*

"A chignon would look more sophisticated. I think a man of Mr. Kesner's station would find that agreeable."

Cordelia couldn't have that. "Curls on top and some trailing down." She never liked it pulled tight on her head.

In no time, the Armstrongs' carriage stopped in front of the Kesner mansion.

Before Father got out, he tapped Cordelia's hand. "Remember to remain near Mr. Kesner. Don't allow one of the other young ladies to wander off alone with him."

"If he wants to slip away with one of them, however could I stop him, Father?" If she wanted to occupy all of Lamar's time, she could.

Her father sighed, presumably at her ineptitude, and stepped out.

Now, Mother patted her hand. "Do the best you can, dear." She exited as well.

All Cordelia would need to do is latch onto his arm. The sisters, Prunella and Colleen, would do all they could to unseat Cordelia, but they were no match for her—if she wanted Lamar. Poor Fancy, on the other hand, was unfortunately almost as vapid as Cordelia acted. With any luck, Cordelia wouldn't have to speak at all—or giggle.

After everyone had arrived, Lamar sat at the far end of the table from his grandmother. Had she or Lamar chosen the seating arrangements? Each person seemed to be strategically placed to the Kesners' advantage. Father sat on Mrs. Kesner's right in the seat generally reserved for the male guest of honor. Since there were only two male guests, Mr. Moseley sat in the second ranking male seat. Likewise, Mother had the female guest of honor seat on Lamar's right and Cordelia on his left in the second ranking seat. Show the utmost respect to the parents and get the daughter. Cordelia had other plans.

The four Moseley women sat in the two center chairs on each side of the table. Certainly, the Moseleys understood the importance of the seating arrangements. However, it didn't stop the two Moseley sisters from talking around Cordelia and her mother to speak with the gentleman in demand.

Prunella leaned forward to gaze at Lamar. "Lamar—

you don't mind if I use your first name do you? You may call me Prunella or Pru or Nellie."

The other Moseley sister beamed at Lamar. "And you must call me Colleen. Or...Coll?" She tilted her head as though confused. "Or Leen?"

Her sister glared across the table at her.

Mrs. Moseley's eyes widened at her daughters' boldness. Likewise, Mr. Moseley glanced down the table.

Fancy smiled and shrugged. Wise of her, though she likely didn't realize it.

Cordelia was interested in how Lamar would answer, considering he'd invited her to use his given name the day they'd met.

Lamar took a slow breath. "Miss Moseley. Miss Moseley." He nodded to one sister and then the other. "First names at this stage in our acquaintances would be highly inappropriate and poor etiquette." He glanced at Cordelia, obviously acknowledging the contradiction.

She understood his reasoning in denying the pair. He clearly didn't want to encourage the young ladies. So why had he offered the use of his first name to Cordelia upon their first meeting? He had clearly not been keen on her.

Prunella shifted in her seat. "Oh, of course. I never meant to suggest anything malapropos."

Malapropos? Did she truly believe that using a formal word like that would ingratiate her with Lamar?

Cordelia pitied him. He obviously didn't care for all the attention he received from the Moseleys. Likewise, she found their fawning distasteful. They appeared desperate. However, Lamar remained a true gentleman by being cordial and polite. Too bad she wasn't interested in finding a husband.

Mrs. Moseley apparently decided to assume control of the conversation from her daughters' disastrous attempts. She praised them both and touted their accomplishments, conspicuously leaving out her niece.

Did the vapid young woman realize she'd been abandoned to fend for herself?

Evidently noticing the discrepancy and being a good host, Lamar addressed Fancy. "What about you, Miss Moseley? You've been quiet."

She tilted her head in a shy manner. "Oh, I wouldn't want to bore you with silly lady interests."

Lamar gave a nod of what might be approval to the young lady for not wearying him. "Self-restraint is often underrated."

Fancy let out a small giggle.

Ugh. Was that how Cordelia came across when she behaved that way?

The young woman narrowed her eyes ever so slightly at Cordelia, revealing a more cunning side. Was she biding her time until her cousins took themselves out of the running with their bold behavior? Then theoretically, she could swoop in and snatch her prey.

Cordelia glanced at Lamar. Was he aware of Fancy's tactic? Could she warn him without giving away her own pretense?

Ten

ON SATURDAY, DRESSED IN A FLOWING gown suitable for the mother and daughter garden party, Cordelia stood in front of the mirror in her hotel room. All this money wasted on luxury accommodations. How many needy people could this feed? Her parents were generous people, and their resources were theirs to do with as they wished, but this kind of extravagance didn't go unnoticed by the underprivileged.

If her inheritance from her grandfather wasn't in a trust carefully managed by her father, she could do so much more good than with her little allowance. She merely needed to wait a few months longer until her twenty-fifth birthday, then she would have access to *her* funds. Hence the reason Father was so intent to marry her off. She would instantly become someone else's headache to deal with.

The only other way to free her money, would be to get married. At which time, her new husband would have complete control over everything that was hers. She couldn't let that happen. It would be easier on everyone if she had command of her assets, and if she were independent. If father didn't do something to block her. He could choose to put it in a permanent trust with someone else always in control.

The Lord had called her to help people and her trust fund was the best way to do that. Fortunately, her parents were just as eager as she was to keep the knowledge of her inheritance from any potential suitors.

Her mother entered from the main part of the suite Cordelia shared with her parents. "You look lovely. Mr. Kesner won't be able to take his eyes off you." Though not that shallow, her mother did believe potential suitors were.

Cordelia smiled. "You think so?"

"Of course. Those Moseley girls won't have a chance. They will have traveled all this way for nothing."

Cordelia sighed heavily for effect. "Too bad he won't be there. This is a mother and daughter tea. No men allowed."

"Oh, I'm sure he'll be about and steal glances at you every chance he gets."

Cordelia doubted that. "I hope so." She forced glee into her voice to appease her mother, but the extra beat of her heart hinted at her true feelings. What was wrong with her? She'd never had these kinds of oversentimental feelings about a man before.

"I think he's taken with you."

"Truly?" *Was that real excitement in your question? Stop it, Cordelia.*

"I do. How do you feel about him?"

Oh, dear. Her zeal was going to get her ushered off to the altar if she wasn't careful. "I don't know. I don't think he's right for me."

"He comes from a good family and has an impeccable reputation. We have asked around town, and he doesn't dally with every woman he meets. And believe me, if he wanted to carry on with every available lady in this town, he could."

Not even when they practically throw themselves at him as Nan had done that first day. Her friend had told her how he had pulled away from her and excused himself while remaining polite.

Her mother stood behind her and studied Cordelia in the mirror. "I think you might be too picky when it comes to choosing a husband." She fussed with Cordelia's cascading curls. "If Mr. Kesner gets away, you might not have a choice about the next. Your father is growing impatient. He truly does know best when it comes to these things."

Cordelia's stomach tightened at the thought of her father compelling her into marriage. "He wouldn't truly force me, would he?"

"You have to understand, a man wants to provide for and protect his family. A father needs to know his daughters are going to be taken care of after he's gone. Your two younger sisters are already settled with solid husbands. It's a duty your father takes very seriously. Finding a good husband is how he can ensure a future for you."

"But when I have my trust fund, I can take care of myself."

Mother gave an indulging sigh as though dealing with a small child who had asked to have her birthday every month. "Unfortunately, that's not how the world works. Maybe someday, but it's not how it is today."

Well, the world needed to change. Women were just as intelligent and capable as men. Perhaps that was intimidating to them. It shouldn't be. Adam and Eve had been the Lord's perfect plan to work side by side as equals, each using the strengths God had given them.

Later at the Kesners' after all the mothers and daughters had arrived, Cordelia counted at least fifty ladies of all ages mingling on the lawn. Tables and chairs had been situated near a tent canopy with tables of food.

Cordelia smiled at seeing the friendly face of Lily Hammond from the quilting circle with her two daughters, around ages six and eight. Cordelia remembered the thrill of putting on a special dress at their ages. She crossed over to the pregnant mother sitting in a chair. "I didn't expect to find you here. Shouldn't you be home resting?"

"I'm doing well. My girls missed attending last year. I couldn't disappoint them again. Doc said it would be all right as long as I took it easy. Edric gave the girls strict orders to not let me do a thing, so they're waiting on me hand and foot. It's more restful here than at home." Lily gave a small laugh.

Cordelia nodded. "I suppose it would be."

The woman's two girls ran to her. The oldest held a plate piled with finger sandwiches and fruit. "I brought you food to eat."

The younger one had a plate with cake and cookies on it. "I brought food too."

The girls set their offerings on the table before Lily.

"These are my daughters Estella and Nancy. Girls, this is Miss Cordelia Armstrong."

They both curtsied and said in a sing-song unison, "Pleased to meet you, Miss Armstrong."

These adorable girls tugged at Cordelia's heart. She curtsied back. "I'm pleased to meet you both too." She hoped to have a daughter as cute as these someday—if she had any children at all. "I'm going to go say good afternoon to Miss Henny."

Cordelia had learned, that like herself and Lily, this was Henny's first time to attend this event as well, having recently reconnected with her daughter.

Mother intercepted Cordelia. "Have you seen Mr. Kesner? I can't find him anywhere."

Why should he be here? He was likely as far from this gaggle of women as possible. "He's not a mother *or* a daughter." Cordelia giggled.

"I know that, but this *is* his home. See if you can find him before the Moseley girls do." Mother studied her for a moment then wiggled her hands in a shooing motion. "Go on. Go find your future husband."

Cordelia obediently strolled off in the direction of the rose garden. She wasn't sure if she felt sorrier for herself or for Lamar. Why did parents and grandparents feel the need to hurry their young into marriage?

Maybe she should make more of a show of being interested in him. Perhaps plan a picnic or some other outing. That wouldn't be so bad. After all, he was a nice fellow.

She leaned forward and drew in the scent of a pink rose. Sweet and soothing. Peaceful, off by herself.

As she approached the end of the roses and prepared to return to the festivities, the voices of the three Moseley girls drifted over from the other side of a hedge. Cordelia froze. Which way should she go?

One of the girls said, "I am the best choice to marry Mr. Kesner." That could be Colleen.

"No, I am." If she wasn't mistaken, that sounded like Fancy.

"It's obvious we can't all marry him." That would be Prunella. "When we determine which one of us he seems most interested in, the other two will aid her efforts to get him. It's better that one of us marries him than someone else."

No doubt Prunella planned to win this game of "catch the groom".

"I should be the one to become Mrs. Lamar Kesner."

Sure enough, Prunella had staked her claim.

"I don't think so. Why you?"

"I'm the oldest."

"By twenty-seven and a half days." Clearly, Fancy wasn't going to let her cousin run away with the potential groom.

"I'm still older."

Poor Lamar. Was he aware of how eager these ladies were to be his wife?

"We certainly don't want him to take a liking to that simpering Armstrong girl." So that was what Fancy thought of her.

Cordelia edged along the row of perfectly manicured hedges to put some distance between herself and the Moseley girls. They obviously had their sights set on Master Kesner. Did he favor any of them? He could do so much better.

She headed across the lawn. Glancing over her shoulder, she saw the girls meandering and pointing, as though they were trying to determine which way to go.

Cordelia ducked behind a tree. When the Moseleys wandered the opposite direction, she bolted toward a large building, keeping the tree between herself and where she thought the trio was.

Lamar stood in the loft above his workshop. So far none of the Moseley ladies had discovered him here. Surely, they would hunt for him. He had made sure to escape long before Grandmama's guests arrived and planned to remain secluded for the duration of the event. A strategy that had served him well in years past.

When the main door to the workshop creaked open a fraction, he stepped into the shadows but kept a view of the level below.

Cordelia squeezed through the opening.

His eyes had adjusted to the dim interior, but it would

take several minutes before hers did.

What was she doing here? Should he call to her? He was about to but halted upon hearing the voices of two or more of the tenacious Moseley young ladies milling about.

Cordelia glanced around frantically. Apparently, she'd heard the Moseleys too, so she must have come to hide from them as he had. She hurried to the large wicker basket he would use on his hot air balloon and hoisted herself to a sitting position on the rim. When she lifted her legs, presumably to climb in, she tumbled back in a heap. With no time to right herself before the others entered, she pulled her feet down and dragged the layers of her dress on top of herself.

She resembled a lump of frilly laundry.

When the entry door opened fully, he stepped deeper into the shadows but where he could keep watch on the drama—or comedy—about to ensue.

All three Moseley girls scuttled through the door. After glancing around, they all heaved a sigh in unison as though they were one. Couldn't they have an independent thought?

The younger of the two sisters said, "He's not here."

"That servant assured us he would be here." The cousin.

The older sister spoke now. "Father will see to it the servant is properly reprimanded."

"Where do you think he could be?"

"Maybe he went to the stables?"

"Let's go." The trio left.

That was a close call. Time to head down and let Miss Cordelia know she hadn't gone completely unseen.

Cordelia listened intently for any sign that the Moseley girls had changed their minds and decided to take another perusal of this building. Their voices drifted into the distance. Fortunately, this oversized basket was lined with canvas so they hadn't been able to see her through the gaps between the weaves.

Time to unfurl herself from this uncomfortable

position. Placing her palms on the wooden floor, she pushed herself up slightly but froze. Was that a footstep from within the workshop? She listened.

Whistling suddenly flitted through the air.

Someone was still in here? Who? It couldn't be any of the Moseleys. Had Lamar Kesner been in here after all? It had to be him. She remained perfectly still as the whistling progressed closer.

Please don't see me.

The footsteps came nearer.

Holding her breath, she dared to peer through a grommet in the canvas lining.

Lamar's profile hovered just beyond the wicker. He moved away.

She slowly released the air in her lungs.

He seemed to be walking about the area. An occasional tool clinked to punctuate the tune. How long would she have to remain crumpled like this before he left?

He ventured closer again, leaned his backside against the basket, and poked his elbows out to rest on the lip of it.

She didn't dare breathe.

He spoke. "How long are you going to remain there?"

Who was he talking to? Was someone else present?

He spun around and gazed straight down at her. "What possible reason could you have to hide from that trio of charming ladies?"

He obviously knew she was in here the whole time.

Her embarrassment slipped right into indignation, and she extended her arm. "Be a gentleman and assist me." She giggled as he would expect that.

"First tell me why you were hiding."

"Who said I was hiding?" She gave a goofy smile. "I lost my balance and toppled in."

He pointed to the second level. "I saw you from there. You definitely climbed in on purpose. Granted, your tumble inside was less than graceful."

And he'd merely watched? She gritted her teeth. "Oh, just help me out of here."

He chuckled.

"Never mind. I'll do it myself." She shifted around onto her hands and knees and stood. Then, backing to the edge opposite him, she hopped onto the lip.

Like before, she tottered on the rim.

Lamar hurried to the other side. As she lost her battle for balance, he caught her. "Whoa, there." With one arm around her waist, he tucked his other behind her knees and lifted her. After a few seconds, he lowered her feet to the ground but didn't remove his arms.

Standing in his embrace for a long moment, she enjoyed his gray gaze. His steely eyes exuded power and strength that seemed to hold her captive. She couldn't let this man get entangled in her thoughts, so why couldn't she pull away? She wanted to, didn't she?

The voices of the Moseley girls approached again.

With the haunted expression of a hunted animal, Lamar cleared his throat and let his arms fall to his sides as he stepped away.

She felt the loss of his nearness. What had that been? She shook the feel of his arms comfortably around her from her mind. How could she have allowed herself to slip out of character for even one instant? She wouldn't make that mistake again.

When the Moseleys entered, Prunella spoke. "There you are, Mr. Kesner. We've been looking all over for you."

He gave a tight smile. "Here I am. I trust you ladies are enjoying the party."

"We are now."

The trio descended on the poor man, edging Cordelia to the background.

Prunella touched the sleeve of his shirt. "We decided you should take each of us on an outing."

Lamar's gray eyes widened as he pulled away. "I..."

Cordelia hated that these ladies were cornering him and forcing him to either accept their scheme or to be rude. She stepped next to him. "Oh, he can't do that. He's going to help with a project the quilting circle is doing." She turned to him. "Isn't that right, *Lamar*?" She purposely used his first name to show Prunella Moseley and the others that she was closer to him than any of them. She giggled for good measure.

Prunella opened her mouth, apparently aghast. "A gentleman *does not* belong at a ladies' sewing circle."

Good point. Even though Lamar questioned her with a quirk of his eyebrow, he hadn't rebuffed the idea. Now she needed to invent something fast, so she ventured forward. "Well, not typically, but we're making a bachelor quilt." Where had that come from? Not a half-bad idea. She realized she'd devised a scheme just as calculating as theirs, but this was for his own good. Wasn't it?

Prunella narrowed her eyes. "You aren't having men sew, are you?"

"Of course. It will culminate at the Founder's Day Festival where we'll sell it to the highest bidder. We are still working on the details."

Lamar extended his hands. "Sorry, ladies. My time is spoken for." He hooked Cordelia's hand around his arm. "If you'll excuse us, we have some planning to do." He escorted her from the building.

The more she thought about it, the better a bachelor quilt sounded. Certainly, no one had already conceived such an idea, so it wouldn't interfere with other events or fundraisers. Before Friday when the ladies regularly met, she needed to think through a few of the particulars. If she mentioned the quilt to his grandmother, Lamar would have little choice but to participate.

Once out of earshot, he sighed heavily and released her hand from his arm. "Thank you for rescuing me."

Surprisingly, it had been her pleasure. He might not be so appreciative when he realized he would be hand stitching part of a quilt. She couldn't wait to see that.

Eleven

THE NEXT DAY, LAMAR RODE TO the Atwood Hotel atop his horse. Still being early, he should catch Cordelia. He had to admit she was persistent. She kept up her pretense even when he suspected she knew he knew she was putting on an act. What he still couldn't figure out was why. An alluring puzzle.

Today, the Armstrongs hadn't arranged to come over to Lamar's. Therefore, this would be a perfect opportunity for the young Miss Armstrong to slip away per her custom, though Thomas hadn't caught her sneaking away in recent days. Lamar would make sure to not lose her this time.

A footman approached and took hold of Edelweiss's halter. "Would you like me to unsaddle and stable your horse, sir?" Now that the hotel was fully open for business, a replete staff saw to the needs of guests and visitors.

"No, thank you." Lamar dismounted. "Could you keep her here? I won't be long."

"Yes, sir." He stroked the horse's neck. "I'll tether her by the trough."

"Thank you." Lamar started for the entrance but stopped. "Do you happen to know Miss Cordelia Armstrong by sight?"

"I do, sir. Her type of beauty is hard to miss. She is always very kind."

Though he wanted to ask this man, it wouldn't be appropriate to inquire if he found her vapid or confident. "Do you know if she is still in the hotel?"

"I do. She left more than an hour ago."

That was awfully early but fit with her clandestine actions.

The chances of Lamar locating her were slim, but he could check at the White Hotel. "Was she with anyone?"

Had Thomas arrived before she left?

"No, sir."

So, she *was* still off on her surreptitious endeavors.

"Did she take a carriage?"

"No. On foot, but she had her parasol. She informed me it was a nice day for a walk."

"Thank you." Lamar swung into the saddle again and rode toward the White. Unfortunately, she had arrived and left from there as well. Would it do him any good to roam the streets of town? It hadn't afforded him success before.

He rode out to Thomas's to see if his friend had collected any more information. When he arrived, Thomas was nowhere to be found, so Lamar headed into town again and to the White Hotel. He secured a table facing the doorway in their dining room so he could wait for Cordelia to return to change her clothes.

Hungry from having a light breakfast so long ago, he ordered biscuits covered in a sausage gravy, coffee, and a slice of rhubarb pie.

Halfway through his meal, Thomas swaggered in and sat across from him. He pulled the pie toward himself, snagged the spoon from beside Lamar's coffee cup, and took a bite. He puckered his lips. "More tart than usual. Just the way I like it." He took another bite.

Lamar brandished his fork over the table. "Help yourself."

Thomas waved his hand to garner the attention of the server. "Could I get a cup of coffee, sweetheart?"

When the waitress glanced to Lamar, he nodded. "And a fork for him."

She left, then quickly returned with the utensil and coffee. "Shall I bring another slice of pie?"

Lamar shook his head. The savory portion of his meal had satiated his hunger.

Thomas took a swig of coffee then another bite of pie.

Lamar set his cup on the table. "By the time I reached the Atwood, Miss Armstrong had already departed."

"I know. She hightailed it out of there around seven. I followed her to the White where she donned different clothes, then to Aunt Henny's, and then out into the woods. I came to find you. Thank you for not making me hike all the way to your house. My feet are tired."

Had Lamar understood him right? "You know where she is?"

He drained his coffee cup. "Yep."

"Right now?"

"Yep." Thomas took another bite of pie.

"Let's go before she disappears."

Thomas waggled his fork over the table. "She'll be there a while. I want to finish my pie."

"That was *my* pie."

Thomas took another big bite, leaving only the crust rim, and slid the plate forward.

Lamar set money on the table and stood. "Were you tailing her on a horse?"

"On foot, and my feet haven't recovered yet."

"I'll go to the livery and rent a horse for you."

Thomas stood and gave a dramatic bow. "My feet thank you."

Once they were both on horseback, Thomas led the way out of town.

No wonder Lamar hadn't been able to find her on the streets of Kamola.

Thomas veered off the trail and dismounted.

Lamar did the same. "Are we lost?"

Thomas shook his head and put a finger to his lips. He tethered the horses to a tree branch and motioned to follow him.

What was Thomas doing? Cordelia certainly hadn't come all this way.

Thomas crouched behind some bushes and pointed through the underbrush.

Lamar squinted. Movement in the distance appeared to be people, at least four or five different groupings in a sort of encampment but not Cordelia. He whispered, "I don't see her. Why have you brought me here?"

"She's there. In the shade of those trees with the children."

Lamar studied the group. He recognized the dull, brown dress before he did her, because her face was hidden behind her wide straw hat. "What is she doing here?"

"Helping them."

Colored people, Chinese, Indians, as well as white people all separated themselves by their race but lived in proximity to each other near a water source, a healthy flowing creek. Some in canvas tents, a couple of wagons, and one teepee. "Who are they?"

"Immigrants mostly. People the good townsfolk don't want near them."

"And she's aiding them?"

"Yes, along with the tall blond fellow and the pretty blond lady..." Thomas pointed to the pair. "...brought a wagon with a few provisions. Also, Aunt Henny and Mr. Hammond came with their own rig. They distributed what individuals would accept. The rest, they piled on the ground. I saw one person sneak to the stash while no one was paying attention. By the size of the pile now, I would say that several more people have liberated items from it."

Leaving supplies made no sense. "Why don't they simply take everything at first?"

"They may not have much, but they are proud people."

Lamar shook his head. "I don't understand. If Cordelia and the others are giving all this away for free, why not accept it? You certainly didn't have any trouble taking free food from the Atwood kitchen, and you have less need than these folks appear to have."

Thomas chuckled. "My pride was banished years ago. They feel guilty for not being able to provide better for their families."

Lamar studied the encampment. "They seem to be separated into various races. Why not move their dwellings closer together? They could better assist each other that way."

With a shake of his head, Thomas blew out a breath. "They don't trust one another."

"Then why not camp someplace else?"

"The creek." Thomas inclined his head. "This has the best access to fresh water and level ground."

That made sense to a degree. "What's to stop one of the groups from blocking the water supply from the others?"

Thomas gave Lamar a sideways glance. "Aren't you just full of questions. If they did that, the rest would band together against them, denying them access altogether."

That made sense. "How do you know so much about how they think?"

"I've spoken to a few of them on occasion, those who have ventured into town, and people like them. To simply give them things chips away at their dignity."

Lamar never imagined people lived this way. No permanent home. No employment. No security for the future.

Thomas tapped Lamar's arm. "We should go before someone spies us." He retreated a few paces.

Lamar straightened to his full height. "I'm going over there."

"That's not a good idea. You'll spook them and send them scattering to the four winds with the way you're dressed. They'll think you're an overlord come to kick them off the land."

He didn't have the right, but the person who owned this property did. "To whom does this land belong?"

Thomas shrugged. "Someone who doesn't come out this way often?"

Lamar didn't want to chase anyone away, but he *was* going over to get a better understanding of what was going on. He removed his tie and put it in his suit jacket pocket. Then he took it off along with his hat, handing them to Thomas. "Is that better?"

Thomas rolled his eyes. "You still look like an overlord."

Lamar turned up his shirt sleeves a few times and ruffled his hair, then waited for approval.

"Overlord."

What more could Lamar do?

Thomas closed his eyes and shook his head slowly. "I'm not going to talk you out of this, am I?"

Lamar needed to make a closer inspection at what was happening and to ensure Cordelia was safe. "What if there are bandits in one of the groups?"

"I doubt that." Thomas removed his tattered hat and placed it on Lamar's head. "You won't be fooling anyone, but at least they might be able to see that you're trying."

"Thanks."

"I'll put your things on your horse and return the rented one to the livery."

"Aren't you coming with me?"

"Nope. You going over there will be bad enough. Two strange men tromping where we don't belong will frighten them for sure."

"Mr. Hammond and the large blond man are there."

"They had defenseless women accompanying them."

How would that make a difference? Lamar didn't want to unnerve anyone, merely learn more about these people and Cordelia's involvement with them. "I appreciate you finding out about all of this for me. I'll see you back in town." He turned toward the encampment.

Cordelia sat on the ground with the children scattered around her, telling a story of woodland creatures helping each other even though they weren't the same species. The best way to curry favor with the adults was through their young. It was encouraging to see the little ones had less trouble mingling with different nationalities than the adults. Hope for the future.

Several children's eyes widened. A few stood and shuffled backward.

She motioned with one hand. "It's all right. There is nothing to be afraid of." Her plea didn't quell their fear. She heard no shouts from the camp behind her as to a danger like an animal attack, but the area did seem oddly quiet.

Then one parent after another called their children who quickly obeyed.

Now, she knew something was wrong.

As she turned to look toward the rest of the camp, a deep-voiced man spoke. "Good afternoon, Miss Armstrong." Fancy men's shoes stood next to her.

She let her gaze travel the length of his fancy clothes. *Lamar?* What was he doing here? *Oh, dear.* How had he found her? She forced a giggle. "I thought you were going to call me Cordelia."

He raised his eyebrows. "Your little act isn't going to work on me anymore."

She hoped he wasn't yet fully convinced, so if she remained firm in her behavior, he would soon doubt himself. Rather than outright denying it, she would distract him. She held out her arm. "Do be a gentleman and help me stand."

He took her hand and assisted her to her feet, but when she tried to free herself, he held fast.

Dutch came over. "Release Miss Armstrong." His tone left little room for argument.

Lamar held her gaze. He apparently didn't plan to acquiesce.

Oh, dear. "I'm fine, Dutch."

Her friend didn't retreat but neither did Lamar.

With her hand still held captive by one man, she turned to the other. "You have nothing to worry about." She kept her attention on him until he yielded and joined Nan a few feet away. Most of the residents had withdrawn to the fringes of the encampment, their dwellings, or disappeared altogether. She swiveled her head back to Lamar. "You've scared everybody off."

"That wasn't my intention." His grip on her hand loosened, but he didn't outright release her.

She was reluctant to pull free, so she left her hand in his. "Then what are you doing here?"

"Trying to figure out where you keep disappearing to. Now I know."

He knew she had gone off before? "How did you find me?" Too much time had passed from when she'd left town and arrived here for him to have followed her. He would have come out of hiding before now.

His mouth ticked up on one side. "I have my ways."

That told her nothing. "I must ask you to leave. You have frightened everyone."

He tucked her hand around his forearm at the same time he stepped to stand beside her. "Tell me about these people."

"Why do you want to know about them?" She narrowed her eyes, fully alert and suspicious of the man.

"Does it matter? I just do."

"It does matter. These people don't need any more trouble. Their lives are hard enough."

"Who owns this land?"

Obviously not him. "I don't know." She hadn't thought of that before. If the owner found out people were squatting on his land, he could cause all kinds of trouble for them. However, they hadn't been bothered so far.

He guided her to the middle of the settlement where Henny, Saul, Dutch, and Nan stood. He shook Saul's hand and gave a nod to Henny then indicated the other two. "Introduce me to your friends."

Cordelia gestured toward her large friend and self-appointed protector. "You already sort of met Mr. Mulder. Dutch, this is Mr. Kesner."

Lamar stretched out his arm. "Pleased to make your acquaintance."

Dutch squeezed Lamar's hand and didn't let go. He appeared to be tightening his hold, likely to assert his dominance. Lamar didn't flinch and appeared to be returning the action.

Men!

"Stop it, both of you."

After a moment, they released their grips.

Cordelia expected such behavior from Dutch as she had seen it before but not out of someone like Lamar. Why should he care? Surprisingly, his attention thrilled her. She indicated her other friend. "This is Miss Barwick."

He dipped his head toward her. "A pleasure to be officially introduced. I trust you had no lingering issues from your tumble a few weeks ago."

Cordelia swallowed hard. He recognized Nan.

Nan's eyes widened as she smiled sweetly. "A pleasure to meet you. Cordelia has told me all about you."

"Has she?" Lamar glanced at Cordelia. "I hope at least some of it was favorable."

"Let's just say her final assessment has yet to be made."

Were the pair of them flirting? It shouldn't bother Cordelia, but it did. How to stop it without sounding jealous, because she was definitely *not* jealous.

Lamar returned his attention to Cordelia. "Now, introduce me to some of the people in this community."

Why did he want to meet them? "I don't think..." At the raise of his eyebrows, she trailed off.

"Please."

"You aren't going to make them leave, are you?"

"As far as I know, neither my grandmother nor I own this land, so we have no jurisdiction over it."

"You could tell the owner."

"I won't." He placed his free hand on his chest. "You have my word."

She had little choice but to comply. She walked slowly toward a teepee where three natives stood. "This is Running Bear. He's Kittitas, part of the larger Yakima tribe. Running Bear, this is Lamar Kesner."

Lamar stretched out his hand as though to shake. "Pleased to meet you."

The brave kept his arms folded across his chest. *"Áay."*

Cordelia smiled at Running Bear. "He said hello."

Lamar lowered his hand and dipped his head. *"Áay."* Nearly perfect pronunciation.

How considerate of him to use Running Bear's language. "This is his wife, Little White Dove."

He dipped his head toward her. *"Áay."*

She smiled. *"Áay."*

With a simple hello, he had charmed Little White Dove. Did he do that on purpose? Or was it part of his charismatic personality?

Cordelia indicated a five-year-old boy. "Their son Little Bear."

"Áay."

Little Bear planted his feet and folded his arms, mimicking his father.

Cordelia moved to a pair of Chinese men. "This is Chang and Fu. They're brothers."

"How do I say hello to them?"

"Ni hao."

Lamar faced the men. *"Ni hao."*

Neither man spoke but both bowed, seemingly pleased.

She introduced him to the small band from the Netherlands led by Borga, the few black people in the makeshift village, and a group from Ireland.

"Why do they all stare at me with such suspicion?"

"You have the power to catastrophically disrupt their lives." She hoped he didn't.

"Where are they traveling to?"

"Traveling to?"

"They can't continue to live on someone else's land." He held his hands out from his sides. "They have to be on their way to someplace."

Typical thinking of well-off individuals. "They have nowhere to go. This is where they are for as long as they can remain here safely."

Being raised in privilege, he couldn't understand that not everyone had a "place" to call their own.

Henny, who had been a few steps away, joined them and interjected herself into the conversation. "I think we've been here long enough. We should leave these people in peace."

Cordelia agreed. "I want to stay and let everyone know that they have nothing to fear."

Henny inclined her head. "You and the others go. Saul and I will smooth over any ruffled feathers."

Cordelia nodded then turned to Lamar. "You can ride with us." She would not allow him to stay any longer, stirring up fear in these people.

"Thank you, but I have a horse tethered among the trees. I'll meet you at the White Hotel." Lamar strolled off.

Did he know about her having a room there? Or was it merely a slip of the tongue? Did he know all her secrets? That couldn't be good.

A part of Cordelia ached at his leaving but looked forward to seeing him in town.

When Lamar reached Edelweiss, he slipped on his coat

and swapped out Thomas's hat for his own before swinging into the saddle. He goaded his horse into a trot and reached Kamola quickly. On his way through town, he noticed Thomas on the boardwalk in front of the White Hotel.

His friend must have figured Lamar would come here.

Lamar stopped and tossed Thomas his hat.

Thomas plopped it onto his head. "I felt downright naked without it."

"Thanks for letting me borrow it." His friend had been right that it had likely made the people less fearful of him.

"I'm a little surprised you returned in one piece."

"I was in no danger. The people of the encampment were more scared than threatening."

"I meant the lady. Is she angry with you?"

"Irritated at best." Lamar could handle a little irascibility.

"Was it worth it?"

"Definitely." Lamar inclined his head. "I'm headed over to the land office. Do you want to come?"

Thomas shook his head. "I've had enough of town for a good long while. What business do you have at the land office?"

"I need to find out who owns the land."

"Why do you want to go and do that? Causing difficulties for those people won't ingratiate you to the lady."

"I don't plan to cause any problems for them, but if the land owner gets wind of them there, it could mean trouble. I simply want to see if the man is a reasonable fellow or not." Lamar turned Edelweiss toward the land office.

When he arrived and dismounted, he straightened his shirt, donned his tie, and smoothed his hair before replacing his hat. He strode inside.

Mr. Jenkins sat behind a messy desk with papers and maps piled in disarray on it. He wrote in a ledger and didn't immediately acknowledge Lamar.

Lamar cleared his throat in case the man hadn't heard him enter.

"One moment." Mr. Jenkins wrote one final numeral, blotted the ink, and closed the book before lifting his gaze. "What can I do for you, Mr. Kesner?"

"I need information on the ownership of a piece of land." Lamar described in as much detail as he could about the property's location but feared it wouldn't be enough for identification.

Mr. Jenkins stood and retrieved a large tube of paper from a tall wood box housing several others. He unfurled it atop everything else on his desk. He traced some invisible line on the map. With a tap on it, he muttered to himself and opened a filing cabinet drawer. The paper rolled up on itself.

Lamar stepped closer and uncurled it enough to find the place Mr. Jenkins had indicated. Surprisingly, it seemed to be the right spot.

Mr. Jenkins removed a folder and swung back around to his desk. He eyed the paper Lamar still held open. "Thank you." The file landed atop the map.

How Mr. Jenkins could find anything in this disarrayed space was beyond Lamar's imagination, but he evidently could, so why question it?

"That parcel is part of a larger section of land belonging to the O'Gillis family."

Though not generally a disagreeable fellow, Mr. O'Gillis wasn't known for being particularly charitable nor tolerant of trespassers. His son Ian, on the other hand, would use the people squatting on the land to his advantage and possibly to manipulate Cordelia.

Relief had washed over Cordelia when Lamar hadn't been waiting for her outside or in the White Hotel. At the same time, disappointment niggled within her at his absence. Nor had he appeared in the lobby after she had changed into her designer gown again. She could safely return to the Atwood without having to deal with him or account for her actions, which would give her time to figure out how to approach her explanation of her activities.

Nan headed across the lobby with her. "You're falling for this one, aren't you?"

"What? No. Why would you say that?"

"You're different with him. You gaze at him like a star in the night sky you want to wish upon."

Cordelia had felt the shift inside her toward Lamar at the hotel's opening gala then again at his workshop, but she couldn't yield to it, even if she wanted to. God had called her to help the less fortunate. She couldn't do the Lord's work if she had a husband to control her every move. "You are seeing things. I can't afford to fall for Mr. Kesner or anyone else."

Nan shook her head. "Is your will stronger than your heart?"

"What is that supposed to mean?"

"A person can control a lot of things, but rarely the heart."

"I did with Percy."

"He was different. He wasn't your heart's match." Her friend opened the door.

Cordelia would merely have to work harder at repelling Lamar from her heart and drive any thoughts of him from her mind.

Outside, Dutch helped her into the wagon alongside Nan. It wouldn't be prudent to be seen about town traveling in a wagon alone with a man. Nan provided an acceptable buffer.

A half of a block away from the Atwood, Dutch stopped to let Cordelia off. Before he could assist her down, Lamar appeared, seemingly from nowhere. "Allow me."

Oh, dear. Cordelia hesitated then accepted his offer. She had little choice, as it had been much of this day.

He gripped her waist and lifted her easily to the ground.

When she turned to send her friends on their way, Dutch had his eyes narrowed at Lamar. She tried to capture Dutch's attention. "Thank you. I'll see you two later."

Her protector made no move to leave until Nan gripped his forearm and whispered to him. He snapped the reins, propelling the wagon into motion, but kept his warning glare on Lamar.

Lamar poked out his elbow toward her. "May I escort you to the Atwood Hotel?"

Again, she had little choice, so she tucked her hand around his arm. Not knowing what else to do, she giggled.

"You can drop the giggling act. I know better now."

Did he truly? Or were his suspicions merely stronger now? "You know what?"

He eyed her sideways. "Shall I tell your father where you were today?"

She heaved a sigh. "Very well." She'd had to try.

"I'm glad you're reasonable." Lamar tilted his head toward her. "Why do you pretend to be simple? You obviously aren't."

She supposed it was pointless now. "People expect a lady of my station to be compliant, soft spoken, and to care only about fashion, marriage, and supper parties. And, of course, to be a pretty decoration on a man's arm. No brains or opinions of her own. Vapid."

"You played the part well. That's exactly what I'd thought."

"I merely give them what they are expecting. I suppose you're going to inform my father what I've been doing."

"I haven't decided."

Yet, Cordelia sensed he had decided, but what, she didn't know. "Devise an excuse to break this arrangement my parents and your grandmother have concocted, and you can be free of me. I'll go along with whatever you choose."

"Why would I want to do that?" He thanked the

doorman for opening the door and escorted her inside.

"Why would you want to continue with a situation foisted upon you by others?"

"Because you suddenly became interesting." He turned and simultaneously extended his arm. "Mr. Armstrong, so good to see you."

Cordelia's father shook Lamar's hand. "Mr. Kesner." Father glanced at her. "Your mother was worried about you."

Father's way of wanting to know where she had been.

"My fault, Mr. Armstrong. We ran into each other. I'm sorry for keeping her so long."

She released her captured breath. Why was Lamar covering for her? What ploy was this? And what would he require in return for this favor?

Lamar swiveled to face her, holding her hand in his. "It was a pleasure and enlightening to spend time with you. I eagerly anticipate our next encounter." He kissed her hand. "Good day." He wheeled around and strode toward the exit with the confidence of a man who had been given the world.

What would Cordelia do now?

The leverage he presently possessed could make life very difficult for the downtrodden and for Cordelia. How would he wield this power?

Twelve

IN THE WAKE OF CORDELIA'S UNAUTHORIZED disappearance yesterday, Father refused to allow her to attend the quilting circle today. He wanted her to be available should Lamar call on her. She had dressed and gotten ready, on the off-chance he would acquiesce. The trouble being, Mother was siding with him this time. Cordelia could be assured that one of them would be keeping her in their sights *all* day.

After dropping her embroidery bag onto the settee, she proceeded to tug off her crocheted gloves one finger at a time. Regaining her parents' trust would take a while. Though she had returned with Lamar, they knew she hadn't left with him. For if she had, he would have called for her via one of her parents. Her goal had never been to deceive them, only to assist the less fortunate. If they knew what she was up to when she disappeared for extended periods of time, they would forbid her from helping those people.

Cordelia tossed her gloves onto the bed as she crossed to the open French doors and walked onto the balcony. A new complication had been added to her life. Lamar Kesner. Though grateful he hadn't exposed her secret, she did wonder what he planned to do with the information about the outcasts.

Soon Mother joined her. "Your prayer has been answered."

She mostly prayed for a way to escape, which she doubted was what Mother spoke of. "Have you and Father changed your minds about allowing me to attend the quilting circle?"

Mother gave her a withering look. "Not after yesterday. Honestly, Cordelia. I can't imagine where you wander off to all the time."

Cordelia appreciated their lack of creativity in this area. "I don't see why you won't let me go. The ladies were very nice." She wanted to tell them of her idea for a fundraiser. "I promise not to go anywhere else. Like last week, you can send a driver with me."

"When you vanish for hours on end, we worry about you. You have always had a propensity to meandering aimlessly, ever since you learned to walk. There are many unscrupulous people who wouldn't hesitate to harm you or hold you for ransom."

Cordelia had never liked being confined. "If you aren't permitting me to attend the quilting circle, then what prayer of mine has been answered?" Perhaps relinquishing control of her trust fund for her to use as she wished? Even more doubtful than allowing her to attend the quilting circle.

"Leaving your room."

Though pleased, Cordelia sensed a catch. "Leave for where?"

"You'll have to ask Mr. Kesner. He's come calling for you." Her mother smiled broadly.

Cordelia's heart danced. Lamar? *Wait. Stop it, Cordelia.* She shouldn't be eager to see him. He could ruin everything for her. So far he'd kept her secret. But for how long? She shouldn't go with him, but what choice did she have? If she refused, he could tell her father what she'd been doing. One false move from her and he still might.

Mother proffered the hat that matched Cordelia's dress. "Come now. Don't keep him waiting."

After pinning on the hat, Cordelia snatched the crocheted gloves she'd tossed onto the bed. Her game of cat and mouse just turned more precarious. She slipped on the gloves and fastened the little pearl buttons at her wrists then trailed her mother into the adjoining rooms.

With his hat in his hand, Lamar stood with her father, talking. As though sensing her presence, he turned and bestowed a warm smile on her.

Cordelia's breath caught at the sight of him. Her heart rejoiced at the same time her stomach twisted with trepidation at what he must be telling her father. She needed to stop reacting like a silly schoolgirl. Especially now that he had knowledge he could use to try to bend her to his will. She curtsied. "Good morning, Mr. Kesner. We weren't expecting you."

"It's a mite better morning now that you're here." His expression enlivened, sending her heart skipping about.

No, no, no. Stop reacting to him in any way.

Father raised an eyebrow. "Mr. Kesner has called for you."

Lamar stepped forward. "I know I've surprised you, but I'm hoping you'll agree to spend a portion of your day with me."

"She would be delighted to." Father eyed her. "Wouldn't you, Cordelia?"

She couldn't very well turn him down with Father and Mother so eager for her to be courted by Lamar. As well, it would give her the means to escape her hotel room. She dipped her head. "I would be honored." Maybe after an hour or so she could convince him to part ways with her. She couldn't use her normal ruse of shopping for clothes to rid herself of an unwanted suitor because he was wise to that ploy. If she could persuade him to go off on his own, then she would still be able to attend the quilting circle.

Mother gave her a parasol. "Here you go. You wouldn't want the sun to parch your delicate skin."

"Thank you, Mother." Cordelia preferred shade to the blazing sun.

Lamar motioned toward the door. "Shall we?"

She preceded him from the room.

He escorted her along the corridor to the elevator. "Let's not forget, I know your secret, so please refrain from inane giggling. It's not becoming."

How could she, when he held such power? "Let's not forget that you are a gentleman. I trust you will behave as such."

A twinkle danced in his gray eyes almost like sparks of light. "Always."

That remained to be seen. However, his treatment of her today would reveal a lot about his character.

Once downstairs and outside, he replaced his hat as he guided her to a waiting buggy with the Kesner crest on the side. After helping her into the open vehicle and climbing in, he set the rig into motion.

She pushed open her parasol, blocking the beating sun. "Where are you taking me?"

"You don't know?"

Had Mother said while Cordelia hadn't been paying attention? "How should I?"

"I'm surprised. This was your idea."

"Mine? You're blaming me for this?" Even though he was taking liberties, she enjoyed the banter. Much nicer than acting like a witless female, but if Mr. Kesner thought he could match her in a game of cleverness, he'd best think again.

He glanced at her sideways. "Blame?" He paused as though weighing the word. "I think that's accurate."

Lamar had suddenly become insufferable, and yet intriguing.

"Are you going to tell me where you're taking me, or not?"

He chuckled. "You'll see."

His laugh both warmed her and comforted her.

After a few minutes, she couldn't stand the silence. "If you won't tell me what our destination is, tell me why you have a hot air balloon basket in that large building on the Kesner estate."

He guided the horse around a donkey cart full of cut wood. "I'm surprised you know what that was."

"I'm not so sheltered that I haven't seen hot air balloons before. Do you have a balloon to go with it or only the basket?"

"I have built two fully functional balloons. This will be my third. It will have the most modern heating apparatus technology." He tilted his head toward her. "Don't tell my grandmother you know about it."

"Your grandmother doesn't know you have a hot air balloon? How can you keep something so large hidden from her?"

"She knows. She merely prefers I don't announce it to..."

"To a prospective bride?"

"Yes. Not that I assume we'll marry. I have no such plans."

"Good, because neither do I." A part of her was relieved he wasn't going to push for a marriage between them, yet disappointment swirled within her. Did he not find her worthy of considering for a wife? Then she heard her own vapid giggle in her head. The point of her act had been to make sure he wouldn't be interested. As he had said, she played the part well. Now that he knew she had been deceiving him with her pretense, he would be even more unlikely to wish to court her. Why did that trouble her so much?

Soon, he pulled to a stop in front of Miss Henny's boarding house.

She frowned at him. "What are we doing here?" This is where *she* wanted to be, but why would he come here?

"The quilting ladies do meet today, don't they?"

"Yes, but..." She had given up the expectation of being able to attend today.

"I seem to recall you saying something about a bachelor quilt. Whatever that is." He climbed down and held up his hand.

Was he serious? She took his assistance. "Why would you come willingly?"

"You did tell the Moseley girls I was helping you. This is me helping."

Did he believe this would be the sum total of his involvement? If she could figure out the logistics, he would be doing a whole lot more.

Time to part company from this charming lady, but before Lamar could, a woman called from down the road, "Cordelia."

He turned to see her friend approaching.

Cordelia greeted her. "Nan."

Lamar pinched the brim of his hat. "Miss Barwick, it's a pleasure to see you again."

The young woman blushed and dipped her head to him. "Thank you. It's good to see you as well." She focused back on Cordelia. "I was afraid you might not make it."

"I felt the same." She indicated Lamar with a swivel

of her wrist. "Thanks to Mr. Kesner, I'm here."

Lamar had suspected she might have difficulty escaping the hotel today.

She went on. "He's agreed to be of service with our fundraising event."

That was his cue to depart, so he tipped his hat. "I will leave you ladies to your gathering. I'll return this afternoon."

Cordelia hooked her fingers into the crook of his elbow. "Oh, but you must come inside so the ladies know you are a willing participant."

He had already concluded with all the assistance he had imagined would be required of him. Now, he got a sinking feeling he'd stepped into something bigger than he planned. "I wouldn't want to intrude. As Miss Moseley said, a man doesn't belong at a quilting circle."

She tightened her hold on his arm. "The ladies will be so pleased you're here. I promise."

Her friend nodded. "I don't know what Cordelia has in mind, but I'm sure it will be a huge success." She headed up the walk.

Lamar motioned toward the buggy. "I can't leave the horse unattended and untethered."

"I'll see to him." Mr. Hammond stood at the horse's head and appeared to be struggling not to laugh.

Where had he come from? And how long had he been witness to Lamar's exchange with the ladies?

Lamar suddenly regretted his actions this day. Simply greet the ladies then he would depart. "I won't be long, so no need to unhitch him."

At the door, Miss Henny greeted them. "Good morning, ladies." She eyed Lamar. "Are you coming in as well?"

Cordelia spoke before Lamar could order his thoughts. "He is. We have a fundraising idea." She made eye contact with him as though daring him to contradict her claim.

If he renounced his participation now, he would be going back on his word. Though sensing he might further rue coming, his desire not to disappoint Cordelia outweighed his discomfort. He'd gone along with her ploy, so he needed to stick with it to the end to keep her from being a liar. He was nothing if not chivalrous.

As Lamar entered the parlor behind Miss Henny, Cordelia, and Miss Barwick, a hush fell over the room. A dozen or so pairs of querying eyes stared at him, an anomaly in this gathering. Like a red dress at a funeral.

He dipped his head. "Good morning, ladies."

Greetings rose from around the room, some almost mumbled as though confused, while others were clearly voiced.

Mrs. Atwood rose from her chair. "Mr. Kesner, what brings you to our humble gathering?"

What indeed. "Miss Armstrong wished for me to come in and bid you all a good day." He glanced at Cordelia. "I'll take my leave now."

She slipped her hand around his forearm. "Not yet. We must tell them about our fundraising plan."

"I'm not privy to the details of *your* plan." Though he enjoyed her touch, he wanted to leave. No, he *needed* to leave.

Miss Henny motioned. "I would offer you a seat, but all of my chairs are taken up by the ladies."

With so many women staring at him, he felt very much on display, like the only slab of beef hanging in the butcher's window surrounded by a pack of hungry wolves. "That's all right. I'm not staying." He willed Cordelia to move this along.

"It will only take a few minutes, then you may go."

She was giving him permission? When had he lost the advantage he'd gained yesterday?

Miss Henny retrieved a small piece of stitched fabric from the arm of the settee. "Cordelia and Nan, why don't the two of you sit?"

Miss Barwick took a seat.

Cordelia remained on her feet. Next to him. No doubt to keep him from fleeing. "I'll stand for now."

Miss Henny nodded. "Please tell us your idea, then Mr. Kesner will be free to get on with his day."

"Has anyone ever made a bachelor quilt?"

Faces around the room appeared as confused as he was. Most shook their heads.

"So, if we made one, we wouldn't be stepping on any toes at the Founders' Day Festival?"

More shaking heads.

One of the ladies asked, "Are we going to make quilts for bachelors? Then they buy them?"

Someone else said, "I don't know if we have time to make a bunch of quilts. We haven't even finished the one we will be donating for the auction."

Cordelia had thought about this long into the night but hadn't come to any definitive conclusions of how such an event would work. However, she had an idea or two. "We don't make quilts for bachelors. Bachelors make a quilt to be sold or auctioned."

This was what she had been getting at?

Lamar swallowed hard. "You expect bachelors to actually sew a quilt? That will never work."

Several ladies voiced their agreement.

"You have me intrigued." Miss Henny widened her eyes. "Go on."

"I haven't ascertained the details. Basically, several bachelors would each piece a quilt block. Then they will sew the blocks together and quilt the layers."

"Wouldn't it be easier if we did it ourselves?" one of the ladies asked.

It would be so much easier for the ladies to sew it themselves, especially for me.

"How will having bachelors sew raise any money? People would merely think we made the quilt."

Cordelia made eye contact with several of the ladies. "The bachelors could pay an entrance fee to participate."

More head shaking and skeptical looks.

"Men can't sew."

Cordelia offered her palms. "We would assist them."

"Why would bachelors agree to do this?"

Cordelia's eager countenance at the beginning of her explanation diminished to defeat. "Like I said, I haven't quite sorted out the particulars. Between all of us, we can come up with a way to make it work."

Most bachelors wouldn't volunteer to participate and certainly not pay to do something they didn't want to do. "Men aren't going to pay to sew. Or to be humiliated."

Cordelia faced him. "How could we convince them to both pay and participate?"

"A pretty face." He hadn't meant to say that aloud, but it wasn't a bad idea.

Confusion marred the expressions around the room.

Cordelia narrowed her pretty green eyes. "Explain."

He was going to regret this. He should cease talking and not open his mouth again. "Bachelors would pay to have a lady help them."

"They would?"

He hated to make the confirmation, because it would put him right in the middle of it. "They would. Also, people, both men and women, would likely pay to watch bachelors fumble about with a needle and thread."

Cordelia's eyes brightened. "That means, it could raise money three ways. The bachelors, the spectators, and the quilt itself."

Miss Henny beamed. "Marvelous idea."

Agreements echoed around the parlor.

Miss Henny gave him a steady gaze. "Mr. Kesner, can we count on you to recruit an additional bachelor or two?"

This was bad enough he would be forced to participate. How could he convince others to do so? "I don't know how successful I'll be, but I'll ask around. If you don't need me for anything else, I'll take my leave."

"You have been a huge help."

"Before I go, what are you raising money for? It might aid in enlisting others to take part."

"The people camped outside of town."

Telling potential candidates that bit wouldn't be a benefit. He would determine what best to say to entice unwilling victims. He dipped his head. "Good day, ladies. I'll leave you to decide on the details." He retreated from the room.

Cordelia escorted him to the door. "Thank you so much for going along with this."

The gratitude in her expression just might make participation worth it. "I wouldn't inform people what you are raising money for. At least not at first. Let them get used to the unorthodox idea first."

"Probably wise. Your involvement will make this so much more successful. I'm sure we'll be able to raise more money because of it."

He might not mind taking part if no one else in town would be privy to it, but the point of him participating was to make more people aware of it and want to pay to see the spectacle. "I'll be back this afternoon." He exited while he still could and returned to his buggy. This was not at all how he'd expected the day to go. However, he knew who was going to join him in this quilting fiasco.

When Lamar reached his buggy, Thomas sat in it. Precisely whom he wanted to see. "Good morning."

His friend shook his head. "As I feared."

Lamar grabbed the side of the vehicle and climbed in. "What has you in a fit of pique?"

"You're up to something. You aren't returning to the encampment, are you?"

"Why would you think that?" He snapped the reins, putting the buggy into motion.

"Because I know you."

Lamar didn't want to be talked out of anything he'd planned today. "How did you know I would come to Miss Henny's at this time?"

"I followed you."

"On foot?"

"Wasn't hard. You were walking the horse pretty slow. No doubt to spend more time with the beautiful Miss Armstrong. Be on your guard or you'll fall into her trap."

"She has no trap. Apparently, she doesn't want to marry me any more than I do her." Which irked him for some reason. He had no interest in a woman who played games.

"And yet, you are still trapped. She says she's not interested in you, which makes you all the more interested in her."

He couldn't deny that, but neither would he admit it.

Thomas went on. "The way I see it is, the little lady has a heart for those people which will cause you to make it *your* mission to do all you can for them to ingratiate yourself with her. The best thing you can do is to leave those poor people in peace."

He could have done that and probably would have until he learned who the land holder was. "The O'Gillises own that acreage."

"How do you know?"

"I inquired at the land office."

"This could mean trouble."

"Exactly. If Mr. O'Gillis discovers there are squatters on his property, he'll run them off. If his son learns that Cordelia has a soft spot for them, he'll use it to his advantage. You should have seen the way he looked at her during the hotel opening gala."

"Ian? Not good. How are you going to keep him from learning about them?"

"I have a couple of ideas. I'll let you know when I settle on something."

"Anything you want me to do, I'll do it."

Lamar grinned at Thomas. His friend would probably live to regret that statement. "I'm glad to hear you say so. We are volunteered to help Miss Henny's quilting ladies with a project to raise money to assist the people at the encampment."

"If it undermines the O'Gillises, you can count on me."

His friend might not be so eager once he learned sewing was involved. But no need to inform him yet.

"I'll let the ladies know they can depend on you."

After Thomas had discouraged him from returning to the encampment, Lamar headed to the Washington State Normal School to recruit one of the professors. Isaac Hughes leaned heavily toward cerebral endeavors and went mute or stammered around the ladies. This might be the right opportunity to force him out of the pages of his books.

Lamar rapped on the doorframe of Isaac's office. "You busy?"

Isaac looked up from the weighty tome lying open on his otherwise clear desk. "Not particularly. Come in." As he stood, he closed the oversized book, then tucked it away on the shelf next to his desk, aligning it perfectly with the others. Isaac was fastidious about everything being in its proper place. One thing put to right before starting another, even a short conversation. "Please have a seat." He retook his chair.

Lamar sat. After a few pleasantries, he broached the topic which had brought him here. "I've offered to help Miss Henny with a fundraising project. Would you be willing to join me on it?"

"For Aunt Henny and charity? Of course."

Miss Henny's popularity in town made people want to do for her regardless of the reason. If Isaac knew he would not only be sewing but also working closely *and talking* with a young woman, he would run as far from Lamar as possible. Lamar had every confidence, with a little encouragement, Isaac would do fine. Once he had the task at hand to focus on, he would be less nervous with a pretty lady at his side.

Being vague about the nature of this project, thus far, had served Lamar well in recruiting a couple of his friends. If Lamar had to participate in this farce, he wanted to be assured he wouldn't be alone. Also, he wanted Cordelia's endeavor to be a success.

Cordelia knotted off the thread on the border sash of the quilt the quilting circle was donating to be auctioned at the Founders' Day Festival. She had been glad to contribute since she hadn't brought along her embroidery like last time. The top of this beautiful star quilt was nearly complete. It should fetch a good price. The proceeds were going toward paving the main streets in town. The quilt the bachelors would make wouldn't be nearly as exemplary as this one but, nonetheless, for a worthy cause.

Mr. Hammond peeked in the parlor. "I don't mean to disturb you ladies, but Mr. Kesner is here for Miss Armstrong."

Cordelia lifted her head. "He is?" The quilting circle usually stayed for at least two more hours.

Mr. Hammond bobbed his head. "He's waiting out front."

Miss Henny gave her a nod. "That's fine. You go. We have everything well in hand."

Cordelia stood. "Thank you."

Nan stood as well. "I'm going to leave with her. Thank you, Aunt Henny, for your hospitality."

On the porch, Cordelia glanced at her friend sideways. "You don't have to leave because of me."

"You know Dutch. If he's left to his own devices too long, he gets twitchy." Nan descended the steps next to her. "Besides, I want to get another gander at your beau."

"He's not my beau," Cordelia said in a hushed tone.

Nan chirped her disbelief and reached the buggy first. "Good afternoon, Mr. Kesner."

Lamar had climbed down a moment before she reached him. "Good afternoon, Miss Barwick." He dipped his head to her then turned to Cordelia. "I hope you don't mind my arriving early, but I'm expected at home, and your father won't be happy with me if you arrive alone. He'll think I abandoned you."

"True, but I would be the object of his displeasure."

He flashed a mischievous smile. "We can't have that."

Nan stepped aside. "I should be getting back to the hotel."

Lamar proffered a hand. "We'll give you a ride."

"I don't want to trouble you."

"What kind of gentleman would I be to make a lady walk?"

Cordelia hooked her arm with Nan's. "It's settled.

We'll take you." Which meant less time alone with the handsome bachelor. His nearness was a danger to her heart.

Lamar assisted them both in, squishing Cordelia between the two. Perhaps Nan being along wasn't as favorable of an idea as Cordelia had imagined. The scent of a spicy cologne wrapped around her, drawing her closer. She blocked the aroma and the bearer of it from her mind.

Soon Lamar stopped in front of the White Hotel. "Wait for me to assist you, Miss Barwick." He shifted to exit but halted.

Dutch appeared at the side of the buggy and lifted Nan to the ground.

Lamar leaned forward. "Mr. Mulder, it's a pleasure to see you again."

Dutch glared. "Mr. Kesner."

Cordelia couldn't understand Dutch's issue with Lamar. She would need to speak with him about it the first chance she got.

Lamar drove away. "Is there something between you and Mr. Mulder?"

"What? No. Why would you think that?"

Lamar shrugged one shoulder. "He acts jealous. Is he the reason you try to turn suitors away?"

"No. I have absolutely no romantic feelings for Dutch, and I doubt he has any for me. You have nothing to worry about where he's concerned. Nothing at all."

Lamar smiled. "Good to know."

Oh, dear. She had protested too much, but there *wasn't* anything between herself and Dutch.

At the Atwood Hotel, Lamar escorted her inside where Father stood speaking with a hotel staff member. He immediately broke off his conversation and crossed to them. "Lamar, welcome. I trust the pair of you had a pleasant day?"

Cordelia could read in her father's tone, expression, and the way he carried himself, he was also saying, *I'm glad you didn't lose my daughter. She has a tendency to wander away.*

Lamar dipped his head. "Quite enjoyable. Your daughter is enchanting."

Father raised his eyebrows, evidently disbelieving the statement.

She could be enchanting when she wanted to be.

Lamar patted Cordelia's hand on his arm. "Be ready soon after sunrise tomorrow."

"Why so early?"

"I have a big day planned for us." He flashed her that mischievous smile again. "Would seven o'clock be more to your liking?"

Evidently not wanting Cordelia to turn Lamar down, Father spoke. "She will be fully prepared for your arrival."

With a nod, Lamar left.

Though she couldn't think of any activity which warranted rising by dawn, she was intrigued.

Thirteen

THE NEXT MORNING, CORDELIA FIDGETED IN one of the many hotel lobby padded chairs. She lifted the lid of the picnic basket sitting at her feet. Since she was leaving so early, Father had instructed the hotel kitchen to prepare a casual breakfast with an array of foods for her and Lamar. Strawberries, blueberries, cheese, egg salad sandwiches, cookies, and a few other things deeper in the bottom of the container.

"Would you leave that be?" Father sat in an adjoining chair, reading a newspaper he'd had sent in from back East. "Its contents haven't changed in the last two minutes."

After letting the lid drop, she straightened with a sigh. Where was Lamar? She tilted her head just so, to keep the wide brim of her hat from bumping against the back of the chair and knocking it askew. Now, she could glance at the entrance.

Again.

Father pulled out his pocket watch and flipped it open. "It's ten of seven. Now sit still. He'll be here."

She wasn't worried, not really. He'd always been punctual, even arriving when she least expected him. She fidgeted only because she was anxious to know what Lamar had planned at this hour.

One of the hotel's livery men entered from the front door and went to the registration desk. The livery men only came in from there on the behest of a patron. Milton, at the desk, pointed across the lobby to her father. Must be hotel business.

The livery man crossed to Cordelia and her father. "Sir, a carriage has arrived for your daughter."

Cordelia jumped to her feet.

Father gave her a stern look. "Cordelia."

She lowered herself into the chair again.

Father spoke to the man. "Is the gentleman not coming inside?"

"There isn't any gentleman, merely the driver. He's come from the Kesner estate."

Father set the paper aside and stood. "I'll see what this is about. You remain here." He walked toward the entrance.

Stay put? Not possible. She stood and hoisted the basket.

The livery man took the hamper from her. "Allow me, miss."

"Thank you." She hustled after Father, reaching him as he sized up the impressive enclosed carriage with the Kesner crest on the door.

Father spoke. "Where is Mr. Kesner?"

The driver stood at attention next to the conveyance. "Master Kesner sent me..." He inclined his head toward Cordelia. "...for Miss Armstrong."

Father swung around and rolled his eyes at her. Returning his attention to the driver, he said, "Why didn't he come himself?"

"He was needed elsewhere."

Intriguing. The more she learned about this man, the more she wanted to know. Cordelia approached the vehicle. "We don't want to keep Mr. Kesner waiting."

The driver opened the door.

She hesitated for Father's approval.

He gave a reluctant nod.

Cordelia climbed in before he could change his mind.

The livery man placed the picnic basket on the floor.

When the door closed her father spoke to the driver. "Tell Mr. Kesner I expect him to come personally to call for my daughter next time."

"Yes, sir."

The conveyance rocked slightly as the driver climbed to his perch. Then it lurched into motion.

This was both puzzling and exhilarating. She never would have imagined Lamar to be so fascinatingly mysterious.

After tugging off a glove, she ran her hand over the

luxurious deep-green velvet seat. Soft. The tan silk, which covered the walls, was ruched together into circles on the front, rear, and roof. He'd obviously sent one of their finest vehicles. Was he trying to impress her? Unsure how she felt about that, she pushed the thought aside to contemplate at another time.

At the Kesner estate, the driver steered past the main house, then the carriage house, the stables, and the large building she'd hidden in to escape the Moseley girls. The well-maintained drive went through a wooded portion of the property. Still, he didn't cease. Where was he taking her? Was she still on Kesner land?

Eventually, the trees parted, revealing a field. In the center sat a huge floating balloon.

Cordelia's breath caught at the rainbow striped monstrosity.

The vehicle rolled to a stop several yards away.

She didn't wait for the driver to climb down and assist her. Instead, she flung open the carriage door and stepped out, her gaze held captive by the colorful sphere confined by an enormous net. As though pulled by an unseen force, she moved toward the structure.

Lamar seemed to be giving instructions to the handful of men scattered about.

One of them with a scruffy beard inclined his head toward her.

Lamar turned with a smile. "You made it."

She had apparently surprised him. Good. That might keep him mentally off balance. "Did you doubt I would?"

"It is pretty early."

She would normally only be rising at this time. "What lady doesn't enjoy a little intrigue when it's dangled in front of her?"

"I know plenty of ladies who would have found a request to be ready so soon after first light to be rude and unacceptable."

"Are you implying I'm not a lady?"

His eyebrows shot up. "What—? No. I—"

Oh, he was fun to tease, but that wouldn't attain her an excursion into the air. "Do say you will allow me to go for a ride in your hot air balloon."

"And here I thought it would take a great deal of cajoling to convince you to go with me."

Why did people—both men and women—think ladies were altogether frail and unable to cope with the unordinary. "Contrary to what some believe, few women actually faint at the least provocation of an unconventional task." She snapped open her fan and strolled past him.

He fell into step beside her. "Have you ever fainted?"

She huffed a breath. "Sir, you insult me." She swung around to face him. "Are you going to take me up or have you wasted my time?"

"I have found that time with you is never wasted." He stared at her large hat. "Before we go. There's an open flame. Would you mind—"

Lifting her arms, she yanked out the two hatpins, then tossed the hat and pins into the grass. She refused to allow the norm of women wearing hats to keep her from this adventure.

He chuckled. "...removing your hat."

"Let's go." At the side of the basket, she gripped the rim to hoist herself up. She hoped she didn't tumble in as she had last time.

"Wait."

He wasn't going to deny her a ride, was he? What else did she have on that he might disapprove of?

He motioned to the other side of the square, wicker container. "Over here."

She rounded the structure. "Steps. Ingenious." Had those been next to the basket when it was inside that building and she'd fallen in on her backside?

"I wouldn't want you to go headlong inside."

She touched her upper chest with her gloved fingertips. "I would never do something like that. I'm a lady."

His eyebrows twitched. "Of course not." He offered his hand, assisting her up and in.

Exhilaration coursed through her body, causing her skin to tingle all over. She was about to fly high into the air and see the world as God might. Not exactly like God, but closer than being earthbound.

The carriage driver handed Lamar the food hamper. "The lady had this with her."

Lamar lifted the lid a crack to peer inside.

Cordelia extended her arms. "It's a picnic breakfast. Since we were leaving so early, Father thought it might be nice. I can put it in here."

With an approving nod, Lamar lifted it over the rim, setting it on the floor. Then he gave instructions to his ground crew before climbing inside. He checked the lines of the balloon net where they attached to the basket. Seemingly satisfied, he fussed with the heating mechanism then pulled a wooden handle on a chain, causing the burner flame to shoot higher with a hiss into the opening at the bottom of the silk.

She gasped at the blast of noise.

Lamar glanced at her with concern. "It's all right. This is safe. I don't want you to be scared."

"I'm not afraid. I wasn't expecting such a loud sound." This could possibly be the most exciting thing she ever did.

He pulled on the burner chain for a longer blast than before. "Cast off."

Several lines were released from their moorings in the grass.

The balloon didn't move.

Once again, Lamar pulled on the chain.

"Why aren't we rising?"

"Give it a few more seconds." A smile spread slowly across his face. Then the basket creaked as it rocked slightly, lifting slowly off the ground.

A small squeak escaped from Cordelia. She had just left the earth, never having imagined she would do such a thing.

The balloon rose almost to the treetops and hovered there.

Lamar motioned with his arm. "You can see Kamola over there."

She peered between the trees in the direction he indicated. The town seemed both bigger *and* smaller than from the ground. Smaller because the buildings seemed to have shrunk to a toy-like size. Yet bigger, because she could see so much of it at once from the downtown area buildings to the normal school to the acreage of the Atwood Hotel to the sprawling ranches beyond. The beauty of the world God had created took her breath away.

After taking in the panoramic view for several minutes, she realized they had stopped. Was this it? Was this all there was to a balloon ride? Shouldn't there be more? "We don't seem to be moving. Shouldn't we still be rising? Does it need more hot air?"

"We remain tethered to the ground."

She glanced over the side. Sure enough, a rope trailed from one corner of the basket all the way down to where four men stood, staring up at them, somewhere between five to ten stories.

"Why are we tied to the ground?"

"I didn't want you to get frightened by floating too far."

"I don't have a weak constitution. I want to fly as high as we can go."

He raised his eyebrows. "If you're sure."

Though a slight apprehension squirmed in her midsection, she wouldn't miss this opportunity and nodded eagerly.

His instant smile reassured her and touched her heart.

He pulled on the chain twice, causing two short bursts of flame to shoot into the opening of the balloon. Then he hauled in the three untethered ropes, coiling them in the corners and another two blasts of the burner.

With a hand signal to those below, he heaved the last anchor line up, allowing it to pile in one corner.

After another moment, the balloon returned to floating upward as well as in a gentle horizontal direction.

A thrill skipped through her as she ascended higher and higher into the air. Exhilarating!

"Why didn't we go up as soon as you made the flame bigger?"

"There is a delay between the heat being created here and it rising all the way to the top." He pointed inside the silk. "Once reaching the top, it lifts us."

"So, the more heat you add, the higher it goes."

"Correct."

"What if you want to go down?"

"That can be done two ways. First, simply allow the air inside to cool naturally. The other is to pull this rope which opens the vent at the very top of the silk." He pulled on the rope.

The balloon descended.

He released the rope and pulled the burner chain.

She pointed to a metal canister strapped to one of the sides of the basket with a tube snaking from it to the burner mechanism. "I assume that's gas to feed the burner."

"It is." He almost sounded surprised she knew that. "I have a second canister on the other side I can switch to, by turning this lever to the right."

The balloon drifted closer to town.

"How do you steer?"

"You can't truly steer a hot air balloon, not like you can a horse or a boat. The wind currents travel in different directions at various elevations. If I want to head in that direction, I take it up until I catch the air current traveling that way."

Every so often he pulled the chain, releasing the gas that fed the flame.

"Can we do that?"

"Sure." He blasted the flame for a longer burn, waited, and another one. He did so until the balloon changed course ever so slightly.

But they weren't traveling to where he'd said they would.

"I thought we were going that way."

"Patience. It takes time for all the heat to rise and carry us."

In another minute or so of rising, the balloon headed the way he'd said.

"How do you know how high to go?"

"I can feel the shift and the balance in the basket as well as seeing the direction of the ground below."

"May I try?"

"Of course." He motioned her over. "Take hold of the handle here."

She wrapped her hand around the wooden grip.

"Give it two short bursts."

She tugged on the chain, but it didn't budge. How had he made it appear so effortless?

He enveloped her hand with his, helping her with the chain. The flame shot up. He helped her tug it again. "It's a little tricky to figure out how hard you need to pull it."

The scent of his cologne tickled her senses. His nearness rattled her brain. This would not do. She freed her hand and stepped away. "Thank you for letting me pilot."

"You can try again if you like."

"No, thank you. I'll leave the flying to you." She didn't dare stand that near him again. Instead, she gazed across the vista of trees toward the river and the Cascade mountain range beyond. How would she ever be content on the terra firma again after seeing the world like this?

She leaned her head over the side and looked straight down to see how far up she was. Everything seemed so small.

Her head felt as light as this balloon. Was that because of the elevation?

Darkness crowded the periphery of her vision, narrowing her focus.

The landscape moved in waves and ripples. Why did everything appear so odd?

She concentrated on taking deep breaths.

Suddenly, strong arms latched around her waist and pulled her away from the edge. "Whoa. Don't tumble overboard."

She gulped in air. "I must have gotten a little dizzy for a moment."

"I find it best to focus on the horizon rather than the ground." He put a bent finger under her chin and forced her attention to his face. "Are you all right?"

"I think so. I've never had that happen before."

"You've probably never had the opportunity to be up at this high of an elevation." His piercing gray gaze held her in place.

He certainly wasn't like any of her other suitors. Nothing ordinary about this man, and everything intriguing.

Lamar kept his arms around Cordelia. He had called her name, but she'd seemed to not be able to hear him. Then she'd leaned precariously over the rim of the basket. He'd had to act fast to keep her from losing her balance altogether.

His heart raced. From her being in potential danger? Or was it from her nearness?

Probably both.

Now that he had her here, he was reluctant to release her even though she was safe. He allowed his gaze to linger on her features. Was her skin as soft as it appeared?

A strand of her lovely dark hair danced against the side of her face.

He brushed it back, causing his fingertips to graze her cheek.

She shuddered at his touch.

Her rose petal lips parted slightly.

Would she allow him to kiss her?

He inched closer.

As her eyes widened, she gasped. "Tree!"

"What?"

She pointed behind him. "A tree! We're going to hit it!"

He spun around to face the looming branches, at the same time he automatically reached for the fuel chain. "Hang on." He tugged the chain, opening the valve to release gas to the burner. The mechanism hissed, and the flame shot higher into the balloon. It would take a half of a minute or more for the heat to reach the top of the silk to lift them out of danger.

"Hold on tight." He wasn't going to be able to get them to rise fast enough to avoid the tree. He glanced to make sure Cordelia was indeed safe. He couldn't have her toppling over the edge.

On the side opposite the oncoming vegetation, she stood with her back braced against the corner and her arms gripped over the lip of the basket.

She should be out of harm's way there.

He sent another blast of heat into the balloon. The first tank let out the telltale hiss, warning it was nearly empty. Lamar cranked the lever to engage tank two and gave the heater another blast. The switch had been successful.

The basket rocked to and fro as the side and bottom scraped along the branches. He pulled the chain again for a longer burst. When a larger branch was about to hit the basket, Lamar sat on the rim with his legs out. He held tight to the rope attached to the net encasing the silk and pushed off the bough with his feet.

The basket budged a little away from the foliage.

He swung his legs inside again. Dare he add more heat? Or wait until what he'd already poured into it to rise to the top?

He blasted again to make sure they cleared this tree and several others beyond it.

He had been reckless to have allowed this to happen. Of course, he'd needed to pull Cordelia to safety, but he never should have lingered. Her nearness had taken over all his senses.

The balloon lifted out of the branches, then continued to rise.

Up and up.

Up to where the air current shifted in a different direction. A direction he didn't want to go. If the balloon drifted too far, there wouldn't be enough fuel to return.

He pulled on the vent rope, releasing some of the heated air.

They slowed, then quit rising.

He glanced at the landscape to get his bearings.

Cordelia released the side of the basket. "Are we safe now?"

He nodded. "I'm so sorry for that."

She moved closer and rested a hand on his arm. "It wasn't your fault. I'm the one who foolishly looked over the edge. I never expected to get dizzy."

That was generous of her, but he knew better than to allow himself to get distracted, for even one moment when in the air. "I'll get us back as soon as possible."

She gave his arm a squeeze. "You don't have to do that. The balloon isn't damaged, is it?"

"No, but I used a lot of extra fuel."

Her eyebrows lifted. "Do we have enough?"

"I don't know." He hoped so. "It depends on the air currents. If they are blowing in our favor, we should make it."

She nodded. "If not, we'll be walking into town."

What could he say?

He piloted up and down to make the best use of the currents. After fighting with them for quite a while, he knew the second gas tank had to be near empty. He pointed. "I'm going to make a landing in that field."

"Are we out of fuel?"

"Not yet, but I don't want to run dry and have us drop on a tree or house, or in the river."

Once over the tree line, he opened the vent, causing the balloon to descend rapidly. "This could be a little bumpy." He didn't have the option of alternative locations or rising to try to ride the current back around to here. He had one attempt at this. "Stand at that end to balance the weight."

She stood where indicated and watched the terrain.

He opened and closed the vent to guide them to a location he thought might be a good place.

Lower and lower.

The meadow looked less level the closer it came.

A few feet from the ground, Cordelia leaned over the rim. "We're going to make it."

"It's going to be bumpy."

A bottom corner of the basket banged the ground, rocking it and nearly knocking Lamar off his feet. Cordelia didn't seem to have as much trouble as she held onto the side. After a couple more brushes with the terrain, the basket rested in the meadow at a precarious angle. He extinguished the burner flame.

The slope caused Cordelia to skitter to his end of the basket.

He hooked his arm around her waist to keep her from falling.

He wished to stand there, holding her. Instead, he scooped her into his arms, lifting her over the rim of the listing basket. So much for impressing her with his aeronautical skills. He climbed out as well. "Would you mind giving me a hand deflating the silk?" He hated asking, but this would go so much better with a second person.

"Of course. What do you need me to do?"

"Pull on the vent rope." He handed her the wooden handle at the end of the line.

She tugged on it.

The balloon deflated, causing the silk to become wavy.

As it slackened more and more, Lamar pulled on the net over the silk, drawing it down and away from the basket until it rested on the ground. With his head hung, he made his way back along the length of it to where Cordelia waited. This had been humiliating. "I'll walk into town to rent a buggy, then return for you as quickly as possible."

"You don't have to do that. I can walk as well."

"I can't ask you to trek all that way on foot. Kamola has to be at least two miles away."

"Then it's serendipitous I brought a picnic breakfast. Shall we eat?"

How could she be so calm? So agreeable? "You aren't upset about this debacle?"

"Why should I be? I rode in a hot air balloon, and you allowed me to fly it. I don't think I've ever done anything so exciting." She motioned toward the balloon basket. "Do you mind getting the food?"

He retrieved it, then helped her spread a blanket on the prairie grass.

Cordelia unpacked the meal.

He had a hard time believing she wasn't furious with him for getting them stuck out here. He was furious with himself. No other woman he knew of would be this agreeable about such a situation. An extraordinary lady indeed.

After eating their fill, Lamar stood. "We should get going if you're still willing to hike into town. Otherwise, I'll go get that buggy."

She smiled sweetly up at him. "No need." She indicated the far end of the field where a wagon and buggy drove toward them.

Of course, his helpers would have been watching the balloon in the distance and came for them. His freight wagon would need to travel here eventually to retrieve the balloon.

Though grateful to not have to abandon Cordelia here, a part of him ached that his time alone with her had come to an end. He would have to plan another outing soon.

Fourteen

THE FOLLOWING WEEK, CORDELIA STOOD IN the arching doorway of the Grand Ballroom in the Atwood Hotel. Her heart leapt at the sight of all the wedding preparations. Staff members scurried around setting up and decorating for the festivities to be held here tomorrow. Everything was coming together beautifully. The bride, Aunt Henny's daughter, was fortunate for such a joyous occasion.

Cordelia's heart ached that she might never have this some day. Some day when the Lord freed her from the work of helping others. She looked forward to that day. But then who would assist those less fortunate, the needy, and the outcasts? Though she hoped for a wedding and a family, she didn't want the poor to be without a champion. They needed her. A family of her own was her sacrifice in serving the Lord. She wouldn't abandon the less fortunate and disappoint God.

She had been able to pacify her own longings in the knowledge she was answering a higher calling in her life. But the desire to marry and have children had begun crowding in on the work the Lord had set before her.

For the first time, His calling on her life had become a burden. Nothing like the Christ had felt before He went to Golgotha, but none the less, a weight.

Heavenly Father, I want to do Your will. Take away this heavy feeling. Please help me not give in to my own selfish desires.

Perhaps someday, women could have a family *and* participate in meaningful work the Lord intended for them.

Mother came up beside her. "Soon, we'll be decorating this room for your wedding. It's not the church back home, but it will suit nicely."

The churches in Kamola were small buildings in comparison.

Cordelia wouldn't tell her mother she was wrong. She didn't want to voice the permanent lack of nuptials in her future, or it would make the loss real and final. "What if Mr. Kesner isn't interested in marrying me?" Which she knew he wasn't.

"Nonsense." With a flick of her wrist, Mother waved that notion away. "He has been coming around more and spending quite a bit of time with you. He will be asking your father for your hand any day now."

Cordelia doubted that. He'd said he had no intention of marrying her. "I'm not so sure." Though on their first outing, he'd said he was interested in marrying. She had even given him permission to bow out. Why hadn't he?

Mother took Cordelia's hand and patted it. "Don't fret, dear. He'll ask. If he tarries too long, your father will talk to him or his grandmother."

"Oh, don't do that."

"Why not?"

Besides putting Lamar in an awkward position, she couldn't flirt with the idea of marriage. If Lamar did propose, she didn't know if she would have the restraint to turn him down, but she would *have to*. God had given her a different calling. "It would be embarrassing."

"Your father wouldn't be the first to prod a groom into action."

"I don't wish to marry anyone who doesn't truly want me." Her heart twisted at the thought of Lamar not wanting her, even though she knew she couldn't marry him. She needed to know she was wanted. Why did it matter so much to her? Had she fallen in love with him while she was trying so hard not to? Couldn't be. The Lord wouldn't allow it. Whatever she was feeling for the kind and handsome Lamar Kesner, it wasn't love. But it was something.

"I've seen the way Mr. Kesner looks at you. There is keen interest in that man's eyes."

Keen interest was far from love.

"You have captured his attention. Hold onto it. Don't

let him waver or allow another young lady to distract him away from you."

Encouraging him to find some other lady interesting was exactly what she needed to do, but she didn't have the heart to follow through with it.

He was to be her escort at the wedding. After that, she would discourage him.

However, she needed him for the bachelor quilt. He would be a strong draw for both the ladies and the spectators.

After the bachelor quilt and Founders' Day then. It would be difficult to keep her heart in check until that time, but she must. Then she would break things off with him.

Her chest tightened at the thought.

In the room designated for the bride, Henny stood behind Geneviève, gazing at her daughter in the mirror. She was such a beautiful bride. "Are you nervous?"

Geneviève shook her head. "I can't wait to become Mrs. Monte Gladwell."

That surprised Henny. She didn't know a single bride who wasn't a little anxious about embarking on this new journey in her life. "It's all right to be nervous. I would guess Montana is a little apprehensive."

Geneviève jerked around to face her. "You do not think he will fail to show up, do you?"

Felicity stood near them. "Not my brother. If he says he's going to do something, he does it. Even if he doesn't want to."

Henny cringed. It would have been better if the young woman had stopped before the last sentence.

Geneviève's eyes widened. "He does not wish to marry me?"

Now, Felicity's eyes widened. "No. That's not what I meant. I merely wanted you to rest assured, he *will* be waiting next to the minister when you walk down the aisle." She turned to Henny with a pleading gaze.

"Of course, he'll be here. He loves you very much and is as excited as you are to be married. You have nothing to worry about." So far, both Henny and Felicity had made blunders which caused the bride anxiety that hadn't been there before.

A knock sounded on the door. Henny went and opened it. Her wonderful son stood on the other side. "Is the bride ready?"

"Yes."

Geneviève hurried over, grabbed her brother's arm, and pulled him inside the room. "Please tell me Monte is here."

His eyebrows dipped. "Why wouldn't he be?"

She gripped his upper arms. "Is he here or not?"

"He's here and as nervous as a chicken at a feather plucking."

Henny sighed in relief. Now, her daughter could breathe easier. Where had her son ever heard something like 'a chicken at a feather plucking'? It didn't matter right now. Geneviève's peace of mind was most important.

Her son shifted his focus to Henny again. "Are you ready?"

"Is it time?"

"It is. I'll walk you out to your seat."

Henny kissed her daughter on the cheek and left with her son.

On the way between the bride room and the ballroom, her son spoke. "It's official. I'm back to being Winston Seymour the third."

"You changed your name?" When Henny's in-laws had whisked her husband and children off to Europe, they had changed everyone's name to make it impossible for Henny to find them. However, a few short months ago, her children had found her. They had come searching after their father passed away.

He nodded. "All legal."

"I hope you didn't do that for me." Though Henny was thrilled.

"I did it for me. A way of taking control of my life and my future."

She was proud of her son for standing up for himself and what he wanted. However, her daughter wasn't of the mindset to change her name back to the one Henny had given her when she was born. Henny was fine with that. Geneviève needed to do what she felt comfortable doing. "I hope you don't completely abandon a relationship with your grandparents. They have done things we don't agree with, but they're still family. Regardless of their behavior, I do believe they love you and your sister."

"Their love is the kind which can choke the life out of a person. As long as neither of them tries to control me, I can be civil." He patted Henny's hand on his arm. "You'll be proud of me."

"I'm already very proud of you."

"I spoke to *Grand-mère.*"

"You did?"

He nodded. "She's here."

"She is?" That was amazing beyond belief. "Your sister will be so happy. Her heart has been breaking a little at her absence. Is your grandfather here too?"

"I didn't see him, and *Grand-mère* didn't say anything about him. I doubt he would come."

Henny was surprised Cora had been allowed to travel here at all, let alone by herself.

"I spoke with her briefly and warned her not to cause a scene or do anything to upset Vivi."

As Winston ushered Henny into the decorated ballroom filled with people, she made eye contact with Cora in the last row. She gave the woman a gentle smile and a nod. Cora gave her a nod back. The most civil she had ever been to Henny.

Up front, Montana stood stiffly. My, he was handsome. A solid fellow who would always take care of her daughter.

Pride welled inside Henny to welcome him into the fold. Her daughter had made a fine choice. Henny sat next to her new husband, Saul.

He squeezed her hand. "Every time you turn around your family is growing."

Henny smiled. "It seems so." After living without them for over two decades, it was nice to have so many loved ones around her now.

After the wedding ceremony, Cordelia waltzed around the dance floor with Lamar. How refreshing to not have to pretend to be dull-witted in front of him. Freeing. "I'm surprised no one has tried to cut in." Very unusual.

"Rumor has gotten around town that we are courting."

"What? Where would they get a preposterous notion like that?" However, a thrill rushed through her at the idea. She needed to tamp down her enthusiasm.

A flicker of pain crossed his expression. "I told a few people."

"Why would you do that?"

"So other men won't try to steal dances and will leave you be. If they think we're courting, they'll be less likely to bother you."

She sensed there was more to it than that. "So, this is a selfless act on your part?"

He smiled. "Not completely selfless. Grandmama is happy and has stopped harping on me."

"What will you do when your grandmother and my parents start planning our wedding that isn't going to take place?" Her mother already was.

"We'll figure out such events in the future. For now, we have only to worry about today and the bachelor quilt. Have you and the other sewing ladies ascertained details?"

"We have." The tasks needed to make the quilt would likely be challenging for him and the other bachelors, but they would have capable, eager young ladies to assist them.

"Are you going to let me in on the plans?"

She would need to tell him sooner or later. "Bachelors will bid on eligible ladies to work side by side with them, guiding them in sewing the blocks. If we recruit enough men, we're hoping for bidding wars as they choose the young ladies with whom they wish to keep company. Three men on each side of the quilt—twelve in all."

"Will there be enough room at Aunt Henny's boarding house?"

"We won't do this there. On the first day of the festival, we'll have a large tent set up where the sewing teams will be established and the individual blocks sewn. The next day, we'll have the quilt stretched on a frame. The men will quilt the layers together with assistance." She hesitated telling him the next part. "We'll sell tickets to spectators who wish to come in and watch the men sew."

"Spectators, huh? More like hecklers if I would hazard a guess." He offered a grin, essentially reassuring her he would be up for some good-natured fun. "That should draw a crowd."

"Oh, I hope so." She laughed. "The third part of the plan for bringing in money is when we auction off the quilt, even if it's not completed. The ladies will finish up anything that still needs to be done at the next quilting circle meeting."

"And how will you approach that the money raised will go to the encampment?"

"We'll tell everyone it's simply for charity and leave it at that so we don't need to explain."

"You actually think someone will pay money for a slovenly constructed quilt men sewed? You'll be fortunate if even one of the bachelors has sewn a stitch in his life. If the quilt turns out at all, it will be more likely that the ladies, who are 'helping', did the work."

"They will be instructed not to, no matter how it

looks. I think if men put their minds to the task, they'll do a fine job."

He raised his eyebrows. "I never realized you were a dreamer."

"There's a lot about me you don't know."

"I look forward to learning." He dipped his head toward her.

Did he truly? Or was he merely being conversational? Either way, she needed to ensure he didn't develop true feelings for her. That would make her inevitable refusal to marry him more difficult. If he professed affection for her to her parents, they would pressure her into marriage.

With any of her past suitors, that idea nettled her, but with Lamar, passing him up would nettle even worse.

Why, Lord? Why have You allowed me to have feelings for Lamar? For my sanity's sake... She hesitated and swallowed hard. *...take them away.*

Fifteen

THE NEXT AFTERNOON, LAMAR STOOD IN his workshop, adjusting the valve on the heating apparatus on his hot air balloon. On the day he'd taken Cordelia up, it had sustained minor damage during the hard landing.

Rogers entered Lamar's workshop. "*She* is requesting your presence. *She* is not happy."

When Rogers referred to Grandmama in that manner, Lamar was usually destined to be at the wrong end of a tongue lashing. He hadn't received one of those in years. What had he done to upset her? It couldn't be about Cordelia. Between helping collect items for the immigrants and the arrangements for the bachelor quilt, he'd been seeing her regularly. "Is this something I need to change my attire for?"

"Causing her to wait might heighten her distress."

Well then, he mustn't keep her waiting. Lamar fell into step with Rogers. "Can you give me a hint as to what this about?"

"I don't know the details, but Mr. Thatcher stopped by."

Curious. What business did Grandmama's lawyer have with her today? Lamar wasn't aware of a meeting. Perhaps that was why she was upset. Had he forgotten about an appointment?

Once inside, Lamar headed straight for the parlor.

"Sir?" Rogers had halted. "She's waiting to receive you in the library."

That made sense since she had recently spoken with their attorney. The parlor was for personal use and the library for business. When he entered, Grandmama sat in Grandpapa's leather wingback chair. It reminded people she held the power of her late husband.

Lamar crossed to her and kissed her on the cheek. "You asked for me, Grandmama."

"If you think buttering me up with a peck on the cheek is going to cool my ire, you are mistaken, young man."

Lamar smiled inwardly at the twinkle in her eyes. It already had. "What can I do for you, Grandmama? Rogers said Mr. Thatcher stopped in. I hope it's nothing serious." He sat in the chair opposite her.

"You tell me. Bright received a visit from Mr. Quincy. I'm sure you're aware of the reason the O'Gillises' attorney is calling on ours."

Lamar did. "I have a good guess."

"Bright has informed me that you have made inquiries about purchasing some land."

Not just any piece of property, but why should that ruffle Grandmama's feathers? "There is a parcel I'm interested in. I didn't think you would mind."

"What I mind is having to hear about it from my attorney and not my grandson."

He hadn't told her because she would have wanted to know why that particular acreage interested him. He had hoped the O'Gillises wouldn't cause a fuss, especially since he'd offered full market value for it. He'd thought of offering over the value, but they might be suspicious as to why and go investigate the area. Then they would discover the people squatting there.

She pinned him with her gaze. "Whatever do you want that property for?"

"I have a project I want to work on."

"Your hot air balloons?"

It would be easy to say yes, but it would never win him this argument. "A different project."

She swished her hand in the air. "We have plenty of acreage you are free to do with as you wish."

"For what I have in mind, I need this particular location."

"What could you possibly want to do with that land, you can't do on what we already own?"

"I'm going to keep that to myself for the time being." To confess his plans could put an abrupt end to them.

Grandmama's eyes narrowed slightly. "Tell me, or I'll have the bank hold all your funds."

Lamar chuckled. "We both know that's an empty threat. Not only will you not do such a thing, but you don't have the authority." Though she could withhold certain funds, others he had complete control over.

Grandmama distained not knowing everything that was going on.

"If you don't tell me, I'll go to Collin O'Gillis myself and tell him to refuse to sell to you."

Now it was his turn to narrow his gaze. "You wouldn't do that." Though she did seem determined.

"Wouldn't I?" Her white eyebrows darted up and then back down. "Do you wish to test me?"

Testing Grandmama had never turned out in his favor. She had him trapped. If Ian O'Gillis found out there were squatters and Cordelia was helping them, he would use it to his advantage.

She held him with her gaze. "Or you can tell me what you have planned, and I'll see to it Collin sells to you."

He weighed his options. He could move forward on his own and risk Grandmama undermining his efforts, or he could give her the details of the squatters and she still might undermine the sale. Or... "It's something I have in mind for Cordelia. A surprise."

Grandmama's whole demeanor changed in an instant, and she beamed. "Why didn't you say so? That changes everything." She widened her eyes. "*Cordelia*, is it? Your romance is progressing nicely."

Lamar hoped so.

Cordelia sat in Celeste Dumont's dressmaker shop. Mother had chosen four gowns from the proprietress's fashion drawings to consider for Cordelia's wedding dress. One for each season, depending upon when the wedding was finally scheduled. Which Cordelia knew would be never.

Mademoiselle Dumont had one of her girls model the third dress already made up in a deep green. "This is how the gown hangs on a female body. It would, of course, be sewn in white for you. Drawings can only do so much for a design."

Though the gown was elegant, it would never suit for a nonexistent wedding. "I'm not sure." Cordelia didn't want this poor woman to put in a lot of work for a dress Cordelia had no plans to wear.

Mademoiselle Dumont motioned with her hand. The current model and a new model exchanged places. "How do you feel about this one?"

Cordelia resisted the urge to sigh audibly, so she shrugged.

Mother patted Cordelia's hand and spoke to her as one would an errant child. "These are all beautiful gowns. I'm sure you can choose one. This needn't be a difficult decision."

Cordelia forced a slight whine into her tone. "We aren't even engaged."

"That will change very soon. We must believe that. We don't want to leave your dress to the last minute."

Mademoiselle Dumont crossed to the model and spoke quietly to her. The woman retreated through the curtain to the back room. *Mademoiselle* Dumont raised a finger. "I may have just the one for you."

Cordelia disliked wasting this proprietress's time.

A few minutes later, the same model returned, wearing a pale green gown with layers of ruffles and beading dotted throughout.

Mademoiselle Dumont described the changes that could be made to this design when making it into a white wedding gown. The bodice would be taken in and completely adorned with beading. An overskirt with a bustle would continue the ruffles to the end of the three-foot train. The veil to be constructed of traditional tulle with three rows of ruffled lace in the back and one in the front to coordinate with the ones on the skirt.

The already gorgeous gown would be even more appealing to Cordelia with the suggested changes. She needed to stop this fiasco right now. How could she do that without tipping her hand to Mother that she had no plans to marry even if she wanted to? Mother would tell Father, and he would arrange a marriage without her consent posthaste.

Mademoiselle Dumont moved to stand next to the

model. "I can see you are hesitant. Let's have you try it on to see how it suits."

More likely than not, Cordelia would find it all the more appealing, so she didn't dare.

Mother patted Cordelia's wrist. "Go ahead. Try it on. Let's see how it fits. I can tell by the gleam in your eyes, you fancy this one."

Cordelia couldn't refuse now. Finding an appropriate wedding gown was the whole purpose for this outing. She stood and followed the model behind the curtains and into a large dressing area.

Two other dress-shop ladies helped Cordelia and the model remove their outer clothes, then the pale green gown was put on Cordelia. From her perspective, gazing down the front, it was still every bit as beautiful. She wouldn't get the complete impact until she viewed it in the full-length mirror in the other room.

The one who had modeled this garment fluffed out some of the ruffles. "This looks better on you than it has on any of us."

She had to say that. It was a selling tactic that worked with most people.

The other two ladies held aside the curtains for Cordelia to pass through to the sitting area, then she crossed the threshold.

Mother turned to her, and her smile widened. She clasped her hands together. "It's perfect."

Cordelia had been afraid of that. It needed to be hideous so she could delay this process. She turned toward the looking glass. Her breath caught. With the suggested changes, it was everything she would want in a wedding dress.

Mademoiselle Dumont fitted a veil on Cordelia's head, pulling the front piece over her face.

Cordelia gazed through the netting at herself in the mirror. Her heart ached. She wanted this gown. She wanted to get married in it. She wanted—

She wanted what could never be.

After taking measurements, pinning in the bodice, and fussing with the veil, Cordelia was finally given permission to remove the dress. When she returned to the sitting area, Mother was gone.

Mademoiselle Dumont approached with a pad of paper and a pencil. "Your mother had urgent business and needed to leave. She said for you to pick out a few garments for your trousseau."

Cordelia couldn't do that. "I am so overwhelmed by everything I've seen today. I need time to think about them. The gentleman hasn't even proposed. Hasn't even asked my father yet. I'm afraid of putting the cart before the horse. I think I'll take a walk to consider all your beautiful fashions."

"I understand. Your mother expects you to have chosen some outfits. I will make a list of ones I think will suit you best. That way, if she returns, we can show her our progress." The proprietress truly did understand.

"Merci." Cordelia scurried out the door.

Nan hurried up to her. "I was afraid you were never going to leave the shop."

"Have you been waiting for me?"

"Yes. I thought you saw me through the window."

Cordelia hadn't. "I wish I had. Mother insisted I pick out my wedding gown."

"I would love to hear all about your dress, but we have a problem at the encampment."

"What's wrong?"

"One of the children fell into a fire pit and burned her arm. Her parents are afraid to bring her into town."

"Why didn't you get the doctor and take him out there?"

"With one look at Dutch, he turned us down. We thought if you spoke to him, he might go."

"Of course." Cordelia quickened her pace toward the doctor's.

"Shouldn't we stop at the White Hotel first so you can change into your common clothes?"

"No time. If someone is in need of a doctor, we must get him there as fast as we can."

Dutch met them outside the doctor's office.

Cordelia inclined her head toward him. "We'll return in a few minutes." She dashed inside with Nan.

The doctor stood beside a desk near the entrance,

speaking to a heavy-set nurse in her forties seated at the desk. She wore a sensible gray uniform with a white apron. "May I help you?" Her gaze landed on Nan and recognition transformed her expression. "You're back. Doctor, you have visitors."

The doctor turned to face them. "As I told your friend, I'm not in a position at the moment to leave my office."

Cordelia tried for her most sympathetic look to convince him to acquiesce. "I have money. I can pay your fee."

"That may be, but I have patients who expect me to be here. As I told your friends, bring the person in to town. I'll be happy to treat them here."

Cordelia glanced at Nan to see if she thought there was any chance of convincing the parents. Her friend shook her head, so Cordelia refocused her attention on the doctor. "That's not going to be possible. Won't you please come?"

He hesitated, appearing conflicted. "I have people with appointments. When I'm through, I'll see about coming 'round."

The nurse stood from where she'd been seated, filling out a patient chart. "Doc, you don't need me here. I could go and tend to the patient."

"Myrtle, I don't think that's a good idea." He hesitated. "But I doubt I can stop you."

"That's right, sir." The nurse's smile brightened her face.

The doctor pointed. "You know where my spare bag is."

Defying the doctor seemed to be a matter of course for her—Cordelia was going to like this woman.

Myrtle snagged the medical case from a cupboard and followed Cordelia out.

Dutch pushed off the wagon where he'd been leaning. "Who is she? She is not a doctor."

Myrtle straightened, adding an inch or two to her height. "Nothing wrong with your eyesight." She flapped her hand in the air. "Help me up to the wagon seat and be quick about it."

Dutch's eyes widened.

Cordelia almost laughed. Strangers never spoke to the large man that way. Most tried to pretend he wasn't there.

He helped Myrtle aboard then assisted Cordelia and Nan into the tail end of the wagon. Then he spoke to Cordelia. "You should ride on the wagon seat."

"I'll be fine here with Nan."

Dutch stared at her.

Cordelia hoped he didn't make a fuss.

Myrtle snapped her fingers. "She said she's fine back there. Someone in need of a doctor is waiting. Get up here and drive this wagon, or I'll do it myself."

With no further protest, Dutch scuttled up to the seat and set the horse into motion.

Sixteen

SURROUNDED BY THE OUTCASTS FROM THE Netherlands at the encampment, Cordelia stood next to Nurse Myrtle and assisted the woman with caring for the injured child. Her friend Dutch translated between the people and the nurse. A group of three wagons made up their portion of the community.

A commotion rose from elsewhere in the camp—voices in various languages. Cordelia couldn't tell what was being said, so she glanced up at Nan. "I need Dutch here. Can you peek around the clothesline and see what the trouble is?" The laundry acted as a pseudo-wall, feigning privacy.

Nan nodded before she left but returned a moment later. The color had drained from her face. "There's a man on horseback claiming to be the landowner."

No! Hopefully, he wouldn't force these people to leave, but from the raised voices, she feared that was exactly what he was doing. "Nan, stay here with Dutch and the nurse. I'll see if I can sweet-talk him into allowing these people to stay."

Dutch stepped closer to Cordelia. "I go with you."

Hopefully, she didn't require a protector. Besides, she needed him here to bridge the language barrier. "Thank you, but I'll be fine." If the circumstances dictated it, she could simply call to him.

She scooted around the clothes and linens flapping in the slight breeze.

A red-haired man sat upon a chestnut stallion located in the middle of the camp. The horse pranced in circles as though agitated, tossing its head and snorting.

She smoothed her hand down her dress. "Sir!" At the very least, she could negotiate time for these people to pack up their belongings and move to another location.

The man maneuvered his animal around to face Cordelia. His hard expression softened. "Miss Armstrong?"

Ian O'Gillis? She had met him on a couple of occasions and wasn't impressed during either encounter. If Lamar's glare at this man at the hotel gala was any indication, he disliked him as well. Unsure how to proceed, she defaulted to her vapid persona. "Mr. O'Gillis." She giggled. "Whatever are you doing here?"

He stilled his horse and dismounted. Closing the gap between them, he took her hand. "Miss Armstrong, you shouldn't be out here. Did these people kidnap you?"

How absurd. "Of course not." She'd sounded a bit too defiant, so she added another giggle.

"This is a dangerous place."

"I'm in no peril here." She tittered to prove her point.

He took both of her hands in his. "You don't understand how treacherous these kinds of ruffians can be."

She resisted the urge to pull free. That would only serve to make matters worse. She needed to quell his irritation, not fan the flames of it. "They aren't ruffians. They have been ever so kind to me."

"These people can't be trusted. I'm taking you back to town."

She had no intention of going anywhere with him.

But...

It would garner these people a little time. In a chipper voice, she said, "All right. Let me get something quick." She slipped from his grasp before he could protest and hurried behind the line of laundry.

Red-faced, Dutch appeared fit to be tied. Speaking of tied, she would do just that if he caused trouble, potentially inflaming the situation.

Cordelia was thankful he hadn't interrupted. "Nurse Myrtle, how is it going?"

"I'm almost done with this little one, but I wouldn't mind examining all the children."

Cordelia nodded. "Dutch, Nan, stay with the nurse and return her to town when she's ready."

Nan's eyes widened. "What are you going to do?"

"I'm going with Mr. O'Gillis."

Dutch thinned his lips. "No."

"I have to. If I stay here, he'll make a fuss. I'll try to talk him into allowing everyone to remain here." Surely, he was a reasonable man.

Nan shook her head. "I don't like this."

Dutch glared. "I do not like it either."

Cordelia agreed. "Like it or not, this is the way it has to be."

Nurse Myrtle spoke up. "She's right. The best way to keep this man from making things worse for these people and clearing them out right now is for her to go."

"I'll leave a message for you at the White Hotel." Cordelia darted between the articles of laundry hanging on the line before Dutch could try to stop her.

The outcasts watched from a distance as she crossed the center of the encampment. She gave a smile to hopefully reassure them that all was well. Then she strolled past Mr. O'Gillis. "Kamola is this way, isn't it?"

He hooked her arm. "It's too far for you to walk. I'll take you on my horse."

She was afraid of that. "Does that mean *you* are going to walk?"

He gave her an indulgent smile. "No. We can both ride my stallion."

Of course, that would be his suggestion. "Oh, I couldn't do that." She giggled.

"I can't allow you to walk. I'm a gentleman."

Cordelia wasn't so sure about that from Lamar's reaction to him. "I would really rather walk." Would he capitulate?

He gripped her arm and maneuvered her to his horse. "I insist."

Perhaps she could swing up and pretend the horse galloped away on its own before he got on, with her helpless to do anything about it. She lifted her left foot up toward the stirrup so she would be in the saddle astride.

"Not that foot. Put your right one in there, then I'll help you up."

She tittered as she complied. He gripped her waist, sitting her sideways atop the horse. She resisted the urge to shudder. Before she could goad the animal into motion, he grasped the saddle horn and the cantle and swung up behind her. The perfect position for him to put one arm around each side of her.

A part of her wished it were Lamar's arms around her, even though she had no right to contemplate such a thing. Those kinds of musings would only leave her wanting.

Good thing she was in her fancy clothes, because with him returning her to town she wouldn't need to explain her drab brown dress to her parents. Her parents would want to know what she was up to and ask too many questions.

If she had to present herself as a socialite, she was dressed the part.

Mr. O'Gillis's hot breath fanned the nape of her neck. "It's providential I came along."

No, it wasn't.

He goaded his horse forward. "How did you end up such a great distance from town?"

It wasn't more than a couple of miles. She could say she'd wandered out here, but even her vapid persona wouldn't amble this far. So, the truth it would have to be. "I came with the nurse who was going to help an injured child."

"There is a nurse back there?" No mention of the child's well-being.

Cordelia nodded.

"I'll send someone out here to see to her safety."

Cordelia was confused. Mr. O'Gillis said some of the right things, but she got the distinct impression she couldn't fully trust him. Was that coming from herself? Lamar's reaction to him? Or was it God? "I do hope the little girl will be all right."

"You shouldn't have come. These people are a menace." Still no mention of the injured child.

"No, they aren't. They were very kind to me."

"They are criminals. All of them."

How could he say that? He hadn't even met them. "No, they aren't."

"They are trespassing on my family's land. That makes them malefactors. We will send men to clear them off."

"Oh, please don't. They have nowhere else to go."

"That isn't my concern. They can't simply live on someone else's property without permission or paying rent."

"They aren't hurting anything." It didn't seem as though the O'Gillises used the land, so why should they care?

"They are criminals. They will be run off or put in jail."

Confused no longer—she didn't care for Mr. O'Gillis, but perhaps she could persuade him to change his mind. Turning in the saddle to face him, she batted her eyelashes. "Please let them stay."

"Why do you care what happens to them?"

"I don't know."

His expression changed from that of an adult coddling an errant child to a cat who had cornered a mouse. "You are soft on these people."

"I feel bad for them."

"Do you truly want those people to stay?"

Oh, dear. The turn this conversation had taken wasn't good. "I don't think they have any place else to go."

"Perhaps, we can come to some sort of arrangement."

Doubtful.

At the Telegraph and Post Office, Lamar picked up the most recent copy of the Scientific American Magazine from the counter. Hopefully, this week's four-page edition would have an article on ballooning, heating apparatuses, or air currents. "Thank you, Morton." He headed outside. The sight which greeted him on the street set his jaw.

Cordelia sat stiff as an oak tree atop O'Gillis's horse with his arms around her. O'Gillis appeared as proud as a gentleman who had been gifted the crown jewels.

What was the man up to? And why did he have Lamar's lady with him?

Yes, she *was* his lady even if it wasn't official.

Lamar swung up into the saddle of his own horse and trailed behind. He wanted to race up to him and demand O'Gillis release her. However, since she didn't seem to be in any imminent danger and making a commotion in the middle of town would likely make matters worse, he chose to merely follow.

For now.

O'Gillis rode straight to the Atwood Hotel.

Good. Cordelia would be safe there.

As O'Gillis neared the entrance where livery men stood at attendance, Lamar urged his horse a little faster to reach there a moment before O'Gillis. Lamar swung down and approached Cordelia, holding up his arms to assist her down.

The surprise on her face mixed with concern.

He gripped her waist and lowered her to the ground. "Are you all right, my darling?" Though he'd never called her that before, he wanted O'Gillis to know she was taken—even if she technically wasn't. He would need to remedy that forthwith.

"I-I'm fine."

O'Gillis dismounted and tossed his reins to one of the attendants, then took Cordelia's hand, wrapping it around his arm. "She's with me. I'm taking her to supper this evening."

Lamar held Cordelia's gaze. She would never do that. "Is this true?"

Cordelia nodded. Her stricken expression stabbed at his heart. "I'm sorry. I have to go."

O'Gillis flashed him a smug expression before escorting Cordelia up the steps.

Did Mr. Armstrong know about this? Did he approve? Lamar couldn't imagine the man would want O'Gillis for his daughter. Of course, Mr. Armstrong likely wasn't well acquainted with the man. Lamar watched as the pair entered through the hotel's grand doors. Cordelia glanced over her shoulder at him before she disappeared inside. Her eyes implored him. But implored him to do what? Rescue her from O'Gillis? Or not to interfere?

What was O'Gillis up to? And why was Cordelia going with him? Needing to get to the bottom of this, he entered as well. If Cordelia told him to be on his way, he would go without incident.

He hurried inside and caught up to Cordelia in the

lobby. "Miss Armstrong, may I speak with you?"

O'Gillis kept hold of her hand on his arm. "Don't make a spectacle. She has made her choice."

Lamar wanted to hear it from her and held her gaze.

Her words came out stilted. "I'm sorry if I led you to believe I held affection for you." Her words didn't ring true.

Or was that wishful thinking on his part? "Why are you doing this?"

"This is the way it has to be." Her words seemed to pain her. "Please go."

O'Gillis smirked. "You heard the lady. Run along."

Lamar curled his fingers into fists at his sides as he strode out. The ache in his chest increased while his doubts dogged him all the way home.

He handed Edelweiss's reins to their stable hand Hank. "Would you take care of her for me?"

Hank stroked the horse's neck. "I would be glad to." He led the horse away.

Striding inside, Lamar headed for the staircase. He would change his clothes and go out to his workshop. Though too late in the day to take his hot air balloon up, he could tinker. Better than nothing.

"Lamar? Is that you?" Grandmama's voice.

He stepped to the doorway of the parlor but said nothing.

Grandmama's expression turned stricken. "What's wrong? Are you all right?"

"I don't want to talk about it." Though he didn't really want to, he entered the room. He slumped into a chair and lowered his head into his hands.

"I think you do want to talk about it. As a child, you would say that very thing then linger until you started pouring out your heart. You might as well get it off your chest before it festers."

He didn't want to talk about it. He should leave, yet didn't move.

"I'm not getting any younger."

He lifted his head. "It's over. Miss Armstrong has made her choice, and it's not me." Why did all the interesting ladies end up with other men?

"What? How could that be? Are you sure? She will

find no finer man than you."

"Very sure." He gave her an imploring gaze. "She's with Ian O'Gillis and sent me away."

"Oh, I can't believe she would..." A slow smile pulled at Grandmama's mouth. "This is wonderful."

"*Wonderful?*" How could she say that? Had she gone senile?

Her smile widened. "Don't look at me like that. I haven't lost my mind. At least not yet. I'll let you know when I do."

"I'm sure you will."

She cupped her hands together at her chest. "You wouldn't be this upset if you didn't have true feelings for her. Didn't I tell you she could be the one? It was only a matter of time before I found the right lady for you."

"Didn't you hear me? She's not the one. She chose O'Gillis." Her dismissal of him had caused his low simmering affection for her to flame to life.

Grandmama leveled her gaze at him. "I heard you. Ian O'Gillis is no match for you. Go get her back."

If she chose someone else, he couldn't force her to care for him.

Grandmama's eyebrow quirked up. "Well, go. What are you waiting for?"

"I already spoke to her. She chose him." An ache twisted inside him. He stood anyway and left the room.

Getting to the bottom of this would need to start at the Atwood, but his course of action after that, he didn't know.

Later that evening, Cordelia found Mr. O'Gillis's escort to supper intolerable. He paid her more attention than she wanted and excessively complimented both of her parents.

He pulled out her chair to seat her.

She wanted to refuse but knew she couldn't. When his fingers brushed the nape of her neck, she bristled.

Don't react to him, Cordelia. She would do her best to ignore him as much as possible. Nausea still rolled around inside her from turning Lamar away while pretending to prefer Mr. O'Gillis. Lamar's confused and hurt expression ricocheted around in her mind like a boat getting battered about in a stormy sea.

Father kept his eyes narrowed, and Mother looked distressed.

When they had asked her about her odd choice, she merely giggled. If she confessed to them what Mr. O'Gillis was up to, Father would send him away, and in turn, Mr. O'Gillis would send the outcasts scattering.

She needed to endure this evening then she could figure out how to solve this whole mess tomorrow.

When the waiter arrived at their table, Mr. O'Gillis had the audacity to order for her without even asking.

One way or another, she had to rid herself of this domineering man. He was the type that once he got his way, he would renege on any promises he'd made. She would figure a way out from under his control and keep the people of the encampment safe. She may have to confess to her father all she had been up to, but that wouldn't protect the outcasts. There had to be a way to rebuff this man while not jeopardizing those in need.

A couple passed near the table on the way to their own.

How odd for the waiter to have chosen a meandering route to get them to their destination. A much straighter course wouldn't have taken them near her table.

When the gentleman stood behind the lady's chair to assist her, Cordelia gasped. *Lamar?*

Mr. O'Gillis touched her arm. "What's wrong?"

Cordelia shook her head. "Nothing."

"Something must have startled you, or you wouldn't have gasped. You aren't taking ill, are you?"

He was a bother.

"I was just thinking about the time I saw a snake slither right across my path. I guess that's what made me take a breath. Silly me." She giggled.

He patted her arm. "Nothing to worry about, dear."

Ugh.

She shrugged as she took a drink of water. Over the rim of her glass, she studied Lamar. What was he doing here? Had he seen her? Did she want him to see her?

Then a more important thought stabbed her. Who was the woman with him? She narrowed her eyes then widened them. Nan?

Her friend made eye contact and smiled stiffly.

She should be jealous but wasn't. Was it because she trusted Nan? Or because she didn't feel them being here together was a romantic thing? Or because she didn't care for Lamar as much as she thought she had? That one stung, but it shouldn't.

Why wasn't Lamar turning around to see that she was in the dining room? Certainly, Nan had told him. Cordelia wished she could speak with either one of them to find out what was going on.

When the food arrived, Cordelia picked at her meal, trying to come up with an excuse to wander past Lamar and Nan's table.

Nan said something to Lamar, to which he nodded. Placing her napkin on the table, Nan stood, causing Lamar to get to his feet as well.

Nan strolled through the dining room, making eye contact with Cordelia again.

Thank you, Nan. Cordelia waited a full minute from her friend's departure before she excused herself. "I'm going to powder my nose." She hurried away before Mother could offer to join her.

She headed straight for the lady's lounge, sure Nan would have gone there.

As soon as she entered, Nan hugged her. "I'm so glad you're safe. What are you doing with that terrible man?"

Cordelia was biding her time until she could ascertain a solution. "I have to pretend to be with him so he doesn't kick those people off the land. Is everyone out there all right?"

Nan explained that the girl they had gone to treat would be fine. Nurse Myrtle had examined all the children and a few of the adults, tending to those who needed it. Dutch had convinced most of the residents to remain until they knew for sure they would need to leave. Even so, the trio of Kittitas broke camp and left.

Cordelia couldn't ask for more.

"Mr. Kesner wants to know what happened, why your

sudden change in actions."

"I feel terrible about that. Mr. O'Gillis has agreed to allow the outcasts to stay on the land if I permit him to court me. I'm absolutely sick about it." Cordelia put her hand on her midsection. "You must let Lamar know that this isn't what I want. Please tell him." She needed him to understand her predicament.

"I will. He knew something was wrong with all this." Nan put her hand on Cordelia's arm. "You have really fallen hard for this one."

Cordelia straightened. "I have not. I simply don't care for people to think poorly of me."

Nan gripped Cordelia's shoulders and turned her to face the looking glass. "That is the face of a distraught woman with a whole lot of feelings for a certain handsome gentleman. And you can rest assured that he has been a perfect gentleman. When I asked him if he wanted to hold my hand to make you jealous, he declined. He was emphatic about *not* wanting to give the appearance there was anything more than friendship between us. He merely wants to know what is going on with you and that snake. He's concerned for your well-being."

How sweet. How had she come to care so much for him in so short a time? This wasn't good. She needed to put a stop to these wayward feelings right now. She pushed those thoughts aside and focused on something that didn't matter. "I don't recognize that dress."

Nan smiled and twirled in a circle. "Isn't it lovely. Your beau bought it for me so I wouldn't seem out of place here. He's very thoughtful."

That he was. "I should get back before they begin to worry about me."

Nan nodded. "I'll stay here a moment or two before I follow."

Cordelia's insides twisted. "You go first. My head is beginning to hurt. I'm going to head to my room."

Nan hugged her and slipped out.

After a minute, she exited, glancing around the lobby for any sign of Mr. O'Gillis. She breathed easier that he hadn't followed her.

Loathe to return to the man's company, she crossed

to the reception desk then wrote a note to Father and Mother, asking them to make her apologies. She had a headache and was going to her room, which was unfortunately true. What she really wanted to do was see Lamar, but that was out of the question.

The desk clerk rang a bell, causing an attendant to scurry over. He handed the missive to him. "See that Mr. Armstrong gets this in the dining room."

The bellhop took it with a snappy nod. "Right away."

"Please wait until I'm well in the elevator. Thank you." With the young man's agreement, she headed to the elevator. Once she entered and the doors closed, the pain in her head, neck, and shoulders immediately eased, almost draining away.

Out of polite etiquette, Lamar stood beside his table in the hotel dining room surrounded by the Moseley girls. With Miss Barwick away, they had swarmed his table and weren't taking any of his hints to leave.

Soon, his dining companion returned. She appeared a bit unsure of how to proceed with this crowd of ladies.

Lamar reached out his hand and guided her to her chair. "Miss Barwick, these ladies are each Miss Moseley."

"Oh." Miss Barwick sounded as though she recognized the name. No doubt Cordelia had mentioned them. "Pleased to meet you all."

If she knew them, she might not say that. Or perhaps, she did know and was simply being polite. He thought about taking Miss Barwick's hand to discourage the Moseleys as she had offered that earlier, but he refused to use a deceptive ploy. He dipped his head toward the interlopers. "If you'll excuse us, I think our food is arriving." He held the back of Miss Barwick's chair. When she was settled, he moved to his own seat.

The Moseley girls were slow to move along.

"I did not invite them over." He didn't want Cordelia to return and think he was entertaining them.

Miss Barwick gave him a sweet smile. "I know. Cordelia told me all about them."

He glanced toward Cordelia's table. Fortunately, she hadn't returned yet to witness the spectacle. "Did you see her?"

"I did." She filled him in on the appalling details.

Lamar had suspected O'Gillis was up to no good. He studied the man from across the room. "She hasn't returned."

"She won't be coming back. She had a headache and went to her room. If you ask me, it was an excuse to get away from Mr. O'Gillis."

He shifted his gaze to his supper companion. "Is it serious?"

"Nothing a little distance from that dandy won't solve."

He liked the sound of that. "So, it is as I suspected. She's not willingly in his company."

Miss Barwick shook her head. "He threatened to kick those poor people off the land. She's pretending to allow him to court her for the time being. She'll figure out a solution. Be patient."

Knowing what O'Gillis was up to would garner Cordelia all the patience she needed.

Miss Barwick fussed with her napkin. "Since the purpose for this little outing has been accomplished, would you like to leave?"

He could but didn't want to. "We still need to eat, and our food has already been ordered."

She sighed. "Thank you. I was hoping to be able to wear this gown a little longer before returning it."

"You don't have to return it. It's yours to keep."

Her eyes widened. "I can?"

"Of course. What am I going to do with it? Besides, you deserve it for helping me."

Her eyes watered.

Oh, no. Not tears. What had he done to upset her? He retrieved his handkerchief from a pocket and held it out. "Did I say something wrong?"

Shaking her head, she took his offering then dabbed at her eyes. "You and Cordelia are so much alike."

Cordelia was far kinder and more thoughtful of others than he ever hoped to be. "How so?"

"You give without hesitation. You see a need and fill it without regard for compensation."

"Where Cordelia is concerned, I agree wholeheartedly, but I have done none of that." Though...he did have a new-found desire to be more altruistic like her. For her, it seemed easy and natural. For him, it had to be pointed out. How had he never thought about the actual lives of those in need who went unseen? He knew the poor existed, but it never crossed his mind to do anything for them, not in any significant way. How could he be so callous?

"But you have. You thought nothing of purchasing this dress so I wouldn't feel out of place in this luxurious hotel. Then you have simply given it to me with no expectation of anything in return."

He narrowed his eyes slightly. "Not true. I expected you to accompany me and speak to Cordelia, which you have done."

She gave her head a little shake. "That's easy. You paid for an expensive dress, you picked me up in a regal carriage, and you're paying for supper. While I have done nothing but show up."

"You make me sound selfless. I assure you, I am not. You view the monetary worth of objects and actions as the only aspects of worth. Your character and willingness to aid others is far more valuable than a fancy frock." Because he had vast resources, the cost meant little to him. He supposed, since she likely had limited finances, to purchase such a gown would be a tremendous burden. No amount of money could buy a person an upstanding character. Money certainly hadn't improved O'Gillis's nature.

Miss Barwick inclined her head, indicating the room behind him. "It looks like the dandy has received the news that Cordelia won't be returning to the table."

Lamar resisted the compulsion to turn to view O'Gillis's expression for himself but knew that would make his reason for being here evident. "What's he doing?"

"He's extended his hand toward Mr. Armstrong. My guess is he's asking to see the missive Cordelia had delivered to her father."

Lamar nodded to let her know to continue.

"Mr. Armstrong appears to be contemplating the request. ... Now he's folding the paper. ... And now he's slipping it into his inside jacket pocket."

"What's O'Gillis's response?"

"His hand is still extended as though he expects her father to relinquish the note. ... Now, Mr. Armstrong is turning toward his wife. ... I think she said something to him. ... Mr. Armstrong just got to his feet and assisted his wife with her chair. ... Mrs. Armstrong is standing now. ... He gave Mr. O'Gillis a nod and is escorting his wife out of the room." Miss Barwick's eyes widened. "What a cad. He didn't even rise out of courtesy when Mrs. Armstrong stood."

Had Mr. Armstrong made a curt remark to him? Lamar could only hope. "What is he doing now?"

"Nothing. Just sitting there, but he doesn't look too happy."

Lamar would love to see his face. He would have to be satisfied with his companion's account of the events.

Seventeen

LATER THAT WEEK, LAMAR SAT AT the breakfast table alone. Grandmama hadn't yet made an appearance, but he hoped she would before he had to leave. He needed to inform her of his plans for today, lest she chastise him again.

Their maid Corrine entered the dining room. "Is there anything else you need, Mr. Kesner?"

"No, I've had enough. Thank you." He set his napkin on the table beside his plate. "Do you know when my grandmother will be down?"

"Right soon, I would imagine. Hazel is helping her get ready."

A bit late for Grandmama to just now be getting dressed for breakfast. He hoped she wasn't ill.

He could wait a few more minutes before he needed to leave. "Corrine, would you tell Rogers to have a carriage brought around for me?" Grandmama should be down by the time it was ready.

"Already done, sir. It's waiting out front." She dipped her head and left.

How? He couldn't recall informing Rogers of his departure time. He pushed away from the table and went into the foyer.

Grandmama descended the staircase dressed not in one of her normal frocks she wore to breakfast, not even a morning dress she might wear if she were receiving a visitor. Instead, she wore a walking suit for going out. When she reached the bottom of the stairs, she eyed him, letting her gaze travel his length. "Good. You're ready. Our carriage is waiting. Let us go." She tapped her cane on the marble floor as she turned toward the door.

"*Our* carriage?" Had he forgotten about a business appointment he and Grandmama had? His meeting was too important to put off. "I'm sorry. I can't accompany you. To ward off any hurt feelings, I want to let you know I'm meeting with Mr. O'Gillis and his attorney, as well as ours, over that property I spoke of."

"I know. We don't want to be late." She swept out the door.

She knew? Dumbfounded, he remained stationary for several seconds before following.

From the carriage doorway, only Grandmama's hand could be seen waving him forward. "Hurry along. Tardiness is poor etiquette."

He hastened down the steps and climbed into the carriage. "*You* are going to *my* meeting with Mr. O'Gillis?"

The stable hand clicked the door shut.

"Of course, dear." She folded her gloved hands in her lap.

The carriage eased into motion.

This was unexpected. "I'm capable of a simple business transaction." He did expect a bit of negotiation before the final price was settled on and the contract signed, even though a price had already been agreed upon, more or less.

"I'm well aware. I have the utmost confidence in your abilities."

"Then why are you coming?"

"Don't worry. I won't say a peep. I'll merely observe."

That would be unlike Grandmama to keep quiet.

Outside the attorney's office for the O'Gillises, Mr. Thatcher waited. Smiling, he doffed his hat to Grandmama. "It's always a pleasure to see you, Florence." He stretched out his arm to Lamar and shook his hand. "Wise to bring her."

"I didn't exactly have a choice. She promised to remain silent."

Mr. Thatcher raised his white eyebrows. "We'll see about that. Shall we go inside?"

Lamar motioned for him and Grandmama to lead the way.

Once inside, they were ushered into Mr. Quincy's office where the senior, as well as the junior, Mr. O'Gillis sat at a long table. Both appeared confident, until the senior O'Gillis caught sight of Grandmama. His expression momentarily faltered, and he stood with a nod to Grandmama. "Mrs. Kesner, I wasn't expecting you." He gripped the fabric at the young O'Gillis's shoulder and pulled him to his feet. "Show respect for a lady."

Grandmama lifted her hand with her cane. "Don't mind me." She crossed to a padded chair away from the table. "I'll be the little old lady sitting quietly in the corner. I could use a cup of tea."

Mr. Quincy nodded to his secretary who scooted out of the room. He motioned toward the table. "Shall we sit."

Lamar eyed Grandmama before taking his seat. If he didn't know she was on his side, he wouldn't turn his back on her.

The secretary returned shortly with a tray in hand. "I didn't know if you took sugar or cream."

"How thoughtful." Grandmama dropped two lumps of sugar and a splash of cream into her teacup. "Thank you, my dear."

The secretary smiled at his grandmother then straightened. "Would anyone else like anything?"

The men all declined.

Lamar nodded to Mr. Thatcher.

He retrieved a file from his satchel. "Per our previous discussion, I have drawn up a contract. I sent a copy to you, Mr. Quincy, to review with your client. If all is well, we can have this signed and get on with our day."

Mr. Quincy opened the folder in front of him with—what Lamar assumed was—a marked up copy of the contract. "My client has a few adjustments to the contract."

Of course, he did. This might take a while. Maybe Lamar should have requested something to drink after all.

Behind him, Grandmama clinked her spoon in her teacup.

The elder Mr. O'Gillis stretched out his hand. "The contract is fine as it is."

"Father?" The young O'Gillis glared at the older. "You were going to gift that land to me."

Collin O'Gillis's features hardened. "It's my land, and I'll do with it as I wish."

"But—"

"Enough."

Ian folded his arms like a pouting child.

The senior Mr. O'Gillis nodded toward the contract in front of Mr. Thatcher. "Send it across the table so I can sign."

As Mr. Thatcher did just that, Mr. Quincy intercepted it. "Allow me to give it a quick perusal." He appeared to skim it for the important points he already knew were in there. He eyed Mr. O'Gillis. "This is what we reviewed. Are you sure you want to sign it?"

Lamar indicated the contract. "Will Ian agree to and sign that final paragraph?" It would free Cordelia from the young O'Gillis's clutches.

Ian leaned forward on the table. "He will not."

The elder Mr. O'Gillis studied Lamar. "This agreement is between me and you. Leave my boy out of it."

Mr. Thatcher tapped the papers in front of him. "It's part of the contract. The bank has been instructed not to release the funds indicated until they hear from me that the contract has been honored in full."

Ian fumed, but in the end, his father got his way.

The bank draft was signed as was the deed to the land which were then exchanged.

Surprised at how easy that had been, Lamar stood. "Pleasure doing business with you." He faced Grandmama and assisted her to her feet.

She set her teacup on the long table. Her tea didn't appear to have been touched. "Thank you, gentlemen." She glided out of the room with little need of her cane.

Lamar glanced back at Ian. "See to it you fulfill your portion of the contract by the end of the day."

At the carriage, Lamar shook Mr. Thatcher's hand. "Thank you. I'm a little surprised the O'Gillises gave in so easily." Then he swung around to Grandmama. "Is that why you insisted upon coming? You knew your mere presence would sway him?"

Grandmama straightened, giving her unapologetic expression. "I know you are perfectly capable of standing up for yourself and of making sound business dealings, but I didn't see why this should be any more difficult than it needed to be. The outcome is the same, simply more efficient. I didn't want him to fleece you. You offered and gave him a fair price."

"What do you have on him?"

"Why would you think such a thing?"

Because Collin O'Gillis had come to bargain yet had capitulated too easily. Experience had taught him, no amount of prodding would cajole Grandmama into divulging her secret if she didn't want to. He kissed her on the cheek. "Thank you."

"You're welcome. I would do just about anything for my favorite grandchild." She held up her hand. "But if you tell anyone, I'll deny it. I wouldn't want to hurt the feelings of my other grandchildren."

Lamar suspected she said the same thing to all of his cousins. "I won't say a word." He could keep a secret as well as she could.

After leaving Grandmama at home, Lamar set out on Edelweiss to find Thomas. It didn't take long to locate his friend standing on the boardwalk with a burlap bag slung over his shoulder, likely supplies. "Thomas, I have a job for you."

His friend narrowed his eyes. "Working doesn't suit me." He wiggled the fingers on his free hand. "Delicate hands."

Lamar swung down. His friend did plenty of work around his cabin or else it would collapse on him under the winter snow. "Did I say this job entailed *work*?"

"Most jobs do."

"This one doesn't. All I require from you is to accompany me to the mercantile. I need your help selecting appropriate attire so I don't appear like an *overlord* when I go to the encampment."

Thomas stared at him for several seconds before his eyes widened with what appeared to be understanding. He slapped his thigh and doubled over laughing. "You're serious." He held his midsection with one arm, but it did nothing to curtail his laughing.

What was so humorous about Lamar's request? "Are you quite through?"

Struggling to catch his breath, Thomas wiped tears from his eyes. "Why do you want to go and bother those poor people?"

"I don't want to bother them. I plan to help. I want to determine what they need most—not merely today but into the future." It's what Cordelia would do.

Thomas sighed deeply. "First, nothing you purchase new, even cowhand clothes at the mercantile, will disguise your aristocracy. They would look unused, and you would still be viewed as an overlord. Second, even if you managed to put together the *right* outfit, you can't waltz in there and expect them to tell you everything you want to know. They have, no doubt, been shunned and treated harshly by regular society, so they won't talk to you. Third, a luxuriant beard appropriate for such an endeavor doesn't grow overnight." He combed his fingers through his six-inch long whiskers. "Perfection like this takes time."

His friend made sense—except the excessive facial hair part—but what other way was Lamar going to acquire the information he needed? "How did you learn so much about people such as them?"

Thomas held his hands away from his sides. "I live a charmed life."

"So then, what should I do?"

"O'Gillis will never give you permission to encourage people to remain on his land."

That was why Lamar had taken care of that. "He won't be a problem."

Thomas scowled. "He's always a problem, and where his family's land is concerned, he will be a bigger louse than usual."

"I've removed him from the equation."

Thomas rubbed his hands together, and his eyes twinkled with mock delight. "Sounds devious. Was it painful? Please tell me it was painful."

Lamar chuckled at his friend's impish glee. "Not painful in the way you mean, but it did hurt him. I took away his ability to manipulate Cordelia."

Thomas's eyes widened. "You bought the land?" A

smile stretched beneath his whiskers, and he continued before Lamar could confirm. "You bought the land." He removed his hat and slapped it against his thigh. "Sneaky. That's so much better. He must be livid."

"He certainly wasn't happy."

"What did Miss Armstrong have to say? Did she bat her eyelashes at you—" Thomas demonstrated "—and tell you how wonderful you are?"

Lamar glanced away and rubbed the back of his neck. "I haven't told her."

"You better be quick about it."

Lamar cleared his throat. "I'm not planning to tell her. At least not for a while."

His friend narrowed his eyes. "Why not? She would be *so* grateful, she would write your name on every line of her dance card."

Lamar suspected as much. "That's exactly why I'm not telling her. O'Gillis used the land to force her into a courtship. I don't want her to think I'm doing the same—because I'm not."

Thomas rubbed his hand across his whiskery jaw. "Dangerous game. She could either appreciate your actions and motives and be thankful or hate you forever for keeping this from her."

Lamar knew that too, but it was a risk he had to take. "Once I know how to help the people at the encampment—not just for a few days or weeks—but henceforward, I'll tell—no, I'll show her what I've done."

"And she'll be so grateful, she'll fall into your arms."

"I'm hoping to have her in my arms before that. Will you help me find more suitable clothes for this task than what I currently have?"

Thomas clasped Lamar on the shoulder. "I'll do you one better. I'll go to the encampment and acquire the knowledge you desire."

"How?"

"By setting up camp and becoming one of them."

"You think that will induce them to confide in you?"

Thomas rubbed his hand across his whiskery face again. Something he often did when thinking. "Possibly. Even if they don't tell me directly, I can observe what some of the people need. By living among them, I can ascertain who plans to stay for the winter and which groups intend to move on."

"How long will that take? One? Two nights?"

Thomas shook his head. "As long as it takes. It's hard to say. At least a week. Likely more. Trust won't come easily for these people."

Lamar shook his head. "I can't ask you to do that. Besides, it doesn't seem time efficient."

"I'm volunteering. I'll be able to determine a few things right away. Others will take a while."

"You would do that?"

Thomas shrugged. "Why not? It won't be so different from my place. I can throw a tarp over a rope or tree limb as a makeshift tent. Might even be fun."

His friend's idea of fun and Lamar's differed vastly. "I appreciate this."

Thomas gave a sly smile. "I'll think of some way for you to return the favor."

No doubt. "Let me know if you need *anything*."

Thomas raised an eyebrow. "What? So, you can buy something *new*?"

Lamar extended his arms. "That's all I know how to do."

"We'll have to work on that."

That afternoon, Cordelia strolled along the boardwalk with Nan. "How are you and Dutch settling in at Miss Henny's?" The pair had relocated to the boarding house nearly a week ago. With Miss Henny's daughter having married and moved out, taking her lady's maid with her, two additional rooms had been freed.

"I love living there. It's so homey. Her son and Professor Tunstall are both quite handsome and attentive." Her friend wiggled her eyebrows.

Oh, dear. "Nan, be careful about getting tangled up with the single men residing at the house." Cordelia was sure Miss Henny wouldn't allow anyone of low morals to board at her place. She had questioned even allowing

Cordelia to help others until she knew the truth.

"Oh, don't worry. I have no interest in either of them romantically, but it is fun having the attention. Aunt Henny has warned them both, and I doubt they would cross her."

Cordelia was glad to hear that. "How does Dutch like living there?"

"Hard to say. He hasn't said much either way."

"So, typical for him. Silent and brooding."

"Pretty much. He either stays in his room or leaves the house altogether."

"Where is he today? I'm surprised he's not standing nearby as guardian."

Nan chuckled. "He can overdo it a little. He went to the encampment. The people there from his home country have quite a pull on him."

"It must be nice for him to speak with people with whom he has so much in common." Cordelia liked the idea of someone she trusted out there. "He can keep all of us apprised if anything arises."

"He says it has been quiet, and the people have settled down about being kicked off the land."

"He assured them I'm doing all I can to keep them on the land, didn't he?"

Nan nodded. "At least to the people from the Netherlands and those who speak English. I don't know if Chang and Fu understand much of what anyone says, but they're smart and seem to grasp what's going on."

"I'm glad to hear that. I'm also relieved Dutch can go so often."

"He goes more than he needs to. With his desire to be with people from the Netherlands, I wouldn't be surprised if he decided to stay with them."

That made Cordelia's heart ache at losing her friend, but at the same time, it pleased her that he had found people like himself. "If he chooses them, I won't try to stop him."

Nan planted her hands on her hips in what appeared to be mock annoyance. "Well, I might." She lowered her arms. "I'm happy for him. He always seemed so lonely. I think he misses his home country and the people. He belongs for once."

Cordelia agreed but stopped mid-thought when a rider approached on horseback.

Mr. O'Gillis reined in. "Cordelia dear, we must talk."

She was *not* getting on a horse with him again. It rankled when he used her first name. Adding *dear* made it doubly irksome.

Nan linked her arm with Cordelia's in a supportive gesture, comforting her.

He flicked his gaze to Nan then returned it to Cordelia. "Privately."

Could she refuse without repercussions to the outcasts? She might as well get this over with. Sighing deeply, she patted Nan's hand. "I'll only be a minute."

"I'll be right over here." Though hesitant, Nan stepped away and a few feet to the side yet close enough to intervene.

Mr. O'Gillis narrowed his eyes as he swung off his horse. After tethering the animal, he guided Cordelia farther from Nan. "I don't appreciate that woman's attitude."

Cordelia didn't appreciate his. She forced a smile. "What did you wish to speak to me about?"

He set his jaw in a hard line. His gaze darted around as though he were disinclined to speak to her, almost coerced. His reluctant expression held hints of anger, as though being forced to eat something distasteful.

Should she wait or prod him again?

With one last glance toward Nan, he squared his shoulders then turned his focus on Cordelia. His face hardened into a more calculated resolute countenance. "It has come to my attention that our courtship might not be in my best interest."

A forced relationship was far from actual courting. She blinked. What had he said? Not in *his* interest? Was he breaking things off with her? Dare she be excited about that? Or was this some sort of trick? Would he now kick the outcasts off the land? "What about the people by the river?"

"I couldn't care less about them."

She knew that. "What are you going to do? You aren't going to make them leave, are you?" Cordelia hated feeling and sounding so desperate.

"Not my problem."

What had he meant by that?

He smirked. "We are through. Please don't beg. It's unbecoming."

The way he said that almost sounded as though that was what he wanted. She was disinclined to indulge his ego.

"I'm off to California. Business, you know." He strode to his horse, mounted, and trotted away.

What just happened?

Nan rushed to her side. "What was that about?"

Cordelia wasn't sure. "He broke off the *courtship*."

"That's wonderful."

"Is it?"

"Of course, it is." Nan gave her an encouraging nod. "This is what you wanted."

Cordelia pinned her friend with a hard look. "What is he going to do about the outcasts?"

Nan's expression fell. "Oh, dear. He's going to cause trouble, isn't he? I'm sure Dutch will let us know if anything happens out there."

The one good thing to come from this was that Mr. O'Gillis would be gone—at least for a while. Cordelia wanted to be happy, but dread coiled inside her.

Eighteen

ON FRIDAY, CORDELIA SAT IN THE Atwood dining room with her parents. She set her knife and fork across her mostly empty breakfast plate. "I don't see why I can't go about town. I told you Mr. O'Gillis broke things off. I won't be seeing him anymore." Hopefully, he wouldn't change his mind and return to Kamola soon.

"I think it's best if you stay at the hotel today." Father pinned her with a hard gaze. "No pouting and no sneaking off. I'll task your lady's maid to keep an eye on you. If you disobey, it will be her job you've sacrificed."

Helena didn't deserve that. Cordelia resisted the urge to expel a large sigh.

Father knew how to force her to behave. He softened his expression toward her. "I'm doing this for your own good. It's my responsibility to keep you from harm."

Trapping her in the hotel wasn't protecting her.

Mother set her teacup down. "Don't fret over it. It looks like rain. You don't want to get caught in a downpour."

"I could take an umbrella."

Lamar strolled up to the table. "Good morning." He nodded to each of them. "I hope you are all well."

Everything within Cordelia reacted to his presence with delight.

A smile pulled at Father's mouth as he stood and shook Lamar's hand. "Good morning. We are well. Please join us."

"Thank you for the tempting offer, but I was wondering if I could borrow your daughter today."

He'd come for her? Cordelia didn't think he would ever want to talk to her again after choosing Mr. O'Gillis over him, regardless of the reason. Obviously, Nan had successfully convinced him she had been coerced. She turned imploring eyes on Father.

"Of course. She may go with you."

Lamar dipped his head to Father. "Thank you." He held out a hand to Cordelia. "Would you do me the honor of joining me?"

She placed her hand in his and rose to her feet. Her heart reacted to his touch and nearness.

Mother tilted her head. "Don't forget a shawl and an umbrella."

Cordelia didn't want to take the time to go all the way upstairs. She wanted to leave while Father was inclined to allow her to do so.

Lamar addressed Mother. "No need to worry. I have an umbrella if we should need it and a blanket in my carriage. If that's acceptable?"

Father nodded. "Of course. Go and have a lovely day."

Lamar offered his arm which she eagerly took. He escorted her through the lobby to the exit then outside to his carriage.

Clouds hung dark in the sky—rain for sure before day's end.

He nudged the horse into motion. "Thank you for agreeing to come with me."

"I must admit I was surprised. I wasn't expecting you."

"It is Friday. I figured you would want to sew with Miss Henny and the other ladies."

Oh dear. He didn't know. She swallowed hard.

Lamar steered the carriage onto the street. "I hope you're not disappointed I came."

"No, not at all." She was disappointed with herself for taking advantage of him. "Please stop the carriage."

"Why?"

"Please."

With a gentle tug, the horse halted. "What's wrong?"

"You came in good faith to see to it I could attend the quilting circle. I was so eager to escape from the hotel, I didn't even realize that was your reason for coming. I got word yesterday that Lily Hammond had her baby. Miss Henny cancelled the group for this week so she can help her new daughter-in-law. At least, I think that's the relationship. Henny's married to Lily's husband's father—

so yes, she would be her daughter-in-law."

Cordelia was babbling, but she couldn't seem to stop herself. She was so relieved to have Mr. O'Gillis gone and to have been able to leave the hotel. "I have taken terrible advantage of you to make my escape. I'm sure you were expecting to leave me at Miss Henny's and go on about your business. I still want you to do that. I can stroll around town—if you'll allow me to borrow your umbrella." She took a breath. "Oh, do say something."

He chuckled. "I was waiting until you were quite through."

How embarrassing. "I am. I'll be quiet now."

"Are Mrs. Hammond and the baby doing well?"

"Oh, yes. She had a boy. I don't know if they have named him yet."

"If you aren't going to Miss Henny's, that means, I have you all to myself for the whole day."

"You aren't upset with me?"

"Of course not. This is really the first chance you've had to inform me."

She took a deep calming breath. "Thank you for understanding."

"Well, since our plans have changed, what would you like to do today?"

"I don't want to encroach on your time any more than I already have. What had you planned before I messed things up?"

"Only to tinker in my workshop on my hot air balloon, but I don't need to do that."

"I wouldn't want to keep you from your work."

"It would be unchivalrous of me to abandon you now that I have you. I'm at your service."

Knowing he'd had plans, she felt bad to keep him from them. "I could go with you and watch." Anything to be free of expectations.

"That wouldn't be very romantic."

Oh, no. As lovely as romance with Lamar sounded, she couldn't allow anything of that nature to develop between them—at least on his end of the relationship. It was already too late for her. "What about going to the encampment?" About as unromantic as it could get.

Seemingly caught off guard, he hesitated before speaking. "If it does rain—and I'm sure it will—being out there would be a bad idea."

He was right, of course. They could get trapped there or end up in a muddy ditch.

"Then that leaves your workshop."

He gave her a sideways look. "You truly want to go there?"

"Why not? It could be interesting." And no chance of it being romantic.

"Very well." He prodded the horse into motion again.

When Lamar drove alongside his stables, he stopped. "Hank, would you follow us to my workshop and take care of the carriage? You can hop on if you like. I would rather Miss Armstrong didn't to have to walk."

Cordelia pointed toward the oversized building nearly a quarter mile across the yard. "It's not that far. I can walk."

Lamar glanced at her shoes. "Are you sure? The ground can be uneven."

"I've walked there before."

Lamar was well aware of that excursion. "As the lady wishes." He climbed down and helped her. So refreshing that she didn't claim to be a helpless female incapable of doing anything. He offered her his arm. When she slipped her hand into the crook of his elbow, he couldn't believe the satisfaction with that simple action. As though every one of his senses had come alive and alert.

Though he hadn't known Cordelia all that long, less than two months, he sensed he might not mind spending the rest of his life getting to know her.

Whoa there, Lamar. Don't fly off in that balloon before you've checked all the riggings and have enough information for that kind of flight. Simply enjoy the lady's company today.

Once inside, he pointed to the balloon basket. "Probably best to steer clear of that. I wouldn't want you to fall in." He couldn't help but tease her.

She appeared to suppress a smile. "I would never dream of it." She strolled toward the far end of the building where the heavy rope net that encapsulated the colorful balloon envelope lay stretched out on the floor. "What are you doing with this?"

"I inspect each knot and all along the ropes for any weaknesses."

"Have you found anything?"

"There are a couple of spots I wouldn't mind shoring up."

She tilted her head. "Don't you have one of your staff do that?"

"I prefer to do it. I like seeing to the details." He knew every inch of this balloon.

Upon her insistence, he showed her where the potential defects were and even repaired the worst of the offenses. She seemed genuinely interested.

Cordelia pointed to something behind him. "It appears as though your household staff is invading."

Lamar swiveled around. Framed in the large door opening were, indeed, many of the staff approaching, each carrying various items.

Rogers led the charge. "Luncheon, sir."

The entourage set up a small café table with a linen covering, chairs, a slender crystal vase with a single rose, dishware, a carafe of coffee, china pot with tea, a pitcher of lemonade, and several dishes of various foods.

Someone had obviously informed Grandmama of his and Cordelia's presence.

Once everything had been put in place and the others began their retreat, Rogers addressed Lamar. "Is there anything else you require?"

Lamar hadn't required any of this but was grateful for it. "It appears we have more than we need. Thank you." He wouldn't have thought to concoct a lavish spread like this. Often when working on his balloon, he forgot to eat lunch all together. When he got hungry enough, he would have suggested that they go inside to eat, but this was much preferred. He would have Cordelia to himself.

Rogers dipped his head and left.

Definitely a pleasant surprise.

Cordelia lifted a silver lid off of a platter of sliced fruit and cheese. "When did you arrange all this? You didn't know we would come here."

When he'd left this morning, he never would have guessed he would be in his workshop with her. "As much as I would love to take credit for this elaborate display, this would be my grandmother's doing."

"How did she know we were here? Or does she always send an extravagant meal to you?"

"She never does anything like this. Perhaps the plate of cheeses and fruit or a sandwich." At least when he was out here alone she didn't. Grandmama must really like Cordelia, as did he. "Either she witnessed our arrival, or one of the staff informed her. Are you upset about this?"

"Not at all. I'm actually quite hungry."

"As am I." He smiled. "Shall we eat?" He held a chair for her.

"Since your grandmother went to a great deal of trouble, I suppose we should." She sat. "Thank you."

He lifted the silver dome covering her plate before removing his and seating himself.

Grandmama had gone all out for this. Roasted new potatoes nestled next to a baked quail with asparagus in a cream sauce. A meal to impress. She must have had cook start on this as soon as they drove by.

Motioning toward the smaller service table, he took a step toward it. "It appears as though we have coffee, tea, lemonade, and water. Which would you prefer?"

"Lemonade, please."

He poured some for each of them. He felt he should apologize for such an extravagant display and so much fuss but thought it might be best not to draw too much attention to it. Focus on the lovely lady across from him.

At the end of the meal, she dipped her head toward him. "You have a bit of sauce on your upper lip."

With his tongue, he licked at it but didn't taste the wayward cuisine.

She picked up a napkin then, leaning across the small table, dabbed at his face. "Got it."

Her touch quickened his heart. "Thank you." His words came out husky.

When her gaze lifted to his eyes, she whispered, "You're welcome."

He found himself inching closer to her.

With an intake of breath, her eyes widened, and she turned away.

He had embarrassed her. Best not to highlight that. He took the carafe. "Would you like some coffee?"

"Yes, please."

After pouring for them both, he took a sip. Cold. He stood. "I suppose you'll be wanting to return to the Atwood."

She set her napkin next to her plate as she looked toward the large open doorway. Rain pelted down in sheets. "It appears the clouds have ceased to hold back."

"I hadn't noticed until now."

"Me either."

He could run through the deluge and get a vehicle. "What would you like to do? I could retrieve a carriage."

"In this storm? That's not necessary. Before the food arrived, you mentioned something about cleaning the blast valve."

"You remembered."

She flashed a smile. "I'm surprised too, but it sounded interesting. I could help you."

Very surprising. He showed her the tools he would use and explained the process before starting.

She handed him tools as he needed them without him having to point to any of them. She had evidently committed each one to memory.

More intriguing all the time.

Hard to believe she was assisting him and seemed to be enjoying herself. He flicked his gaze to her. A streak of dirt marred her rosy cheek. Should he tell her? Most women would be embarrassed. If he didn't let her know and she later discovered the smudge was there, she would also be embarrassed and likely be upset with him.

"Why are you looking at me like that?"

Caught. *Because you are the most enchanting lady I've ever met.* He'd best confess. "I was debating whether it would be worse to inform you about the bit of dirt on your face or not tell you."

Straightening, she lifted grease-stained fingers toward her face. "Where?"

He wrapped his hands around hers. "I'm afraid I've failed as a host, and allowed you to get soiled from helping me." With her hands still enclosed in his, he guided her to his workbench where he gave her a towel to wipe the dirt off. He took a second cloth and dabbed at the blotch on her cheek, smearing it. He'd made a mess of this outing. Her parents would be displeased with him.

When she stilled, he shifted his attention to her green eyes.

As before, every sense in his being flamed to life, only this time tenfold. He dared not move lest he rupture this wonderful moment. He would wait for her to turn away as she had done before.

However, she didn't, seemingly as helpless as him to dispel what was happening.

The tether between them pulled him ever nearer.

With the back of his fingers, he caressed her cheek. Then her mouth.

She shivered under his touch but didn't retreat.

He cupped her face with his hands and pressed his lips to hers.

She leaned into him with a sigh.

He sighed too and wrapped his arms around her.

Her lips were soft and warm.

Why had he waited so long?

That night, Cordelia fought with her covers as she tossed in bed. Finally, she threw off the bedding as she slipped to the floor, kneeling in the darkness. She hadn't been so reverent in a very long time. Maybe she would get her desired answer this way. She interlaced her fingers. *Lord, I want to be with Lamar, but I also want to do as You wish, to help people in need. I can't do both. It's impossible. Either take the desire to build a life with Lamar away or release me from the calling to minister to the outcasts.*

She waited.

No change.

Then, in an almost audible voice, she heard her Lord.

I Am the Great I Am.

She took a slow breath to contemplate.

God competed with no man.

There was but one choice.

God.

Yet, her longing for Lamar remained. She understood. She was to obey the Lord's calling regardless of whether or not her feelings for Lamar diminished.

With an aching heart, tears flooded her eyes. "Yes, Lord."

Nineteen

HENNY STOOD AT THE KITCHEN TABLE, packing a basket of food to take over to the sheriff's. With the new baby in the Hammond household, Henny wanted to make sure they didn't skimp on meals. Helping her were the three older Hammond children.

Nancy and Toby, six and five, had abandoned their task of filling a cloth bag with molasses cookies after having eaten two apiece. Now, they chased each other from the kitchen through the dining room to the parlor and back. Since they weren't hurting anything, Henny allowed them to continue. The child laughter warmed her heart.

Eight-year-old Estella carefully wrapped a loaf of fresh baked bread to put into the basket. "Mama and Papa won't let them run inside at home."

Hearing Estella call her new stepmother Mama also warmed Henny's heart. "I'm sure they don't, but with all the rain we received yesterday and last night, it's preferable to having them track in mud. Also, it's better for them to expend some of that energy here before they return home."

Henny had insisted that the older children stay over with her and Saul last night to give the parents time with their new baby, Scott.

A knock sounded on the door.

Henny's husband, Saul, put down the tea towel he was using to dry dishes. "I'll see who it is."

At the same time, Nancy called from the other room. "I'll get it!"

Henny raised her eyebrows. "Looks like you have competition."

"I'll make sure the little ones don't scare anyone off." Saul chuckled as he left the kitchen.

Estella shook her head. "Nancy always has to answer the door. Even when Mama and Papa tell her not to."

"She's just excited." Henny had been a bit like Nancy, taking every opportunity to be around people.

Muffled voices drifted through the house. Soon, they drew closer, until little Toby scooted into the kitchen ahead of the others and tucked in around Henny's hip. He was still shy around people he didn't know well.

Saul entered next. "Look who I found on our porch."

Lamar Kesner appeared in the doorway with Nancy clinging to his back, nearly choking the poor man. "Good morning, everyone."

Lamar needed to find himself a good woman to marry. He obviously loved children, and they seemed to return the affection.

"What brings you here, Lamar?" Henny tied a string around cloth-wrapped biscuits.

"I have a favor to ask of you. Would you be able to keep Miss Armstrong away from the immigrant camp?"

Henny's hackles rose. He wasn't thinking to control the young woman, was he? "I would need to know your motive for such a request." She hadn't seen him since that day he'd turned up at the quilting circle to announce the bachelor quilt. He'd seemed pleasant to the people at the encampment.

"I want to help them and surprise her, but I don't want her to know yet."

Henny supposed that would be fine. "All right. I'll try to dissuade her if she brings it up, but I have no plans to go until after Founders' Day."

"I appreciate that. I'm headed out there now."

Saul pointed. "In those clothes?"

Lamar smiled as though proud. "I am. Some of my older clothes. I roughed them up a bit. I don't want the people to think I'm there to cause them trouble."

Though they were a little less Kesner, they would still cause him to come across as an outsider at the encampment. Too much of an outsider. Henny didn't want to discourage him, but his choice wasn't going to accomplish what he wanted. "Is your shirt silk?"

He glanced down and nodded hesitantly. "It's from at

least three years ago." He rubbed a hand across his stubbly jaw. "I didn't shave this morning either. Grandmama would consider me scandalous. I slipped away before she could see."

The diminutive whiskers that shadowed his face would help but were far from enough.

Saul gripped his shoulder. "Come with me, son. Let's see what we can find for you that would truly cause your grandmother to call you scandalous."

Lamar furrowed his brow. "Is what I'm wearing not good enough?"

"The problem is they're too good." Henny wiggled her hands at him. "Go on."

"I just can't get this right." He set Nancy down and followed Saul.

When Nancy tried to tag along, Henny stopped her. "You stay here."

Nancy shrugged. "All right. Toby, let's go play." She ran into the other room with Toby trotting after her.

Henny and Estella continued to fill the basket. She prayed her husband would be successful in helping Lamar not be so obvious at the camp.

Lamar strolled back into Miss Henny's kitchen in a blue-plaid cotton shirt and gray wool trousers held up with a single strap of a pair of suspenders. "How do I look?"

Miss Henny gaped at his attire. "I was supposed to mend those pants." The hem had fallen loose from one leg and a small tear marred the shin portion. "Isn't that shirt missing a button?" She was woefully behind on her mending. She could catch up after the Founders' Day Festival. "I think you will fit right in."

Saul plopped Henny's old felt gardening hat on his head. "Now, he'll fit in."

"Is this enough?" Lamar held out his arms. "Won't they still realize I don't belong? I'm sure some of them will recognize me from before."

"Likely, but this might be less intimidating for them." Saul surveyed his handiwork.

The pair of them were probably right.

"Thank you for all this. They may not accept me no matter what I wear. I'll be off." Lamar strolled through the house to the front door.

Miss Barwick leaned against it with her arms folded. "You're heading to the encampment, and you are keeping that from Cordelia. I thought I liked you, but now I'm not so sure."

He couldn't afford to make an enemy of Miss Barwick. "It's only for a little bit. I want to surprise her. Please help keep her from the immigrant camp."

She narrowed her eyes. "You're going to tell her eventually?"

"Yes. I promise."

"When?"

"After Founders' Day. That's only two weeks away."

She relaxed her expression. "I suppose I can do that."

"Thank you." Lamar left and swung onto Edelweiss.

He rode to the spot Thomas had stopped at before and tethered his horse. Lamar might be able to disguise himself with different clothes, but he couldn't mask his mare's thoroughbred bloodlines. He patted his horse's neck. "I'll return in a bit."

Edelweiss bobbed her head.

Taking a deep breath, Lamar strolled into camp. Saul had suggested he go to the river and scoop up water to drink to show everyone he wasn't a threat.

As he crossed the camp, the occupants watched him. He nodded and smiled to a few. His friend wasn't among them. Thomas was who he most wanted to see, to get an update on what he'd learned.

At the river, he crouched and dipped his hand in the frigid water. *My, that was cold.* He sipped it.

A deep male voice came from behind him. "What are you doing here?"

Straightening, Lamar turned to face Dutch. "I merely want to see how everyone is doing."

"They do better when people like you do not bother them."

"I mean them no harm." Since Thomas didn't seem to be about, Dutch could be a good ally—if the man was willing. "I want to help. What do they need most?"

Standing with his feet apart, Dutch folded his arms across his barrel chest. "To be left alone so they can take care of themselves and their families."

Lamar figured that, but with their present circumstances, winter was going to be harsh for them. A little assistance could ease the burden and suffering. "Do they all plan to stay throughout the winter?"

"If that landowner does not throw them off."

That was already one thing he'd done to ease their burden. "I can promise you, no one is going to make them leave. They can stay without fear of anyone expelling them. Will you let the people know?"

Dutch narrowed his eyes. "You are sure of that?"

"Positive."

The big man's shoulders visibly relaxed. "They will be happy to hear."

Progress toward gaining this man's support.

But assuring them they could stay was far from all they would require to survive the winter. "They could probably use firewood."

"They gather what they need. They do not want charity. Leave them alone." Dutch strode away.

By the guarded expressions on the residents' faces, Dutch was likely going to be the most helpful person here. Unless... He scanned the area. Still no Thomas.

He walked over to a lean-to that hadn't been there on his previous visit. The occupant wasn't home. The belongings appeared as though they could be Thomas's. Since there were no other vacated dwellings, Lamar would assume this was where Thomas was living. Where had he gone? Perhaps hunting or fishing.

After walking around the camp and greeting each person not in hiding, Lamar headed back to Edelweiss. He would return another time to catch his friend.

Next to Lamar's horse stood Thomas. What was he doing *here*? Why wasn't he at the camp?

Lamar closed the distance. "I was looking for you in the encampment."

"I know. It's best if we aren't seen together. If the people find out we know each other, I won't learn anything for you and might as well skedaddle."

Made sense, but how else was Lamar supposed to get an update?

Thomas sized up Lamar, even circling him. "These aren't your clothes and don't appear to be recently purchased. They have a natural wear to them. Who's your tailor?"

"The senior Mr. Hammond helped me. Do they meet with your approval?"

"The hat really sells it."

"It's Miss Henny's." Lamar rubbed his hand across his prickly jaw. "I skipped shaving to help too."

Thomas squinted and leaned in closer. "So you did. Almost missed that."

"I thought whiskers would make me appear more unkempt."

"You call those whiskers?" Thomas stroked his bushy beard.

Lamar didn't appreciate his friend's teasing. Time to move on from his appearance and get to the business which brought him here. "I spoke with Dutch and told him no one would make these people leave."

"Did he believe you?"

"I think so, but he wouldn't tell me what else anyone could use. When I asked about firewood, he said the people would find what they needed. Then he walked away. No discussion. Nothing. Gone."

"Dutch is a good man. He mostly sticks with the band from the Netherlands, but pitches in wherever he can."

Lamar sensed the big man had a good character. "Have you learned anything useful? These people require more than simply allowing them to remain on the land. I'm going to make sure they all have enough firewood and somehow get them to accept food to last them through the winter."

Thomas lifted a hand. "Hold up. You can't go showering gifts on them like you do rich folks."

If Lamar offered an expensive gift to someone like one

of the Moseley girls, they would take it greedily. He shook his head. "I don't understand why the people who *need* help the most are reluctant to receive it, and the people who don't *need* it, would accept it and expect more."

"A lot of poor people are proud. By giving them things, you're telling them they aren't capable of taking care of themselves and their family. That they aren't good enough."

Lamar could understand that. Most people wanted to take care of their own. "So how do I help them while leaving their pride intact."

Thomas stroked his beard. "I've been thinking about that and have an idea, but I don't know if you'll like it. It's not something you can throw money at and be done with it. You willing to hear my plan?"

If money wasn't the answer—and Lamar wasn't convinced it wasn't—then his friend's solution must cost time. Everything cost one or the other and often both. "Of course."

Cordelia met Nan in the Atwood Hotel dining room for lunch. Cordelia had sent a hotel carriage for her friend.

After ordering, Nan gazed around the dining room. "This is a first. The two of us in public like this. With no worries of who sees us together."

It was different and refreshing. "We do attend the same quilting circle."

"That we do."

"It's sort of public." Though not really the same thing. Only a limited number of people would see them. Here, anyone could walk in and witness them together.

"Are you going to tell me the purpose of this meeting?"

Before Cordelia could answer, Mother stopped by the table.

"Mother, this is Nannette Barwick. She's one of the ladies from the quilting circle." If not for the friendly group's connection, Cordelia wouldn't have ventured to meet Nan where her parents could readily see them.

Mother smiled. "Miss Barwick, I'm pleased to make your acquaintance."

Nan returned the smile. "I'm pleased to meet you as well."

Mother squinted slightly. "You seem vaguely familiar. Have we met before?"

Most likely, Mother had seen Nan in more than one city they had visited and certainly back in Connecticut.

Nan giggled. "No, we've never met. Maybe I resemble someone you know."

Mother hesitated. "Perhaps. You ladies have a nice luncheon." She strolled away.

Cordelia blew out a breath. "That was close. If I had been you, I would have told her she'd never seen me before."

Nan tilted her head. "She asked if we had met. Which we haven't. Has she seen me before? Many times. Most recently could have been in this very dining room the other night with your Mr. Kesner."

Cordelia liked the sound of *her* Mr. Kesner. "Oh, I hope she doesn't remember that. It could cause unwanted tension. She would fear you are trying to steal Lamar away from me."

"I wouldn't worry overly much about it. When someone thinks they have met you or seen you, I believe it's best to confirm that they do indeed recognize you. Their mind has a positive response to their quandary and is satisfied. On the other hand, if you give them no acknowledgement of their recognition and deny what they believe, their mind continues to search for the answer."

"That's smart of you."

"Thank you." Nan leaned forward. "Now, tell me about your rendezvous with Mr. Kesner."

"It was so unexpected. You should have seen it. The table with the fancy linen and tableware. All the delectable food." Cordelia described the whole meal in detail. "He could have easily taken credit for the whole thing. How was I to know if he'd given a signal to the stable hand or spoken to him quietly? Yet he didn't claim responsibility. He gave his grandmother all the recognition. That was so sweet."

Nan tilted her head. "You sound like a woman in love."

Even Cordelia heard the wistfulness in her voice. "I know. But I'm not. We met less than two months ago. I can't be in love. It's been too short a time. I have no business having feelings for him or anyone when God has given me a different calling."

"You have sacrificed so much. Don't you think it's enough? Surely God will release you from this duty, allow you to live a normal life."

"I stayed up late, praying about this, begging to be discharged from my duty. Not only didn't I get that sense, but the urging to minister to the outcasts was even stronger."

"Maybe you should give him a chance."

Cordelia didn't dare. "If my parents suspected for one minute I might like him, they will start planning the wedding. As you know, my mother has already begun the hunt for a gown. I've managed to slow her progress by being indecisive, but if she senses my attraction to him, my freedom to help others will come to an abrupt end."

"I think he's different from your previous beau."

Cordelia wanted nothing more. "In my experience, men will promise anything, using very convincing arguments, then after the ceremony, everything changes. It happened to my cousin and a couple of my school friends." She wished society worked differently.

"With your parents pushing and his involvement in the bachelor quilt, you can't ignore the poor man."

"I'll do the best I can." She recalled being in his arms and the feel of his lips on hers. She had wanted to stay there forever and pretend the rest of the world didn't exist.

"Why are you blushing?" Nan smiled. "Did something

happen between you and the handsome Kesner boy?"

Cordelia wasn't sure if she should say but nodded anyway. "He kissed me."

"Oo-oo." Nan's face brightened. "Tell me all about it."

"His expression revealed what he was about to do. My head screamed 'No! Run away!', but my heart held me in place, welcoming his touch. I liked it. A lot."

Nan sighed. "I can picture it. What are you going to do?"

"The only thing I can do. Avoid him at all cost."

"I don't see how that will be possible unless you leave town." Her friend's eyes widened. "Are you leaving town?"

Cordelia shook her head. "But after Founders' Day, I may have to." Staying away from him would be challenging, but she had to do everything in her power to resist the pull he had on her and pray more fervently.

Lord, I'm not strong enough. I feel my fortitude waning. Help me remain steadfast in Your calling.

Even with her pleading, she longed to feel Lamar's warm soft lips on hers, one more time.

Twenty

ON MONDAY, LAMAR DROVE A WAGON full of tools into the immigrant encampment. Time to put his and Thomas's idea into action.

The residents eyed him suspiciously as he came to a stop and set the brake. Thomas said this plan had the best chance of working, but there were no guarantees. Adults stood at a distance with small children tucked safely behind them.

Lamar jumped down and motioned. "Come closer."

No one moved. A couple of men folded their arms across their chests.

This wasn't going to be easy. At least his friend stood among the others, as one of them—part of the strategy. He might as well get started. "The owner of this land wants to make it profitable. He would like to hire people from this camp to cut timber and construct buildings and other things." He'd decide it would be best if he didn't claim ownership yet. It would encourage the people to be more willing to accept him and his assistance. "Who here has any experience with either?"

No one volunteered. However, Dutch seemed to be speaking to the Netherland people.

Thomas raised a hand half-staff. "I built my cabin, and I'm handy with an ax."

"Wonderful. I can use your help. Anyone else." Lamar scanned the crowd.

With Thomas's willingness, other adults whispered to each other.

Dutch stepped forward. "I do not live here, but I wish to work." His volunteering would give courage to others.

"Thank you. No worker will be turned away. Who else?" He studied the leery faces. Would he have only two volunteers? The only two who weren't actually a part of the community. Thomas said it might be hard to win their trust and not to push them. So be it. Lamar would start with two. He pointed to Thomas and Dutch. "Come forward both of you, and I'll tell you where to get started."

Both men strode toward him.

Lamar stuck out his hand. "Dutch, welcome aboard." He shook the man's large hand then turned to Thomas. "I'm Lamar. I don't believe you were here the last time I was."

Thomas shook his. "Thomas."

They had decided not to announce their connection too quickly so the community members would continue to trust Thomas.

His friend flicked a finger in the direction of the bovine tethered to the back of the wagon. "What's with the cow?"

Lamar smiled. "I'm glad you asked." Lily Hammond and Nicole Keegan had donated the cow. "The workers will be well fed. Can't have anyone collapsing from lack of food." He ensured his voice was loud enough to carry but not obviously so. "As part of the pay, every family who has at least one member working for me will receive a quart crock of fresh milk. Each day, they work, they can refill their crock."

Thomas raised an eyebrow, which Lamar understood as his approval. Not something they had discussed, but Lamar figured it would be acceptable to the immigrants. He wouldn't be giving them food. They would be earning it.

Thomas tipped his head to something behind Lamar he wanted him to see. "Looks like you're making progress."

Lamar spun around. Four men and one woman, with a baby on her hip and two more little ones not far behind her, approached. Lamar nodded. Maybe this would work after all. He waited until the small group gathered around him. "I'm going to need someone here at the camp to be my foreman." He indicated his friend. "Since Thomas was the first to volunteer, I'll name him as foreman—on a trial basis."

Thomas dipped his head. "I don't know how good I'll do, but I'll try my best."

"I can't ask for anything more." He shifted his attention to the others. "As for the rest of you, can you tell me what skills you have?"

Dutch immediately translated for two of the men.

The two Chinese brothers joined the group.

Lamar addressed them. "Do you speak English?"

They both nodded, and one replied. "Speak little."

That was fortunate, because Lamar didn't know Chinese. "Thomas, there's a ledger in the back of the wagon. Would you use it to write each worker's name and their skills, so I can best utilize them?"

His friend narrowed his eyes. "What do you need us to build? I can write things down later."

Lamar wanted the information upfront but nodded. "You're the foreman. First, I need a pen and barn for the cow."

The mother with the three children raised her hand. "I do not have a husband to work for you, but my son and I know how to milk the cow." She had a heavy Irish accent. Her son didn't appear to be more than eight or nine.

Perfect. "Of course. Thomas, if it's all right with you, we can give her charge over milking and tending to the cow."

His friend pulled a face. "Better than me having to do it." He softened his expression as he turned it on the young mother. "What's your name?"

"Molly Ferguson. My bairns can use the milk."

Molly along with her children were all thin slips of things. They would have a hard time lasting the winter without some meat on their bones.

"You and your children will have milk." Lamar would see to it.

She shook her head. "I won't take any of the milk from my wee little ones."

Now wasn't the time to argue with these people. "Let Thomas know if you would rather be paid with money or food and supplies."

Thomas organized the seven other men and headed to the timberline to cut the first of the trees. Before long, a rough corral was built, and the beginnings of a barn-shed-shelter structure had a foundation. Both would suffice while sturdier ones were constructed.

Phase one had begun. He wished Cordelia were here to see what was taking place. Soon enough. He must be patient.

On Thursday evening, when Cordelia and her parents entered the hotel dining room, her gaze went immediately to Lamar Kesner seated at her parents' reserved table. She struggled to control her dancing heart. It had been so long. Then she noticed his grandmother with him. How had she missed the elegant matriarch?

Avoiding Lamar hadn't been as difficult as she'd thought. Until now. He had been conspicuously absent from her life this week. To have him at supper with her and her parents was both a relief and a worry. He hadn't been around since they'd kissed. Early on in the week, she'd come to the conclusion he'd regretted his actions that day, which had comforted as well as saddened her. Both yearning to see him and wishing him to stay away. She was a mess full of contradictions.

He held out her chair. "Miss Armstrong, you're looking quite fetching this evening."

Father assisted Mother.

"Thank you." Cordelia sat as he pushed her chair in. "I wasn't expecting you at supper."

With a dip of his head, he took his seat. "I ran into your father in town, and he invited my grandmother and me."

She wouldn't be surprised if Father had hunted Lamar down. Father had spoken several times about Lamar's absence and wondered if he'd lost interest in Cordelia. She had prayed he both had and hadn't.

To protect her heart, she interacted minimally throughout the supper conversation. No more than a nod, a smile, or a brief agreement was required from her. Fortunately, her parents kept Lamar and his grandmother engaged with lively discussions.

Or was that *unfortunately*? Her parents seemed to be more and more enamored with him, as was Cordelia. No one seemed to notice her lack of engagement, which was beneficial for her. She could enjoy his company without risk.

After supper, Lamar stood and offered his arm to her. "Can I entice you to stroll with me in the hotel gardens?"

She shouldn't but couldn't really refuse.

When Cordelia hesitated, Lady Kesner spoke. "A stroll would be lovely." She waved her fingers as though dismissing them. "I have business to discuss with your parents."

It wouldn't be wise to be alone with this alluring bachelor, especially after the last time. What other choice did she have with everyone else against her? Cordelia placed her hand on Lamar's forearm and stood. "I would like that." Her heart rejoiced.

Across the lobby, Lamar opened the exterior door for her.

The evening air had cooled from the heat of the September day. The bright, early-fall blooms of red-orange chrysanthemums, yellow daisies, and purple floss flowers gave the ornamental grounds a festive appearance. However, she couldn't enjoy them with the despair swirling in the pit of her stomach.

After a few more steps, he spoke. "You were quiet during supper."

So, he'd noticed. This would be the point where her alternate personality would have giggled. Instead, she shrugged. "I enjoyed listening to the banter. Your grandmother's quite a spirited lady."

"She's quite something. Never a dull moment." He escorted Cordelia to the gazebo near a pond. "I have something for you." He retrieved a red velvet pouch from his pocket.

Even though she knew she shouldn't, she took it. He had bought her a gift? How sweet.

"Open it." He looked as eager as a child on Christmas morning.

If she did, she might be irrevocably opening her heart to him. She pulled at the drawstring top then slipped out an ornate silver hair comb. "It's beautiful." She couldn't allow this and dropped the comb back into the velvet bag.

"I can't accept this."

He removed the comb from the pouch. "Of course you can." He darted his gaze to her hair. "May I?"

Her will dissolved, and she nodded.

He tucked it into her tresses with a smile. "Beautiful."

She suspected he might not be talking about the comb.

He put the velvet bag into his pocket. "I must beg your forgiveness for being woefully negligent in my courtship duties to you."

Though she liked the idea, she couldn't afford to have him thinking of this as a courtship and where *that* would lead. "You're not negligent. You don't have to spend time with me."

"But that's what couples do when they're courting."

"Are we courting?" She needed him to doubt it. It would be easier when she broke things off with him. "From the start, neither of us wanted this match. Nothing has changed."

"Hasn't it?"

Her feelings for him might have, but her resolve to help the poor rather than marry hadn't. She had no choice. 'Twould be best to be honest and straightforward. She mustered her courage. "The Lord has called me to minister to the underprivileged."

"I understand that, but what does it have to do with courting?"

"Everything." A twilight breeze brushed over her bare arms, causing a shiver to ripple her body.

"You're cold." Lamar quickly removed his dinner jacket and draped it around her shoulders.

She wanted to refuse, until his warmth enveloped her. "Thank you."

"Now, tell me why helping others and courting are incompatible."

"Because, men don't want a wife to do such things."

"I wouldn't make you stop giving aid to people."

He might say that now, but it would never last. "My cousin's husband said a similar thing until they married. He said she had to focus on their family and nothing else. Same story with some of my friends from school."

"I won't be like that. You can do both."

She wanted desperately to believe that. "I can't."

"Are you saying God told you to never marry?"

Cordelia nodded.

He clasped her hands in his. "I have received an entirely different leading."

"You don't understand. Please don't make this harder than it has to be."

"Is there nothing I can say to convince you?"

She didn't dare respond, and shook her head.

After a moment, he jerked away. "*You* are the one making this hard."

"I never wanted to hurt you." Her vision blurred.

His expression hardened. "Too late." He strode away.

An acute pain slashed through her chest, knocking the wind out of her. "Lamar."

He didn't turn back or hesitate.

Her heart had been ripped from her chest. The tears from her eyes rolled in rivulets down her cheeks. She pulled his jacket tighter around herself. He'd forgotten it. She needed to gather herself before returning inside. For now, she would draw comfort from the warmth he'd left behind.

Still in his evening attire—minus his jacket—Lamar puttered around his workshop. He'd taken a hotel carriage home to leave the Kesner one for Grandmama. A single oil lamp dimly lit the interior, casting macabre shadows on various surfaces, leaving some areas cloaked with menacing blackness. An apt reflection of his mood.

In the past, the ladies he'd found most interesting had given their hearts to another man. This one had given hers to a whole community of outcasts. Was he going to once again lose an intriguing woman? Perhaps the Lord was telling him to remain single.

He shifted his gaze toward the ceiling. "Then You're going to have to make Grandmama give up her quest. She's relentless." Maybe he should travel the world in his balloon. His grandmother would have a hard time setting him up then. No doubt she would find a way.

The crunch of carriage wheels on the dirt drive outside caught his attention. Who could that be? He strode to the small door he'd entered through to peer into the night.

One of their livery men assisted Grandmama. She must have come directly from the Atwood. She rarely ventured out here. If she wished to have an audience with him, she usually summoned him.

Lamar mentally sighed. He didn't have the energy to spar with her. "Grandmama, what brings you to my shop?"

She gave him his jacket. "You forgot this." She strolled past him and into the building. "You abandoned me."

Hardly. He followed in her wake. "You were in good hands, and I left you the carriage."

She sat on a rolling stool.

So, this was to be an extended visit.

Her hands lay folded primly in her lap. "Tell me what happened."

He hitched his hip against the hot air balloon's wicker basket to appear casual and draped his jacket over the rim. "With what?"

Grandmama waggled her finger. "Don't play with me, young man. With Miss Armstrong. You were pleased to have supper with the Armstrongs, the young Miss Armstrong most of all. She is a lovely lady. The pair of you are well suited."

Suited or not, Cordelia's position was clear. "She doesn't plan to ever marry."

Grandmama didn't comment but appeared to be waiting for him to say more.

"This relationship between her and me, with hopes to lead to a union, was only ever her parents' desire. Not hers."

Grandmama waved a hand in the air. "Nonsense. I've seen the way she gazes at you. Are you going to be put off by a little slip of a lady? You didn't let Mr. O'Gillis stand in your way."

"That was different." He had been able to buy his way

out of that. Cordelia wouldn't be so swayed.

She gave him a withering look that had made him cower in his younger years but not anymore. "Where is my grandson who manages vast wealth and flies around in that dangerous, infernal balloon?"

"It's not that dangerous." He took every safety precaution.

Ignoring his remark, Grandmama continued. "What did she have to say about all you are doing for the inhabitants of the encampment outside of town?"

Lamar furrowed his brow. "You know about that?"

"Of course. Do you think I would allow you to spend a large sum of money without gathering as much information as possible? I don't know everything you have planned to do out there, but I can make a few guesses as well as trusting your judgment. I'm privy to all the goings-on in Kamola."

"All?"

She raised her white eyebrows. "A bachelor quilt?"

How had she learned about that? It was eerie how much she always seemed to know.

"I'll give you a sewing lesson so you can impress Miss Armstrong."

He would pass on that offer. "I've mended places on my balloons. Grandpapa taught me a couple of basics on our first balloon together." He still missed the old man's company and instruction, even if he could be a little brusque at times.

She gave a nod of consent. "Prudent. The less you know, the more help and attention you'll require from her."

He'd thought of that. An appealing prospect. "There's no guarantee I'll be paired with Miss Armstrong."

Grandmama stood and patted his arm. "I have every confidence you two will be paired. The Lord is on your side." She strolled to the door and departed.

His grandmother often left him dazed and in awe. However, she was right about one thing. He wasn't ready to give up on winning Cordelia's heart.

At least not yet.

Twenty-One

THE FOLLOWING MORNING, LAMAR'S NERVES SIZZLED like bacon on a hot griddle as he waited next to his buggy outside the Atwood Hotel.

Upon exiting, Cordelia stopped short.

He dipped his head. "Your carriage, milady."

After a brief hesitation, she continued her descent of the steps. "You've surprised me once again. I wasn't expecting you."

He imagined she hadn't, not after her spurning him last night. "I wouldn't want you to miss your time with the quilting circle."

She looked one way and then the other. "There was to be a hotel carriage. I should tell them it won't be needed."

He'd called Mr. Armstrong, making the arrangements to escort Cordelia. "Mine's the only carriage." He held a hand out to assist her into his vehicle, noting she wasn't wearing the hair comb he'd given her last night.

She took his offered help and climbed aboard.

He followed suit and sat next to her, the reason he'd chosen one of their smaller conveyances. He set the horse into motion.

She straightened the folds of her skirt. "I appreciate your thoughtfulness, but it wasn't necessary for you to come. My parents had already consented to allowing me to attend."

"I made the arrangements with your father." Escorting her was necessary for him so that he could judge her resolve. His conclusion wasn't in his favor. Time for a new subject. "Have the ladies found enough bachelors for your fundraiser?"

She nodded mutely.

After several minutes of her silence, he spoke. "Have

I made you uncomfortable? I don't mean to." But he wasn't exactly sorry. He, too, felt ill-at-ease and still smarted from her rejection.

"No—yes—no—a little."

Good, she was flustered. That meant she cared. At least to some degree.

She clutched her hands tightly in her lap. "I haven't changed my position on us."

Good to know.

"I remain firm."

His high hopes from earlier burned like hot coals in his stomach. "As do I." He ached sitting next to her. He'd thought things would at least return to the way they were before. What had he expected? That she would have changed her mind overnight and fallen into his arms today?

Instead, her outright refusal to consider an alternative burned fresh and hot. He shouldn't have given her a ride. Shouldn't have allowed himself to be so taken by her. Shouldn't be so hurt. But he was. "I have met a lot of women. Only a handful were interesting. The trouble with interesting ladies is their hearts always seem to be spoken for."

"My heart might not be spoken for, but it's not available."

"I see." Oh, her heart *was* spoken for. She merely didn't realize it yet. He would show her. In time.

He left Cordelia at Miss Henny's and flicked the reins with no destination in mind. His original plan had been to go out to the encampment, but he didn't have the desire to now. Should he give up on that whole project? Leave the immigrants to their own devices? That wouldn't be right.

He had allowed Grandmama's little talk last night to bolster his hope, which had withered in the morning light.

The cadence of the horse's hoofbeats and the rolling of the carriage lulled him into allowing his mind to float above his aching heart. High into the air.

That's what he needed—he would plan a ballooning trip. Leave Kamola and his cares behind.

Or he could travel by train back East to visit his

parents and siblings. He hadn't seen them since Easter. But then he would have to field questions about eligible young ladies. Goodness knows, his parents and other relatives knew enough of them to keep a steady parade marching before him for his perusal. He couldn't do that to Cordelia.

He stilled his breathing. Why not? She had already spurned him. He had every right, but the prospect held less than no appeal. Cordelia wasn't like most socialites. He could no more find another lady half as intriguing, than convince Grandmama to quit meddling. He shook his head.

It was then he realized the rhythm of the horse and swaying of the carriage had stopped. The mare had her head dipped, drinking from a trough. Where was he? He glanced around at the modest houses. An unassuming white, clapboard building with a small steeple stood a few feet away. He and Grandmama attended the more formal church near the normal school.

"Can I help you?" A man in farmer overalls with a fistful of weeds in one hand strolled toward his buggy.

He smiled at the groundskeeper. "I'm afraid I wasn't paying attention to where I was going."

The man stroked the horse's neck. "Appears your horse had ideas of her own and plans to have a good long drink. I have some cold tea and cookies the missus made. If you would like to join me, you are more than welcome." He tore the roots off his weeds and offered the leafy parts to Lamar's horse who gladly munched them.

Lamar didn't know this man but felt compelled to go with him. Setting the brake, he climbed to the ground and followed this stranger to the shade of a nearby maple tree.

After sitting in the grass, he poured the brown liquid from a stone crock into a tin cup and handed it to Lamar.

"Thank you." Lamar drank it down, not realizing how thirsty he'd become.

"Would you like more?" The gardener held up the crock.

"No, thank you." He didn't want to take it all.

The gardener unfolded a cloth bundle. "Ginger snap?" Though he didn't think he wanted any, he took one anyway. "Thank you." His stomach growled. He couldn't be hungry. He hadn't eaten that long ago, and he'd had a big breakfast in anticipation of working at the encampment.

Two cookies later, the man brushed his hands together and stood. "Thanks for keeping me company. I should get back work. These weeds won't pull themselves. I don't want the boss catching me being lackadaisical."

Was he speaking of the pastor? Or his wife? Or God?

"Would you like some help?" Lamar had no clue why he asked but found he truly wanted to.

"I won't turn away help." He guided Lamar to the spot it appeared he'd been weeding before and pointed to a burlap sack lying flat on the ground. "You can kneel on that so your trousers don't get dirty."

Lamar knelt. He gripped the stalk of a plant the gardener indicated and pulled. After some resistance, the pesky plant came free from the ground. He tossed it in the heap with the other discards. He hadn't done work like this since he was a boy, as punishment for being party to destroying part of his mother's flower garden.

A few minutes later, the gardener pointed at him with his hand trowel. "If you don't mind my saying so, you aren't exactly dressed for this kind of work. When I first saw you drive up, you seemed troubled."

And confused. Lamar nodded. "I feel doomed to spend my life alone."

"By your clothes and buggy, you appear to have a lot to offer a woman."

"I'm sure I could get anyone of over two dozen ladies in Kamola and more back East to agree to marry me—not that I'm trying to be conceited—but my wealth is a powerful attraction to a lot of people." One of the reasons he preferred to be out West rather than on the East Coast.

"You're looking for something more than a mother of your children."

Lamar thought a minute. "Not even that. Someone I can have engaging discussions with. Someone who has interests outside of fashion and society. Someone who is real and not a fabrication of who society says she should be."

"The problem with having preconceived ideals is that it's hard for anyone to measure up. Does such a person even exist?"

"She does. I've met her."

"Then what's the problem?"

"She's determined to stay single. Thinks God doesn't want her to marry. I've met very few ladies who truly intrigue me. This one has gone beyond piquing my interest. My attraction for her is like...like...like nothing I've felt before. It drives me to do things I never imagined."

"I see."

Well, Lamar didn't.

"What do you like most about this young lady?"

So many things. "She's intelligent, someone to have stimulating conversations with. I think she could always keep me on my toes. Though when we first met, she pretended to be simpleminded." That made him smile. "She's kind and caring. She selflessly helps others. There's a group of immigrants outside of town she's helping. She doesn't even live in Kamola, yet she's doing something to make their lives better. I'm helping too. She doesn't know everything I'm doing. I wanted to surprise her." But now it didn't matter.

"When you picture your future, is she at your side?" The gardener jabbed his trowel into the dirt.

Lamar thought a moment then nodded. "She is." That had never happened with any other lady.

"Now picture your future without her."

Lamar tried. He could feel his face tightening and shook his head. "I don't like it."

"Sounds like you want a true partner, and this one has stolen your heart."

Perhaps. "I think it might be too soon to go that far."

He chuckled. "Love doesn't have a set timetable. Sometimes it grows slowly like a hundred-year-old fir tree. Other times it could be like a flash of lightning."

"Nothing in between?"

The gardener chuckled. "Everything in between."

"How did you know your wife was the right one? Did you have to search a long time?"

"I've been in love with my Karen since I was ten."

"You're fortunate."

"Not everyone's struggles are the same, but we all have them."

"Doesn't seem like it. You found someone so you aren't alone."

"Loneliness comes in many forms. Been married fifteen years." His voice turned despondent. "Karen is still hoping for a baby."

"I'm sorry." That was hard for a lot of people to bear.

After several more minutes of working silently, the gardener spoke. "About the group of immigrants on the edge of town you are helping. If this lady doesn't choose you, will you still help them?"

"I don't understand. I'm doing it for her." So she would choose him.

"Then your generosity has conditions. You will give aid to these people as long as you receive this lady's love in return. It's not a selfless act."

Lamar didn't care for this man's implication. He generally thought of himself as considering others without personal gain. He didn't have expectations from the immigrants, but he did of Cordelia. "I purchased the land they're living on so the previous owner couldn't make them leave." He waited for the man to praise him and tell him his act was indeed selfless.

Instead, the gardener changed the subject. "You seem awfully sure this lady is the right one for you."

"As sure as anyone can be."

"Do you want the very best for her?"

Where was this man heading? "Of course."

"Even if the very best doesn't include you?"

"What? Why wouldn't it?"

"I can't claim to know the mind of God. However, I believe I get a glimpse now and then." He tossed the weed into the growing pile. "I issue you a challenge. Don't pray to get the girl, but pray instead for God to bestow upon her the very best *for her*. Pray also for God to give you the strength to accept whatever that best is."

What if God didn't answer the way he wanted?

The gardener's mouth pulled up on one side. "I can see you are thinking about it."

"I prefer to pray for things when I'm sure of the outcome or have a hand in making them happen. You're asking me to give up all control."

"I don't believe God approves of selfish prayers. When we are willing to give up our own desires, He often gives us something far better than we could have imagined."

Lamar couldn't envision someone better than Cordelia. "And what have you and your wife gotten that is better than the children you wanted?"

"I'm content with our answer lying with the hundred-year-old tree."

"And your wife?"

"She's still hoping."

That must be hard.

"Pastor Matthew, I see you recruited help," a voice called from a few feet away.

Pastor? Rising to his feet, Lamar spun around to face Thomas. Thomas?

The man he'd been working alongside stood and addressed the newcomer. "Good morning, Thomas."

His friend jacked a thumb toward Lamar. "Don't know how much help this dandy will be."

"He's doing a fine job. Haven't seen you in church for a while."

"Been busy."

Thomas attended this church?

Lamar shifted his attention to the man. "I thought you were the groundskeeper."

"I'm that too. I do a bit of everything." The pastor turned back to Thomas. "Have you come to help? Or can I do something for you?"

"I'm here to see this fellow." Thomas clasped Lamar on the shoulder. "No mistaking the crest on his buggy."

Lamar brushed his dusty hands together. "How are things going at the encampment?"

"Doing better. As your work supervisor, I wanted to get a few things with your permission."

"Of course." Lamar addressed the pastor. "Thank you for your advice. You've given me a lot to think about." He walked with Thomas to his buggy.

His friend elbowed him. "What advice?"

"About Cordelia. I didn't care much for it." However, he would be considering it and praying.

"Not everyone is going to tell you exactly what you wanted to hear because you're a Kesner."

Lamar gave Thomas a sideways glance. "People don't do that."

"Don't they? The Kesner name holds sway in this town."

His family name didn't hold any sway with Cordelia.

Thomas hopped into the buggy. "You can tell who your true friends are when you have no money and nothing to offer others. Like you for instance. You are a true friend. I have nothing, and yet you're still my friend. On the other hand, I have nothing and am a terrible friend."

"I disagree." Lamar climbed in and encouraged the horse forward. "You regularly give me honest advice, even when I don't want it."

"You're welcome."

"You have helped me to not scare off the immigrants and instructed me as to how to best offer them assistance."

"You were pretty hopeless on your own."

"And you are managing things for me at the encampment."

Thomas made a face like he'd just guzzled sour milk. "Don't make me sound like a model citizen."

Lamar chuckled. "Don't worry. You have a long way to go before anyone would accuse you of that."

On Saturday morning, Henny opened her front door to Mrs. Kesner. "Florence?" This was a first. The wealthy matriarch had never graced Henny's home before. She felt both honored and unnerved. "Please come in." As she guided her guest to the parlor, she glanced toward the kitchen where she'd left her husband. Saul had either chosen to remain concealed there or had slipped out the back door.

Florence sat regally in one of the wingback chairs.

212 | THE LADY'S MISSION

"You have a lovely home. Is this where you hold your quilting circle?"

"Thank you. Yes. Would you like a cup of tea?"

"I don't want you fussing over me. I won't stay long. Do sit."

Florence Kesner's very nature demanded people fuss over her.

"What brings you to my home?" Henny took her usual place on the settee.

"It's about your bachelor quilt event."

Oh, dear.

"I think it's marvelous."

"Thank you." Henny breathed easier, but even if her important guest didn't like the idea, that wouldn't stop it from taking place. "It was Cordelia Armstrong who came up with it."

"She is such a lovely young lady and the reason I've come. However anyone else is paired up, my grandson must be matched with Miss Armstrong. I trust you to see to that."

Henny couldn't do that—wouldn't do that. "If he doesn't bid for her help yet is paired with her, he'll know some kind of tomfoolery was at play."

"I'm sure he will. Even if he doesn't, I'm too old to care if my grandson knows I've meddled or not. It's for his own good. He'll thank me one day."

"I can't make you any promises." Henny had been afraid of people trying to manipulate things.

Mrs. Kesner smiled. "That means you'll think about." She stood. "I knew I could count on you."

Henny escorted her guest to the door. "Like I said, I can't guarantee they will be paired. The best I can do is assure you I'll pray for God's will in the matter."

"Then it's as good as done."

After Mrs. Kesner left, Saul came up beside Henny. "That was pleasant." He *had* been hiding.

She gave him a hard look. "Was it? Now I'm in a pickle."

"Why?"

She waved her hand toward the door to indicate the woman who'd just left. "A suggestion from a person with clout, like her, is more of a mandate."

Saul's expression turned puzzled. "But she left it up to you."

Henny squinted. "Did she?"

"It sounds like not? Are you going to go against her wishes?"

"I promised myself I wouldn't play favorites or fudge any of the results."

Saul's eyes widened. "I don't know of any other person in Kamola who would cross the great and powerful Mrs. Kesner. What can I do to help?"

"Pray Lamar Kesner is the high bidder for Miss Armstrong."

"Will do."

So would Henny, starting right now.

Cordelia stood next to the settee in her hotel room, pulling on her lace gloves. She had been elated when Lamar picked her up on Friday to take her to quilting circle even though her parents had already given her permission to go. At the same time, she'd felt disingenuous for accepting the ride after rebuffing his feelings.

Mother fluttered in. "Hurry up, dear. The carriage is waiting. You don't want to be late."

"I don't see why I have to go alone."

"Lady Kesner requested an audience with you...alone. This is quite an honor. A good sign."

No, this was a bad sign. She would more than likely be scolded for hurting her grandson. Would Lamar be there as well? Why did everyone insist on making plans for her life? Why couldn't she do whatever she pleased? "I'm ready."

Mother stepped in front of her. "Let me make sure everything is perfect." She ran her gaze head to toe—twice. "I don't see anything she could find fault with. Be off with you."

Cordelia knew of a huge thing Mrs. Kesner could find fault with.

She took the elevator to the lobby, went through the front doors, and climbed into the waiting Kesner carriage.

This is not intimidating...not at all. She had to keep telling herself that.

Cordelia's stomach knotted. No doubt Lady Kesner wanted to convince her to reconsider her grandson. Cordelia had done little else the past few days. Still, the outcome had to be stepping out of the way to put God first. *Lord, help me remain steadfast in Your will.*

The Kesner carriage came to a stop in front of the mansion of the same name. She pressed a hand to her midsection. A flock of birds flapped wildly in her stomach. The door opened, and the livery man assisted her down.

Inside, she was ushered into the formal parlor where she'd first met Lamar. He'd been standing at the mantel, all handsome. Her insides had tingled at the sight of him. Today, the quivering was a different sort.

Lady Kesner stood with a smile, extending her arms. "Welcome, my dear."

Cordelia crossed to her, allowing the woman to grip her hands.

"I can't tell you how pleased I am you came."

Did she have a choice?

Lady Kesner released her. "Please have a seat."

Cordelia did, though she would have rather stood so she could flee if need be.

The older woman poured them both cups of tea and offered a scone. "I thought it was time I got to know you better without the extra people."

That answered the question of whether or not Lamar would show up. But the question about Mrs. Kesner pressuring her was yet to be seen.

"Henny tells me the idea for the bachelor quilt was yours. Very clever of you."

"Thank you." Cordelia got the impression the older woman was giving her a genuine compliment.

"Tell me about this project."

Cordelia proceeded to explain how the event would work.

Mrs. Kesner eyed her for a moment as though she were trying to puzzle something out. "You are far more intelligent than you appeared at our first meeting. I apparently misjudged you."

Cordelia was relieved not to be keeping up the pretense. Let the woman think what she would about the misconception. The less said the better.

"No wonder my grandson is so taken with you."

Here it came. Would it be in the form of pleading or coercion?

"Tell me your interests. What are your dreams for the future?"

Neither pleading nor coercion? What was she up to? No doubt she hoped her grandson was featured prominently in Cordelia's dreams. Although he was, not the way this woman hoped. Should she confess her true interests? Or keep them hidden? If she told her about the encampment, Mrs. Kesner could refuse to allow her grandson to court Cordelia or forbid Cordelia to help those people. Neither prospect sat well with her.

Apparently, Cordelia had hesitated too long without answering.

"Some people find me intimidating, though I try hard not to be." Mrs. Kesner took a nibble from her scone. "I especially don't want you to feel daunted in any way."

Hard not to be. But she did seem genuinely sweet.

"Perhaps we will speak of it another time." Mrs. Kesner sipped her tea.

All in all, the visit went well. Which only served to confuse Cordelia even more.

She honestly liked Lamar's grandmother, making Cordelia's eventual departure all the more painful.

Twenty-Two

FOR THE NEXT WEEK AND A HALF, Lamar did as the pastor gardener had suggested and prayed God would bring Cordelia the best, even if that wasn't him. Every time he thought of her—which was often—he lifted up a prayer for her. In a prodding from the Lord, he included a caveat, to keep his distance from her until the Founders' Day Festival and the Bachelor Quilt event. He didn't know which was harder, staying away from her or praying himself out of her life. Both agonized him.

While spending more time at the encampment, he transitioned from mostly observing and directing to pitching in with the work. His hands went from aching to blisters to calluses. He rubbed a thumb across the hardened flesh of one palm. He'd earned these, and it felt good. His self-worth had increased the more he contributed. Also, he understood the people better.

He'd fondly anticipated this day when he would see Cordelia again, but now that it had arrived, his nerves were twisted and scratchy. How would she receive him? In his absence, had another man stepped in? Would she show indifference toward him?

Lamar drove his buggy toward Thomas's place. Passable terrain went only so far. Today would test their friendship to the brink. Whether it survived was yet to be seen.

When he had gone as far as he could with the buggy, he parked, grabbed the bundle he'd brought, and walked.

Thomas exited his cabin. "I'm ready."

Lamar held out his package. "I brought you a change of clothes. I thought you might want something a little nicer."

Thomas extended his arms out from his sides. "I bathed and put on my best trousers and shirt. People take

MARY DAVIS | 217

me as I am or not at all. I appreciate the offer though."

Should Lamar insist? Doubtful it would do any good. Thomas would likely wish he had changed and probably regret not taking a razor to his face as well. Lamar motioned in the direction he'd left the buggy. "Let's go."

At the meadow where the Founders' Day Festival was being held, many tents and vendor booths were already erected in anticipation of the main activities tomorrow. Lamar left his buggy in the care of Beanpole and a few other young lads who were tending to horses and vehicles for a fee. The festival didn't formally start until the bonfire this evening. However, the Bachelor Quilt would kick things off this afternoon.

Lamar pointed across the meadow. "Aunt Henny is in a tent over there." He had come earlier to help construct the oversized tent for the event—one their family owned for large outdoor gatherings. It had sides that could be rolled up to allow air to flow through it or battened down with door flaps to close out the weather. Or in this case, keep nonpaying spectators from viewing the show.

On his way, he saw Cordelia carrying a pile of fabrics. His pulse reacted at seeing her. He'd feared his feelings for her might have waned with his absence. Not one bit. If anything, they had grown stronger. Without the conscious thought to do so, he headed in her direction. Like a moth to a flame. Would he get burned? "Cordelia. Let me carry those." He took the stack from her.

The sun glinted off the silver comb in her hair, the one he'd given her. "Thank you." Her smile seemed stiff. "You made it."

"Did you think I wouldn't?" Or had she hoped he wouldn't? But the comb in her hair said otherwise.

"That doubt had crossed my mind. We didn't exactly have a cordial parting."

He would never disappoint her. "Bad form to go back on a promise. I'm quite looking forward to this event. Also, as promised, I've recruited a couple of able-bodied bachelors. This is my friend Thomas Spencer. Professor Isaac Hughes should be along shortly." If not, Lamar would go find him.

Thomas removed his tattered hat and clutched it to

his chest. "Pleased to make your acquaintance, Miss Armstrong."

"Pleased to meet you too." Cordelia studied Thomas, squinting. Her head tilted slowly to one side. "I know you. You're that beggar outside the hotel a couple of months ago. I've been wondering how you were. You were also helping the day Lamar took me for a balloon ride."

Thomas nodded. "Guilty as charged. I'm doing very well. Thank you for asking."

She turned her gaze on Lamar. "Have you been helping him?"

Was that admiration he saw in her eyes? Lamar didn't know what to say. Confess he and Thomas were long-time friends? Or skirt the truth? "I've known Thomas for a while." That was somewhere in between.

Cordelia narrowed her eyes. She likely suspected it was longer.

Thomas slapped his hands together. "I've come to aid with Aunt Henny's project. What can I do? Set up chairs? Haul stuff?"

Lamar appreciated the subject change.

Cordelia's gaze widened toward Lamar. "He's one of the bachelors?"

Lamar offered a tight smile with a nod.

With a puzzled expression, Thomas inclined his head. "What bachelors?"

Cordelia shifted her gaze from one man to the other. "You didn't tell him what he was volunteering for?"

Lamar shrugged. "I was vague on the details."

"But he doesn't know?"

He shook his head. "If I'd told him, he likely wouldn't have come."

Cordelia flashed a wide smile. "I think you're going to have an interesting time explaining it to him." She folded her arms. "I can't wait to hear it."

Was she flirting with him? She certainly was being pleasant. Perhaps the time apart had been a benefit after all. However, that wasn't why he'd done it. The pastor's words ran through his head...*He often gives us something far better than we could have imagined...*

Thomas turned on Lamar. "What have you gotten me

into?"

"You want to help Miss Henny support the outcasts at the encampment, don't you?"

Even through his bushy beard, it was evident Thomas pressed his lips together. "I'm not going to like this. I can tell."

Lamar smiled. "Remember you promised. You said you would do anything to assist Miss Henny."

"Exactly what is it I'll be doing?"

Cordelia giggled. How refreshing. "Sewing a quilt."

"What!" Thomas recoiled.

"You likely don't have to worry about it." Cordelia motioned toward the tent. "When word got out that bachelors would be bidding for the company of eligible young ladies to assist them, we had several more volunteers. If your secret bid is lower than anyone else's, you're off the hook."

Thomas heaved a sigh. "I can handle that. One penny."

Lamar clasped his hand onto Thomas's shoulder. "Remember, the money will help the people at the encampment." He shifted his attention to Cordelia. "How is this going to work?" He hoped it wasn't like a cattle auction. That could be humiliating for all involved.

"Each bachelor will receive a piece of paper. After the ladies are introduced, the men will write down the name of the lady they wish to assist them with this task and how much they will donate to the cause in order to have her undivided attention. A gentleman may list a first, second, and third choice. Miss Henny and a couple of the other married ladies will sort through the papers. The high bid will secure her company during the project."

That seemed reasonable. But how could he ensure he would win Cordelia's assistance? Any man would desire her attention. He'd heard O'Gillis had returned to town a couple of days ago. If he'd gotten wind of the auction, he would no doubt try for her as well. Even though the man had consented to not pursue her, he could skirt the agreement by this being a public event.

Cordelia pointed. "Our event tent is over there. If you can give those yard-goods to Miss Henny, I would appreciate that. I'll be there in a few minutes."

Lamar wanted to stay with her. "Do you need any help?"

"No, thank you. I'll see you there."

He continued on. It would be best if he remained at Thomas's side to make sure his friend didn't slip away.

Thomas shook his head. "I can't believe what you've gotten me into. Sewing?"

"In my defense, you never asked what you would need to do."

"Ha! I can't believe I allowed you to dupe me." Thomas stroked his beard. "I should have seen this coming."

Professor Isaac Hughes joined them. "Good day, Lamar. Thomas."

Facing the professor, Thomas walked backward. "Glamour Boy roped you into this too."

"Helping Aunt Henny? Yes. I'm glad to."

"Did he tell you what will be required of you?"

Isaac shrugged. "I didn't ask."

Thomas jabbed a finger in the professor's direction. "Your mistake and mine. We're going to be *sewing* a quilt."

With a sudden stop, Isaac jerked his head to face Lamar, his eyes as wide as saucers. "I don't know how to sew."

Halting as well, Lamar shook his head. These two were making way too much of this. "Don't worry. You'll have a pretty little lady at your side to assist you."

"What?" Isaac's voice cracked.

Lamar patted the air with his free palm. "It's not going to be that bad. You two will do fine. It's for a worthy cause."

Thomas leaned toward Isaac. "All you need to do is bid low. If all the other bachelor's out bid us, we're off the hook. Then we can sit back and heckle." He poked his thumb toward Lamar. "I'll definitely be giving this one a hard time."

"Just so you know, if you want to heckle me, you'll have to pay an admission fee." Lamar started walking again. The other two followed suit.

"It'll be worth it."

Isaac retrieved his handkerchief and dabbed at his

upper lip. "I think I'm coming down with something."

"You'll be fine, Isaac."

"I don't know what to say to a lady."

This was ridiculous. "Do you know how to say good afternoon?"

"Of course." Isaac tucked his still neatly folded handkerchief into his trousers pocket.

"Thank you?" Lamar pressed.

"Yes."

"That's all you need. I promise. When you are first paired with a lady, wish her good afternoon. After that, hold out your sewing and contort your face as though you're confused. When she does anything to assist you, thank her. I promise, you won't have to say anything else. Look helpless, and she will do the rest."

Inside the tent, half of the chairs he'd helped with earlier were occupied by men except the front row. Most of those were taken by unwed young ladies. They must be the ones to guide the bachelors. Besides those in the chairs, a greater number of men lined the rear and side walls. Apparently, they wanted a quick escape route should they deem it necessary. Male bravado only went so far.

Lamar approached Miss Henny in the front beside a table. "Miss Armstrong asked me to turn these over to you."

"Thank you." She took them and set them on the table at the front of the tent. "Where is she?" Her worried expression suggested she might be wondering if Cordelia would show up.

He hoped she didn't decide to abandon this project on his account. "She said she would be along shortly."

"Good. We'll be starting soon."

Lamar rejoined his friends in the center back among the standing men.

Upon entering, Cordelia sat in the ladies' row.

Thomas leaned in. "Who is that lady speaking with your sweetheart? She's not from Kamola."

His sweetheart. He hoped so. "Her name is Nanette Barwick. She's Miss Armstrong's friend."

"Perhaps this won't be so bad after all."

Lamar smiled. A pretty face could get most men to do things they never imagined. It certainly worked for him.

Henny quieted the group then explained how the Bachelor Quilt event was going to work.

Several gentlemen shook their heads and slipped out. Others declined the paper and pencil offered to them by the ladies circulating. Among them, Lamar's two friends, Thomas and Professor Isaac Hughes, but Lamar accepted on their behalf. He was going to make sure his friends honored their commitment.

Even though several unrecruited bachelors had volunteered when they had learned they could spend time with pretty young ladies, Henny had anticipated some of them wouldn't want to participate. But they had their solid recruits like her son, Lamar, two deputies, and the younger of the other two professors who boarded at her house as well as a few other town regulars who had evaded the altar thus far.

Each of the twelve ladies introduced herself along with some skill—besides sewing—she possessed, like cooking and baking. This gave rise to some whoops and whistles.

Cordelia Armstrong, Nanette Barwick, Franny Waldon, Trudy MacVay, Felicity Gladwell, and Silvie Dubois were among the twelve.

"In case anyone was wondering, I will *not* accept any bribes. And no shenanigans." Henny was glad to *not* be participating in this event. If she hadn't married Saul in June, would she have? The ladies in the quilting circle might not have given her a choice. And as long as Saul would have gotten paired with her, it wouldn't have been so bad.

The gentlemen wrote on the papers and dropped them into a large coffee can Henny had decorated.

Henny spoke to the crowd. "Thank you all for participating. Go enjoy the festival. Return in one hour, and we'll reveal which fortunate bachelors are with each of these lovely ladies."

After shooing everyone out of the tent, including the single ladies, Henny and two of the older married women sorted through the papers to make their list of couples.

Henny chuckled at Lamar's paper. His three choices were all Cordelia, and his offer would certainly win him the seat next to her. Just in case, he'd added a contingency of twenty-five dollars over the highest amount if not him.

When she unfolded a paper for Thomas, she wasn't surprised at his low number because of his reluctance. What surprised her was the amendment to the amount and Lamar's signature that he would honor this. He'd also altered Professor Hughes's. He obviously wanted to make sure his friends were beside him.

Henny's son had placed a sizable bid but no lady's names. As of yet, he wasn't sweet on anyone. He had confided in her to put him with any young lady who might not receive any offers.

Her son was such a gentleman.

They had the pairs.

Time for the fun to commence.

Twenty-Three

An hour later in the Bachelor Quilt tent, Cordelia fidgeted as she waited for Miss Henny to read the names. She didn't want to be paired with Lamar, and yet she was apprehensive at the same time she might not be. She had spurned him. He might have taken that to heart and honor her wish for him to leave her be, and that she never planned to marry. Even though she didn't think he truly believed she would *never* wed. She did still hope to someday, just not in the near future, apparently. His absence from her life for the past two weeks had caused a permanent ache to lodge in her chest.

Three more tables had been set up, forming a square. That way the contestants would all face the center to encourage mutual support and camaraderie among the men. Each lady sat on a stool beside the fabric pieces her bachelor would use to complete his quilt block. Next to her was a vacant stool for her bachelor. Also, with the yard-goods were the tools needed, among them scissors, ruler, needle, thread, and a wooden pressing tool.

Miss Henny moved to the front of the room. "If everyone will take a seat, we'll get started." Once everyone quieted down, she unfolded a sheet of paper.

Cordelia held her breath as the proceedings continued.

After several matches, Thomas was paired with Nan. He gave Lamar a sideways glare.

Professor Hughes seemed both surprised and pleased to be put with Trudy.

One lady left, Cordelia.

Miss Henny glanced at her paper. Several men still waited to be called. Including Lamar and Mr. O'Gillis.

The suspense knotted Cordelia's insides.

Lamar stood stoically. Seemingly neither confident

he'd won her assistance nor disappointed he hadn't won another lady's. Had he not bid at all?

Finally, Miss Henny read off the final two people. "Miss Cordelia Armstrong will be helping Mr. Lamar Kesner."

She sighed with relief and dread at having to work so closely with a man she needed to squelch her feelings for. Having missed seeing him for nearly two weeks, she'd also had moments of panic that she might have been successful at turning him away.

He strode toward her, bowed, and dipped his head. "Good afternoon. May I sit?"

My, he looked dashing. The giddiness inside her rose to new heights. She needed to mask her feelings lest he sense how thrilled she was to have him at her side. "Of course. You didn't need to ask." How could her feelings for him be even stronger after his absence? She supposed it could be from relief that he had indeed bid for her. And from Mr. O'Gillis's reaction, he'd fortunately been out maneuvered.

Miss Henny continued. "As for the rest of you, perhaps you'll have better luck at the box social tomorrow. For today, you may purchase an admittance ticket from Mrs. Martin. If you don't, I would ask you to leave at this time."

Half of the men not participating left, while the others lined up for a ticket. Both men and women, who had gathered outside, also purchased tickets and took seats in the chairs around the edges of the tent.

Once the audience was settled, Miss Henny gave instructions that the ladies weren't to do any of the work, not even cutting the pieces to be stitched together. "There are plenty of yard-goods should anything be cut incorrectly. Begin."

One of the men from the audience called out, "Who wants to lay a wager on who will finish first?"

Someone else bellowed, "I'll wager Deputy Cord comes in dead last."

The deputy in question stood with clasped hands, shaking them over one shoulder then the other, as though pleased with the prediction.

Henny, still at the front, raised her hands. "Now, now. We'll have none of that. This is not a contest to see who finishes first. The goal is to complete a quilt for charity."

"A little wager won't hurt anything."

Sheriff Hammond spoke up. "You heard Aunt Henny. Anyone caught placing or collecting bets in here will be escorted out."

Grumbles rippled around the room.

Miss Henny gave a nod to the sheriff. "Do your very best, bachelors. You all have excellent seamstresses to guide you. I have no doubt you will each do a fabulous job."

Lamar rested his hands on the table. "What do we do first?"

"We—you must choose a block pattern. I have selected three for you to pick from." Cordelia unfolded a piece of paper. "I drew a little sketch of each for you. This is the simplest. It's a nine patch. This is an Irish chain. More pieces but not difficult. And this is a wandering star or some call it the Missouri star or the Bethlehem star. The most difficult but not hard." Each lady had chosen three for her bachelor to pick from to make it easier on everyone. "Which would you like to sew?"

"You decide."

"I'm not allowed to do that. You heard Miss Henny. The bachelors have to do everything. That includes choosing the block."

He appeared to think for a moment. "I recall seeing a quilt in our home with little hexagons of fabric in a circle. It was some kind of flower."

"Grandma's flower garden? That might be too difficult. I think it would be best if you pick one of these." She tapped the paper.

"I thought I was supposed to choose. These were obviously chosen by you." He pointed to others around the tables. "It appears a lot of the ones selected by the other teams are similar to the ones here." He tapped the paper. "I want my block to look different. I'm not afraid to try something difficult. Are you?"

Was that a challenge about something more than sewing? Or was he teasing her? But why? To be difficult himself? Or to spend more time with her? Though she deserved the former, she hoped for the latter. "I don't have a hexagon with me, and I don't think any of the other ladies do either. If you don't like any of the ones I suggested, we can figure out a different pattern."

He slid her paper with the three options drawn on it toward himself and flipped it over. With a fountain pen he took from his jacket inside pocket, he drew a hexagon. "Now we have a pattern."

It wasn't that simple. "If the sides and the angles aren't all exactly the same size, they won't fit together properly. It will cause a great deal of frustration. Additionally, even if you had a perfect hexagon, matching all those sixty-degree corners can be challenging."

He gazed deep into her eyes. "I love a challenge."

A warm shiver rippled through her.

He folded the paper with a short edge even with a longer edge and creased it. "How big should the hexagon be?"

"I'm not sure." She curved her fingers on one hand into an open "c". "About like that." If the block they created was a little too small, they could add strips around it to make it match the others in size.

With the ruler, he drew a line and cut on it, making a square. Then he proceeded to fold it several more times to form a strange triangle with points resembling cat ears on the shortest side. He snipped across it, removing the ears and then some. Unfolding the paper, he smoothed it flat.

Cordelia gaped at what appeared to be a perfect hexagon.

He held out the ruler. "To check my work."

"I have no doubt it's accurate." She could tell by merely glancing at it. "How did you do that?"

"A little trick I learned during one of my trips to Europe." He wiggled the ruler. "You know you want to measure it. Go ahead. It won't hurt my feelings."

She did want to check his work, so she took it and measured. Every side was indeed the same. "That's amazing."

From Cordelia's left on the other side of the corner of

the next table, Thomas shook his head. "Showboat."

Lamar seemed to ignore his friend's comment. "Is it the right size?"

"It's a bit small. You will either need to sew a whole lot of these together to form several flowers or make one flower for the middle and build around it with borders."

"How about three in the middle? Then there will be less borders."

She eyed him sideways. "Or you could cut a bigger hexagon."

He pushed the remainder of the paper in front of her. "You saw how I did it."

True, but she hadn't watched closely enough to duplicate it. "We'll work with what you made."

It would take quite a while to cut out all the necessary hexagons, a set for Lamar and a second one for her. She would demonstrate on her block so he could replicate it on his own. Since most of the men had chosen simpler patterns, they had been able to get theirs started. With the ladies sewing blocks too, a second quilt top would be made quickly.

From Lamar's other side, his professor friend said, "I need to take it out." He pulled at his line of sewing.

Trudy MacVay rested her hand on top of the professor's. "Your stitches are excellent. I will not allow you to remove them."

Her bachelor's sewing was so minute, Cordelia couldn't see the individual stitches, and his line appeared as straight as it could be.

Lamar faced the man. "Isaac. The stitches will be on the underside. No one will know."

"I'll know."

"Don't tell anyone, and it will be your secret. Remember Hatcher."

The professor stilled then nodded. "Hatcher."

Trudy slowly removed her hand from Isaac's as though testing him then showed him the next piece to sew.

Cordelia whispered. "Hatcher? That calmed him down."

Lamar leaned closer, his warm breath on her ear. "Isaac had an issue early in his life. He feels a need to do everything perfect and keeps his surroundings in precise order."

Tingles skittered through Cordelia, and she lost her train of thought with Lamar so near, whispering in her ear. She mentally shook the distraction from her head— or at least dislodged it long enough to recapture what she had been going to say. "This event is anything but orderly. Why did he come?" *Focus on the quilt block and not the man sitting next to you.*

"He promised before he knew the particulars."

"You felt the need to trick bachelors to participate."

Lamar inclined his head toward Isaac. "The professor needs to do things he's not so comfortable with. He used to be so much worse. If he survives, the next thing won't be as hard."

It was sweet the way he cared. "And your other friend?"

He poked a thumb toward Thomas. "He deserved it." He picked up the paper hexagon. "I presume I use this to cut pieces of the fabric."

"Yes."

"How many do I need?"

"You wanted to make three flowers, right?"

"Yes."

"Then you'll need twenty-one out of the various prints, seven for each flower. Six for the petals around the center. Then you'll need more of a solid color for the background."

He removed a blue calico, a yellow, and a pink. Then he chose a dark green print and a tan solid color. He meticulously stacked them, aligning one corner of each.

Was he doing what she thought he was doing?

He laid the pattern in his perfectly aligned corner and cut out five layers at once.

Yep, that was what she thought.

The chatter around the table turned to the box social to be held the following day. With some of the ladies teasing their bachelor about what their box lunch might look like. Others, described in detail to ensure their bachelor would win theirs.

Cordelia tried her best to tune out the prattling, and by

doing so, hopefully Lamar wouldn't pay attention to it either. "Make sure you stop your stitching and knot your thread a quarter of an inch before the end. That way, you can fit the corner of the next hexagon into the junction." She held out the ruler to him. "For you to measure the distance."

"I can gauge it without that."

"It's important to be precise. With so many seams, if they are off even a little bit on each one, the block won't fit together properly."

He tied off his thread and cut it. Then he handed the pieced section to her. "You want to check it?"

From her point of view, she could tell his seams were likely accurate, but his self-satisfied air, daring her to check his work, pushed her to measure it. Perfect! "Have you made a quilt before?" She knew the answer.

"Can't say I have."

"How are you so accurate at knowing the measurement without a ruler? And your stitches are really pretty good."

He smiled, melting her heart. "My grandpapa taught me when we were working on our first balloon. He said if the silk got a tear, I couldn't depend on someone else to be around who could stitch it." He jacked a thumb toward Thomas. "But don't tell him."

"I already know that." Thomas had evidently been eavesdropping.

Unfazed by his friend's comment, Lamar continued. "If I were brazen enough to inquire as to how your box-social box were decorated, would you tell me?"

"I would be happy to." She held her empty hands together with the palms up. "What you see here is what it looks like."

"Ah. You're not entering."

She'd had her fill of auctions with just the one for the bachelor quilt. She never imagined it would be so stressful.

Deputy Sammy jumped to his feet and threw his hands into the air. "Done! I won!"

Miss Henny heaved a sigh. "This wasn't a race. But since you've finished, you can stitch the border strips on yours."

"What? But I finished."

Several chuckles rose from the other bachelors.

The deputy harrumphed into his seat.

One by one the blocks were completed. As they were handed in, Miss Henny and a couple of the other married women joined them into rows and stitched the rows together. Later, the ladies would add an additional border around the outside. Then the top would be layered with a batting and backing fabric that would be basted together in preparation for the men to quilt it tomorrow.

Lamar and Professor Hughes were the final two bachelors. Lamar because of the multitude of little seams and numerous corners. The professor because he was so particular about his stitches. Trudy had been exceedingly patient with him as well as encouraging.

If Cordelia were to venture a guess, she suspected the professor's fastidiousness was, in part, a desire to spend as much time with Trudy as possible. He even insisted upon sewing on the border strips as the other men had done. Lamar did the same. Both men claimed to not want to be remiss in their responsibilities.

Lamar finished before Professor Hughes but not by much. He picked up his completed block. "I best turn in my homework." He walked it to where Henny, Agnes, and Dorthea were stitching them together.

However, he returned and retook his seat, inclining his head toward the professor. "I don't want him to feel like an odd duckling."

Again, his compassion for his friend was sweet. Lamar had whispered to her that the professor wasn't very comfortable around ladies. Cordelia sensed that too.

When Professor Hughes finally finished his, Lamar stood with a bow to Cordelia. "Thank you for all your assistance. You were an excellent teacher."

"You were an outstanding student." She was disappointed he would leave her now. "Are you still bringing your balloon to give rides tomorrow?"

"I am. You'll have to come by for an excursion."

"I might just do that."

He smiled. "I'll be counting the minutes." He strolled away.

Long after he'd left, she still gazed at the spot where he'd departed, almost willing him to return to her.

Nan flounced in and sat next to her. "I suspected from the first day, he could be the one."

Cordelia had sensed it as well. "The one or not, I can take no action." Why would the Lord do this to her? *Lord, eradicate my feelings for him. I can't go on like this.* After the festival, she would convince her parents to leave Kamola. Until then, she would pretend this courtship was exactly what she wanted.

No pretending about it.

Cordelia needed to stop thinking about him in such a positive way. "Tell me about Mr. Spencer. Did he say how he knows Lamar? Or how long they have been friends?"

"No. But I got the impression it's been a long time."

Interesting. "He seemed affable."

Nan pressed her lips together a moment. "He's a strange one. There is something not right with him."

"What do you mean?"

"Some of the words he used and his mannerisms didn't fit him. Almost like he was two different men."

"That doesn't sound good. I heard that mountain men or ones who have lived on the streets in big cities can be a rough lot because they aren't used to being around people. They can be ill-mannered without even knowing their words or actions might offend others."

Nan twisted her mouth to one side. "It wasn't that. He was never impolite or uncivil."

Understanding bloomed inside Cordelia. "You're sweet on him."

"What? No. Don't be ridiculous."

"It's all right if you are."

Lamar stood next to the wagon of split wood Grandmama had donated for the bonfire. He had started to help unload it, but many more hands had joined in, making him irrelevant. In times past, he wouldn't have even contemplated pitching in with such a chore. He had to admit to himself, he'd actually been a bit disappointed when he wasn't needed. He'd enjoyed the work at the encampment.

Mr. and Mrs. Armstrong approached. Mr. Armstrong made eye contact. "Mr. Kesner, we are so pleased to have run into you. You must join us this evening for the festival bonfire."

"Please call me Lamar." How would Cordelia view his unexpected presence? Would she appreciate him imposing?

Mr. Armstrong inclined his head in what appeared to be approval. "Lamar, do say you'll join us. We won't take no for an answer."

So, he wasn't really being given a choice. Perhaps Cordelia didn't plan to attend. "And your daughter?"

Mrs. Armstrong smiled. "I believe her words were something along the lines of the bonfire having the potential to be quite romantic. We'll bring everything— chairs, food, blankets." She wiggled her fingers. "See you at dusk."

The pair strolled away.

What should he do? Go or not?

Romantic activity? With Cordelia? He liked the sound of that. Then he could figure out if his impression from earlier was correct about Cordelia having warmed to him. She *had* seemed to have missed him. Nothing she said, but rather a gleam in her green eyes. As well, she had been wearing the silver hair comb he'd given her.

Later, Lamar drew nearer to the bonfire area, where many people had gathered. The Armstrong trio stood next to a quilt stretched on the ground. The elder two greeted him warmly, and that twinkle in Cordelia's gaze still glistened. Almost as though she were pleased at his arrival.

Mrs. Armstrong glanced toward the sky. "I do hope it doesn't rain."

Worry flitted across Cordelia's expression. "I don't think it will."

"I'm sure you're right." Mrs. Armstrong patted her daughter's hand.

The clouds had ebbed and flowed throughout the day but, in the last hour or so, had thickened.

234 | THE LADY'S MISSION

Mr. Armstrong motioned toward the quilt. "There is a basket with food for the two of you and a lap blanket in case a chill comes up, as well as a shawl for you, Cordelia, so you don't get cold."

Cordelia's eyes widened. "Aren't you staying?"

"Your mother and I are exhausted, so we're going to retire for the evening. We aren't as young as we used to be." With a wave, they strolled away.

Lamar held out his hands. "I didn't plan this. Is it all right with you?"

She nodded. "It's fine. If I don't stay, I'll never hear the end of it." Expectation brightened her features.

Not exactly excitement to be left alone with him, but she didn't react negatively.

Lord, if a courtship with Cordelia is not to be—or not to be at this time—give me an indication. I don't want to pursue wooing her if You are only going to take her away from me.

He proffered a hand, which she took to lower herself to the blanket. "Thank you."

The promised chairs must have been forgotten. He sat and reclined on his elbows. This way, he could watch her without being obvious.

Though he longed to kiss her, he couldn't bear her possible rejection right now. He wanted to simply enjoy her company.

Soon, the mound of wood was set ablaze. Even from several yards away, the heat reached them.

After about a half an hour, the first raindrop hit Lamar's hand. Hopefully it was a lone droplet.

Then another and another.

Had Cordelia felt any? She didn't act as though she had.

Murmurs about the precipitation rippled through those gathered.

No denying it now. "The rain has begun."

"Perhaps it will stop."

He liked her optimism. "I hope so too."

One by one, the couples and others around the bonfire stood, gathering their belongings.

The drops increased in number and size, hissing in

the flames. People squealed and ran for their buggies or toward town if they had come on foot.

Lamar stood and held out his hand. "I suppose it's time."

Cordelia tilted her head to look up at him. "It will take a few minutes for the others to get their horses hitched and their vehicles on the move. The temporary corral will be congested with everyone vying to leave. Besides, a little water never hurt anyone." With that, she closed her eyes and laid back, a gentle smile on her face.

"Are you going to lie there and get rained on?"

"It feels refreshing. You should try it."

Lamar had never met any socialite who wouldn't have run for cover and complained about getting even the least little bit wet. He laid on the quilt next to her with his eyes closed as well. It *was* nice to have the cool drops on his face.

When they turned to large splats, Cordelia gasped.

Wiping the water from his eyes, Lamar jumped to his feet and hauled her up. "Dash for that tree. It will keep most of the rain off." He grabbed the quilt and basket.

Cordelia giggled the whole way, but not the annoying vapid tittering when he'd first met her. This was genuine pleasure. However, she hadn't hurried fast enough to outrun the downpour that happened in a rush.

Under the branches of leaves with hints of turning fall colors at their tips, Lamar set down the basket, placing the quilt on top of it. He untangled the shawl and draped it around Cordelia's shoulders. "I don't want you getting chilled."

She snugged it around herself. "Thank you." Water dripped off her dark tresses.

He retrieved his handkerchief that was remarkably dry and dabbed at her rain spattered face.

Wet tendrils lay plastered to each of her cheeks. He dislodged one, then another, brushing them away from her face. His gaze locked with hers. How long would she allow him to regard her in this manner?

Surprisingly, she didn't withdraw. The tip of her tongue slid from one corner of her mouth to the other.

As though coaxed by an invisible thread, he felt

himself being drawn closer to her. He could break it if he had a mind to—but he didn't.

Her eyes drifted closed, and her warm breath fanned his lips.

Would hers be as sweet as when he'd kissed them several weeks ago in his workshop? There must be something about rain that drew them together.

Before their lips met, another couple ran under the tree's leafy protection. With a quick intake of air, Lamar stepped away.

Thomas.

"Mind if we share the tree canopy?" To his credit, his friend did appear a little contrite.

"Of course not." Lamar determined to be content in the knowledge Cordelia had been willing to allow him to kiss her. She had definitely changed her mind about courting.

Staring after Lamar, Cordelia remained under the tree with Nan while he and Thomas fetched the buggy. Disappointment at being interrupted shrouded her, penetrating into her soul. Obviously, the Lord didn't want anything to transpire between her and Lamar. A heaviness pressed in on her.

Nan touched her shoulder. "I'm sorry for spoiling your moment with Mr. Kesner."

Cordelia mentally shook herself back to reality. "I'm glad you did."

"But it appeared as though he was about to kiss you."

Exactly. For one brief moment, she had willed him to do so. Cordelia couldn't allow anything like that to happen again. *Forgive me, Lord.* "You know a romance right now isn't feasible. Perhaps someday." All her hope hadn't been squashed yet. She prayed a husband would be in the near future—and perhaps Lamar would still want her. Perhaps, she was to finish her work with the people at the encampment first.

"God could be telling you that it's all right to be with Mr. Kesner."

"Then He's going to have be a lot more explicit about it. My calling to help the unfortunate was very clear. I've received no leading to stop. And I don't want to. There are so many people in need." Cordelia sighed. The constant struggle to be able to help outcasts had worn her down. More and more she felt like ceasing her efforts. "Pray I stay strong in my convictions."

Nan squinted at her as though trying to work out a possible solution.

Cordelia willed her friend to create a defensible argument.

Instead, Nan's shoulders straightened. "I'll be praying all right."

Guilt crushed in on Cordelia for contemplating a way out of her calling. How selfish of her. Who would stand up for those people then?

Twenty-Four

ON SATURDAY, LAMAR HAD ARRIVED BEFORE dawn at the Founders' Day Festival grounds in the wagon with his hot air balloon. Having rained only long enough to chase everyone away from the bonfire, it had quit after midnight. The sun had come out this morning, further drying the ground and burning off the fog. A perfect day for ballooning.

He would give rides for four bits each with the proceeds going to the migrants. In addition to some of the Kesner staff, he had hired Thomas and three of the other men from the encampment to make ready the balloon.

Lamar studied Thomas. "Are those new clothes?"

Thomas shrugged. "It's all I had that was clean." They were nicer than his usual fare.

Lamar squinted at his friend. "You combed your hair." He jabbed a finger in his friend's direction. "You trimmed your beard." The six-inch length had been neatly shorn to two.

Thomas made a face.

"You almost appear positively civilized."

"Now you're just being mean." Thomas grimaced. "I perish the thought."

"Would your renewed interest in your appearance have anything to do with Miss Barwick?"

Thomas grunted. "Are you going to help with your own balloon or stand around yammering all day?"

Lamar chuckled. Would wonders never cease? One more positive sign from the Good Lord above.

After the sun had nudged above the horizon, the full balloon tugged at the ropes anchoring it to the ground, as though it couldn't wait to greet the wispy clouds above. A small crowd had gathered to see the spectacle.

Lamar smiled at the audience. "Who wants to fly above the treetops?"

The skeptical spectators whispered to one another, but no one came closer.

"That doesn't look safe."

"What if it fell from the sky?"

Lamar understood their caution for something they knew little about. "Adventurous people have been flying in balloons for over a century. From high in the air, a person can view God's creation as a bird does, soaring near the clouds. There is nothing quite like it. The whole town is visible at once. Who wants to experience this breathtaking phenomenon before anyone else?"

Still no one approached.

"The first person to volunteer will get their ride for free." That ought to intrigue someone.

Disappointingly, still no spectators came forward.

Evidently, being a pioneer was not desirable.

Cordelia emerged from the crowd. "I've ridden in this very balloon and, as you can see, returned unharmed."

Lamar hadn't been aware of her there. She must have been tucked in behind others, likely trying to go unnoticed.

More whispers.

Lamar offered her his hand. "Miss Armstrong, perhaps you would like to prove to these fine people that it is indeed safe. Be the first?"

She hesitated. That wouldn't encourage others. Quite the opposite. However, she placed her hand in his. "I would be thrilled to go up again."

A tingle rippled through him at her touch. That was the third time he'd gotten the impression things were going to work out between the two of them. Like Gideon in the Bible, Lamar kept asking God for one more indication to be sure. And one more.

He led her to the steps and helped her in.

Cordelia stood at the rim. "Who will take this adventure with me?"

"I'll go." Ian O'Gillis stepped forward and climbed aboard without permission.

Why did it have to be him? The man was pestiferous. Lamar gritted his teeth, liking nothing better than to refuse him a ride. "That will be four bits."

O'Gillis handed over the money. What was his angle now?

Lamar pocketed it. "Who else?"

"Me."

"I want to go."

"I'll go."

The three Moseley girls spoke at almost the same time.

Lamar cringed internally at their eagerness. Where had they come from? "I can take only one more passenger this trip."

The eldest Moseley sister, Prunella, thrust forth her money and tucked it into Lamar's coat breast pocket. "Sorry, ladies. I've already paid."

Colleen and Fancy both huffed a breath in protest then folded their arms.

Prunella sashayed around to the steps and held out her hand to Lamar.

He took it and helped her in. He received a very different feeling assisting her than he had with Cordelia. At least he wouldn't be alone with Prunella. He climbed in. "Miss Moseley and Mr. O'Gillis, will you stand there and there? I need to balance the basket." He pointed. "Miss Armstrong, over on this side if you please." That put Cordelia closest to him and the other two farthest away— as far as one could be within the confines of a five-foot square basket. He studied his passengers and sighed. This would likely be a peculiar trip.

As Cordelia scurried to her corner, O'Gillis reached for her arm but missed. She gifted Lamar with a smile that warmed his heart then mouthed, "Thank you."

Prunella latched onto Lamar's elbow. "I would feel so much safer next to you."

"But it won't be safer. The basket would be off balance. I wouldn't want you to tumble over the side."

She gasped and scuttled to her designated spot. Mission accomplished.

O'Gillis touched her arm. "Don't mind him. I won't let anything happen to you."

Lamar gave the heater two long blasts then leaned toward the edge. "You can cast off the ropes."

Thomas and three other men untied the ropes from the anchor stakes.

"O'Gillis, will you pull in the two on that side and coil them on the floor?" Lamar did the same on the other side.

The balloon rose immediately, lifting higher and higher.

On one hand, Lamar wanted this ride with Cordelia to last a long time. On the other, he would like to be rid of his other two passengers as soon as possible.

In a smug tone, O'Gillis asked, "How does this work? Do you merely drift on the breeze and hope it takes you where you want to go? Not very practical."

Ballooning wasn't meant to be practical.

Cordelia faced her fellow passengers. "May I answer?"

With a dip of his head, Lamar motioned for her to continue.

"Drifting on the breeze is partially right, but it takes real skill to get the balloon to go where you want it to. It's not haphazard as one might think."

Lamar smiled at her pronouncing him skilled. He loved watching her expound on ballooning dynamics. She had picked up a lot on their one excursion.

She arched an arm over her head. "There are air currents traveling in various directions. Mr. Kesner will keep the balloon rising by adding heat. Hot air is lighter than cold and so the trapped air lifts the balloon."

To punctuate her point, Lamar pulled on the heater valve chain, causing a blast of fire to shoot up into the neck of the balloon.

She gifted him with a smile. "Because we are traveling that way, that's the direction the breeze is moving."

Prunella propped a fist on her hip. "I don't feel any breeze. It's as still as can be."

Cordelia turned wide eyes on Lamar, obviously not knowing the answer. Few people understood the physics of air flow. It hadn't been broached on his other trip with her.

"That's because we're traveling *with* the breeze. It's not moving around us to be felt as it passes the surface of the skin, but rather, we are moving within it, traveling at the same speed."

242 | THE LADY'S MISSION

Prunella shook her head. "That makes no sense at all. If there were a breeze, I could tell, and I feel nothing."

Whether it made sense or not, that was the physics of the matter.

Cordelia studied the view across the treetops. "Does this ever grow old?"

"It hasn't so far." He pointed to garner his other two passengers' attention. "If you turn that way, you can see Kamola." The town seemed so different from this altitude. "And over there are the Cascade Mountains." They stood tall and majestic. He could picture God's hand creating them.

"Oh, my." Prunella put her fingers at the base of her neck. "I've never seen such a thing." She looked one direction then another before shifting her gaze toward the ground. "How high are we?"

"A few hundred feet."

Prunella swayed, then gripped the side of the basket. "Make it stop. I want to go back."

Oh, dear. Vertigo.

"O'Gillis, hold on to her."

"I'll help." Cordelia took a step toward Prunella.

Lamar extended his arm in front of her. "Don't. You'll upset the balance."

O'Gillis wheeled the Moseley girl away from the edge. "Don't look down. Focus on the horizon."

Prunella's face had an ashen pallor. "I want out of here. Make him put this down. Right now!" She stomped her foot.

O'Gillis kept his hold on the young woman's arms. "We are over trees, so I'm sure he cannot. You have nothing to be frightened of."

"Give her something in the distance to focus on. I'll get us in a current that will return us to the festival."

O'Gillis nodded then extended his arm. "Over there is Bald Mountain."

Prunella shook her head.

"Come on. Just take a little peek."

She shot a glance in that direction. Her shoulders that had been tucked up around her ears eased slightly. With each new sight O'Gillis indicated, Prunella appeared to relax a bit more.

Lamar never would have guessed the man possessed even the minutest amount of compassion for a fellow human being. Perhaps he smelled Moseley money. Lamar focused on piloting the balloon toward the festival grounds posthaste. He soon found a current heading the right way and rode it. Remembering the ones at the lower altitudes, he went past the target before descending, which garnered him a glare from O'Gillis. Once in position, he opened the top vent, allowing the balloon to sink faster than he normally would. He needed to cross the flow traveling the wrong direction quickly so as not to prolong Miss Moseley's misery.

More than a hundred feet from the ground, Lamar motioned to O'Gillis. "Toss out the anchor lines."

O'Gillis complied with the two on his side of the basket.

Lamar tossed the closest one overboard, but when he went to attend to the last, Cordelia stood hefting the thick rope over the rim. He tipped his head toward her. "Thank you."

She winked. "Women are capable too."

"No doubt about that." He tugged on the top-vent rope, releasing more of the heated air.

The basket landed a little hard, which earned him another glare from O'Gillis.

Lamar motioned to the men maneuvering the steps to have them placed on the side closest to Miss Moseley.

O'Gillis quickly abandoned ship and assisted Prunella, leaving Lamar with Cordelia. He longed to head straight back into the sky with her, leaving the rest of the world behind, but the line of customers halted that course of thinking.

As Prunella scurried past her sister and cousin, she said, "You do *not* want to go in that horrible contraption. It was awful. I nearly died."

Not even close.

That sent a few customers scuttling away, with them, the remaining two Moseleys.

"Allow me to assist you, Miss Armstrong." Lamar climbed out then helped Cordelia over the edge to the top step. Before she could descend, he gripped her waist and lowered her to the ground.

For a brief moment as he gazed into her green eyes, the rest of the world seemed to fall away and time slowed. Only the two of them existed. Like last night in the rain. He willed her to feel their connection too. In a barely audible voice, he said, "If it were up to me, I would fly away with you." Had she heard?

"Lamar?" Thomas whispered.

Lamar had allowed himself to get carried away. He straightened as he stepped away. "Who's next?"

Cordelia faced the crowd. "I never once felt unsafe. The view from up there is spectacular. Nothing like you have ever witnessed." With a nod to him, she walked into the crowd, taking his heart with her.

Beanpole from the livery came forward, handed over his money, and scrambled aboard.

Dutch approached with three of the older children from the encampment. A thirteen-year-old girl, a twelve-year-old boy, and Molly Ferguson's eight-year-old son. He handed over the fee for the children. "They can go?"

"Of course." Lamar thought about refusing the money but didn't want to make a spectacle of it. The proceeds were all going to the camp anyway, so it was relatively the same.

Later, after many balloon rides, Lamar headed for the box social event. Cordelia had said she wasn't entering, but perhaps she had changed her mind. He scanned the throng. His heart's longing was nowhere to be found.

Soon the announcement for the bidding came and the first decorated container was put on the auction block—Lamar's cue to exit that area of the festival. With a nod to Mr. and Mrs. Armstrong, he left—disappointment mixed with relief. Neither O'Gillis nor any other man would be able to compete for Cordelia's time, but then, neither could he.

He strolled about the grounds.

Thomas sauntered up to him with food on some brown paper. He held up his morsels. "Spicy chicken wings. Want some?"

"No, thank you."

"You're missing out. Chicken wings are under appreciated." He took a bite.

Lamar preferred not to sear the inside of his mouth and his stomach. "I'm surprised you didn't get a box social lunch."

"Naw. Don't want to get a young lady's hopes up."

"Miss Barwick didn't enter?"

"No—I mean, how am I supposed to know? You didn't bid on Miss Armstrong's?"

"She didn't enter either."

Thomas nodded. "That makes us two bachelors on the prowl."

In the not too distant future, Lamar hoped that number to be down by one.

After a bit of meandering, Mr. and Mrs. Armstrong caught up to him. Mr. Armstrong held a decorated box. As with many married couples, the wife submitted one for which the husband won.

Lamar nodded toward the bundle. "Congratulations on winning your wife's entry."

"This isn't for me." Mr. Armstrong held out the package. "This is for you and our daughter. This is hers. When you weren't among the crowd, I took the liberty to bid for you."

Lamar accepted the box, staring at it. "Thank you."

"Is something wrong?" Mr. Armstrong asked.

"I'm a little surprised. Cordelia said she wasn't participating."

Mrs. Armstrong wiggled her hand in the air. "We had the hotel kitchen make one for her, so it should be excellent."

Which meant Cordelia didn't know. "Why would you do that?"

"To allow you and your sweetheart to dine together. We felt terrible for the pair of you getting rained on last night." Mrs. Armstrong tucked her hand around her husband's elbow. "I believe our daughter is in the quilt tent. Enjoy your meal."

Stunned, he stood there for a moment. Should he go to Cordelia and force her to eat a meal with him she had no knowledge of?

He would go but leave it up to her if she would eat with him or not. Either answer would tell him a lot. *Please,*

God, let it be the former.

Was this box lunch the sign he'd prayed for about the timing to move forward with courting Cordelia? He'd expected this answer to take a lot longer in coming. He hadn't even finished helping the immigrants.

Thomas chuckled. "Go get her. You don't want her to faint from starvation."

Turning his attention heavenward to ask the Lord, he halted. How many times must he ask for signs? God would know better than him if this was the right timing. *Thank You, Lord.*

Cordelia remained in the Bachelor Quilt event tent alone, threading needles in preparation for the afternoon session with the men quilting the layers together. Having many needles threaded, the bachelors wouldn't need to take the time to do it. Truthfully, she was hiding. She didn't want her parents pestering her about Lamar. And she didn't know if her heart could withstand being near him, knowing after today he would be out of her life.

All in all, the bachelors had done a fine job with piecing their blocks. Some seams were a bit wavy, but stitched altogether as a whole, it was beautiful, more so than she would have imagined. A sampler representing the assortment of people in town as well as the men who stitched it.

The other ladies had gone to participate in the box social. Gratefully, she had abstained from that endeavor. But if she had entered, who might have won hers? The one man she would have wanted to, was the one she needed her weak will to stay away from.

The stitching together of the layers had been set for this afternoon to give all the festival goers, as well as bachelor quilt participants, ample time to enjoy the festival and all it had to offer. No one expected the men to complete the task in the time allotted, but Miss Henny conveyed her hope that some of them would return to finish as much as possible.

Cordelia crossed to the quilt stretched out on a

wooden frame in the center of the tent. It stood three feet or so off the ground on a stand. She began sticking two threaded needles into each block.

The two middle ones would be the most challenging, as those two bachelors would need to reach over the ones on the edge. Each bachelor would work on their own block and some of the border connected to it. Any parts that weren't done during the event would be finished later by the quilting circle, who would also sew on the binding. However, the auction to purchase it would take place later this afternoon.

As though summoned by her earlier thoughts, Lamar entered, carrying a pink parcel with a substantial green bow.

Her insides shimmied with glee at his presence. At the same time, a burning sensation heated the pit of her stomach. How could he bid on another woman's box? *Stop it, Cordelia. You have no claim to him. Now or ever.* "You know you're supposed to eat that with the lady who provided it." Though she tried for a cheery tone, the words were dirt in her mouth.

His chuckle warmed her. "That would be you."

"What? I didn't enter." Intentionally so, even against her mother's encouragements.

He set the container on the table where she had been working. "Apparently, your parents entered this on your behalf."

Of course, they did. Delight quickly pushed aside her annoyance. "And you outbid everyone else."

"Not exactly. I would have if I had known, but your father did and bestowed it upon me."

"What? Why?" Her parents certainly were determined.

"I believe your mother's words were, 'To allow you and your sweetheart to dine together.'"

His sweetheart. She liked the sound of that. Should she just give in? How could she resist when she was outnumbered by her parents, Lamar, his grandmother, *and* her heart? *Lord, I can't do this.*

I am your Rock.

Lamar lifted the box a few inches to indicate the

lunch. "Will you join me? Or shall I leave this for you?"

She should tell him to take it with him. "I am hungry." *Don't do it, Cordelia.* "I would very much enjoy the company." She seemed unable to turn him down. This might be the last time she spent with him after the quilt was completed. It couldn't hurt, could it? Soon enough they would part ways.

His immediate smile sparked a cozy feeling within her, like snuggling up to a toasty fire wrapped in a comfy, crocheted afghan.

This is a mistake. But it's only lunch. And she did need to eat.

He set the container on the empty end of the long table then proceeded to remove the contents one at a time. He arranged two place settings next to each other, including china, crystal, and linens. No doubt prepared by the hotel's kitchen.

Her parents had spared no luxury.

He rested his hands on one of the chairs at a place setting. "Luncheon is served."

She attached the final two needles before crossing to him and sat in the offered seat. "Thank you."

As he took the one next to her, a thrill rushed through her, hugging her soul. She had to stop this, but her heart wasn't cooperative. Her only recourse would be to leave town.

They ate in silence that was surprisingly neither strained nor awkward.

After finishing, he sat back in his chair. "Thank you for a great meal."

"Remember, I didn't put this together. It's the hotel kitchen staff who deserves your praise."

"And your parents warrant credit for having them do it. I wasn't sure what I was going to eat." He turned sideways to face her. "Speaking of such, I want to extend my gratitude to you for inviting me to participate in this project."

"No, thank you. Because of your willingness, we were able to enlist other bachelors. Miss Henny said, without your support, we never would have convinced enough men to agree."

"How is this next part going to work?" Lamar studied the quilt.

And she studied him. His gray eyes held delight and warmth. He wasn't the self-absorbed socialite she'd first assumed him to be. He was kindhearted and passionate. When she remained silent, he turned toward her and caught her staring. Had he noticed?

She cleared her throat and shifted her attention to the project in the center of the room. "The bachelors will sit closest to their block and sew through all the layers."

"Will you be at my side?"

His question sounded like more than a simple logistical inquiry. "Each lady will be by her bachelor—not *her* bachelor—but the one whom she has been helping." Had it suddenly gotten hot in here?

"As long as you're beside me to make sure I don't do anything wrong"—his voice held a husky tone— "I'll be happy."

Cordelia swallowed hard.

"Even with the rain, I enjoyed the bonfire with you."

She had too. Too much so.

"About last night..."

She didn't want to talk about that. Even thinking about it was weakening her resolve. *Get up, Cordelia, before your determination is completely depleted.* But she wanted to know what he was going to say. *By then it will be too late.*

"When we were standing under that—"

Voices outside the tent drew nearer, returning Cordelia to her senses. She straightened. That had been close.

Two men entered with a padded armchair. One of them nodded to Lamar. "For your grandmother."

"Is she coming?"

"She is indeed."

Cordelia stood. "Excuse me. I need to take care of something before the event starts." She hurried away to the far side of the grounds and pressed her spine against a tree.

She needed to pull herself together and order her thoughts before sitting next to the man she loved for a prolonged period of time while pretending *not* to care for him.

Why had Cordelia thought this bachelor quilt was such a grand idea? He had practically declared his intentions with that near-kiss last night. Then this morning after the balloon ride, she'd feigned not to hear his softly spoken proclamation and not to see the desire in his gray eyes. She had almost climbed back into the basket and flown off with him.

Lord, release me from this calling. She swallowed hard. *If it be Your will.*

He that hath pity upon the poor lendeth unto the LORD.

Her shoulders sagged. *Then help me remain strong.*

Twenty-Five

AFTER A FEW MINUTES ALONE WITH the Lord, Cordelia felt much refreshed, strengthened, and at peace. Determined to simply enjoy the rest of the event and to not struggle over her myriad of feelings associated with Lamar, she took another moment before returning to the Bachelor Quilt tent. This was about the outcasts and not her. She merely needed to get through this afternoon. Then she would slip out of town.

"There you are." Nan came around the tree.

Cordelia sucked in a breath, not having expected anyone. "I'm glad you're here. I need a favor from you and Dutch."

"You know we would do anything for you." They were indeed good friends.

"I'll be leaving town tonight or in the morning. I need you and Dutch to remain here and help the people at the encampment."

"So soon? Why are you going to rush away? Are your parents making you?"

"No." If they knew, they would stop her. "I can't stay around Lamar any longer. Each day I'm here, makes it harder and harder. With my parents, Lamar, and his grandmother all pushing us together, I'm fighting a losing battle this time. The only way to resist them all is to not be here."

"What about the outcasts?"

"That's why I want you and Dutch to stay."

Her friend studied her for a moment. "You can't go without saying good-bye to the people at the camp. There are many who would be hurt."

It might be risky, but Cordelia could do at least that, and she really did want to see them one last time. She nodded.

Nan twisted her mouth to the side. "I was going to wait until after the festival, but it sounds like that might be too late. Dutch is leaving us. The people from the Netherlands at the camp told him of others across the mountains who have settled in the Willamette Valley. Some of his relatives could be in that location. He plans to travel there before winter to find out."

"That's wonderful. I do hope he locates his family." Cordelia would miss him. He'd been a faithful friend. "I'll leave money for his passage by train at the hotel. Let me know if there is anything else I can do to help him get there."

"I wish you would give it to him yourself."

"I'll try, but if I can't, tell him where to find it."

Nan gave a slow nod. "We should return to the Bachelor Quilt event."

Cordelia agreed. Delaying it wouldn't make her trouble go away.

At the tent, only a handful of people had arrived. Soon the bachelors and spectators slowly shuffled in and took their seats. Then Lady Kesner entered with her cane gently tapping the grass and took her chair, like a royal presiding over the event. Even Cordelia's mother had come, sitting beside the grand lady.

Miss Henny stood at the front. "Once again, this is *not* a race." She gave Deputy Sammy a pointed look. "We will be auctioning this quilt later this afternoon, even if all the sewing isn't completed. We'll finish it before delivering it to the highest bidder. You may begin."

With quick instructions, the men took the first of many stitches that would outline blocks and highlight seams.

As the event proceeded, the weight of Cordelia's decision to leave pressed in. The thought sickened her. She placed a hand on her stomach to keep undulating nerves at bay.

Lamar glanced over. "Are you all right?"

"I'm feeling a little peaked."

Taking her hand, he squeezed it. "I think I know what this is about."

He couldn't possibly.

He poked his needle into the quilt, and pushing his chair back, he slipped off the seat and down to one knee.

Her breath caught.

The noise inside the tent trailed off until silent. The only sounds were the voices coming from beyond the canvas walls.

With her hand still in his, he gazed up at her. "Miss Cordelia Armstrong."

She shook her head to discourage him.

He continued. "I'm aware we've only known each other for a short time, but even so, I have born witness to your kindness, generosity, intelligence, and wit. I can think of no other lady who would bring me more pleasure in spending the rest of my life with."

She whispered, "Please don't."

His eyes narrowed slightly as though confused, but he went on. "Will you do me the honor of becoming my wife?"

Why? Why did he have to do this in so public a place? She bit her bottom lip. Why couldn't he have waited until after the Founders' Day festival? Then she would have told him she couldn't allow this thing between them to go on. She didn't dare glance at any of the expectant faces around the room. She couldn't do this right now. Tears flooded her eyes. She needed to get away. She shook her head. "I'm sorry." She pulled her hand free. "I can't."

Without looking at anyone else, she dashed out of the tent.

The voices of her mother, Aunt Henny, and others chased after her. She couldn't stop, needing to get away.

Ahead of her, Father lowered his eyebrows in question.

She couldn't face him.

In another direction, a stranger gave her a concerned look.

She pivoted again, catching sight of the hot air balloon.

Lamar enjoyed going up to get away from the pressures and demands of life on earth. She needed to get away too.

Hiking up her skirt, she ran toward the balloon. She

untied all four of the anchor ropes, climbed up the steps, and tumbled into the basket. Righting herself, she pulled with both hands on the heat chain hard and was able to make the flame shoot up into the balloon.

A handful of people turned and meandered toward her. Would they try to stop her, or were they expecting a spectacle? She couldn't wait around to discover which. She pulled on the gas chain repeatedly, sending flames into the neck of the silk. It was taking too long for the heat to reach all the way to the top.

Finally, the basket tilted slightly as it rose a few inches off the ground.

Thomas reached the basket, grabbing the rim. His hands slipped from the side as the balloon rose a little higher.

Cordelia pulled the chain to add more heat into the balloon cavity. She needed to get away from everyone. Give herself time to think.

Thomas grabbed a dangling anchor rope. "Lamar! Lamar!"

Cordelia leaned toward the edge where Thomas was thwarting her escape. "Please let me go."

He had looped the rope around one of the anchor stakes. "No, ma'am. Pull the rope to open the vent at the top."

She shook her head. "Let go."

He was losing ground. As the balloon rose incrementally, his hands slid along the rope. "Lamar!"

Lamar shook his head. How could Cordelia have refused him? He'd been sure she felt the same as he did. She might as well have shot him in the gut. Then the pain would be over with quickly.

"Lamar!"

He swung his gaze to where Thomas called to him. His friend held one of the anchor ropes of his balloon, but it was inching through his hands.

In the basket, Cordelia frantically waved her arms toward Thomas. What did the fool woman think she was doing? She must be trapped.

Lamar raced toward the balloon along with several other men. With the basket about six feet off the ground, Lamar leapt, hooking one elbow over the rim. The wicker dug into his flesh. He reached up with his other arm, trying to get that one inside. He was slipping. If he lost his grip completely, he would plummet to the ground. Though he wouldn't likely be injured, Cordelia would be left to an unknown fate.

Cordelia gasped. She rushed to his side of the basket, causing it to tilt, and grasped his arm, steadying his hold. It had probably kept him from falling as the hot air in the silk cavity lifted the balloon higher.

The basket rocked as Thomas inevitably released the rope, dropping the few feet to the ground. The balloon rose at an alarming rate.

She grappled at the back of Lamar's jacket, clutching fistfuls of his suit fabric. Almost clawing at it.

He swung his other arm up and in. "Open the vent!" That *would* lower the balloon.

"I don't dare let go. You could fall. I won't let go of you."

But she already had when she'd rejected his proposal.

With both arms over the rim, he flung one leg up, catching it on the edge. Pulling with his leg, he hauled himself up with Cordelia's help and went headlong into the basket. He lay on the floor, chest heaving. He'd made it.

Cordelia stood above him. "Are you all right?"

He nodded.

The balloon rose higher and higher. Faster than it should.

How much heat had she added? She'd obviously been able to pull the heat chain without any trouble.

"You can open the vent now, and we'll descend."

She shook her head. "I don't want to." She turned away.

He needed a moment to catch his breath, then he would do it.

The balloon rose high enough to ride an air current traveling in a different direction.

His lungs still hurt from running to scramble aboard, but he needed to slow their ascent, so he struggled to his feet.

Cordelia stood to one side of the basket with a terrified expression.

He crossed to the controls and reached up for the vent rope.

"Please don't." Her voice was small and almost desperate.

He lowered his eyebrows slightly. "Why not?"

"I don't want to go down."

"Why not?"

She shook her head. "I don't want to be where everyone is."

He understood that. The peaceful sky often lifted his spirits upward, as well. He held his hands up as if she held a gun on him and gingerly approached the middle of the basket. "I'll just lower us a little to catch the right current." When she didn't protest, he proceeded.

The balloon slowed its rising until it leveled off at a safe height.

After a minute, he broke the silence. "Why did you run away? My proposal couldn't have been so unexpected. I know, when we met, I said I wasn't interested in marrying you, but my heart had other plans. If I'm not seriously mistaken, you have feelings for me too."

She mutely stared at him with a wounded look in her green eyes.

The silence twisted his insides. "Say something. Deny you care for me. Anything."

"The problem is I do care for you. All the other suitors were easy to walk away from because I didn't love them. Walking away from you is going to break my heart."

"Then don't." He crossed to her and took her hands. "Marry me."

"I can't."

"Why?"

"I made a promise to the Lord to help underprivileged people."

He studied her a moment, waiting for her to continue. "I don't understand. What does that have to do with us?"

"If I marry, I won't be able to do the work God has called me to."

"Why not?" Her cause was noble. "I still don't understand."

"No husband wants his wife going around with the sort of people God has asked me to help. I would be forced to quit. I made a promise to the Lord. I take promises very seriously."

"I wouldn't make you stop. We can help people together."

"I want to believe that. Truly I do. I had friend after friend who married men making similar promises. Not one of them is doing what they had been doing before." She hesitated then continued. "I feel as though this is the Lord testing me, testing my commitment to Him."

"I do believe this is the Lord's test, but one for *me*. Could I see beyond the persona you projected, to discover your heart? Could I imagine my life differently than how it has always been and how others expect it to be?" He took her hands. "You fear having to give up your work with the needy, right?"

She nodded.

"If I can prove to you I won't make you do that, will you reconsider my proposal?"

"I don't see how that's possible. There's no way to see into the future to know."

"But if I *can* prove to you, will you?"

"Yes."

"Magnificent." He released her hands to work the controls, moving the balloon in the direction he needed.

Cordelia looked about. "Where are we going?"

"You'll see." It took a while, but the destination was just over those trees. Once the balloon cleared the leafy tops, he would need to set down rather quickly.

The balloon was dropping more rapidly than he'd expected. He didn't dare give it more gas. By the time the heat rose, it would be too late to clear the trees. "Hold on. We're going to brush the top of that oak."

She leaned back into the corner and gripped the rim. The basket rocked only slightly as the bottom grazed the upper leafy branches.

He breathed a sigh of relief once clear of the tree. Then he pulled on the vent rope. If they didn't descend briskly enough, they could end up in the water or on the wrong side of it. But if they plummeted too fast, the landing would be rather hard.

The balloon descended with a thump near the creek but thankfully not in the water.

"Are you all right?"

Glancing around, she nodded, recognition gracing her beautiful features. "Why are we at the encampment?"

"To show you what I've been up to." He climbed out and lifted her over the edge. Though he didn't want to let her go, he released her.

Cordelia looked from one structure to the next. She counted five in various stages of construction. Two appeared complete. A sixth one was nothing more than a pile of lumber. "Where did these buildings come from?"

Lamar waved his arm toward them. "Everyone pitched in to construct them." The residents stood around watching.

"They were granted permission from the O'Gillises to build on their land?"

"Not exactly."

She glanced around, clearly noting the construction in varying stages of completion.

"I don't understand."

"It's not their land anymore. I bought it."

Had she heard right? "You did? Why?"

He nodded. "An experiment to see if given a little assistance, people could shape the life they want. I provide the materials, and they each build their own dwelling. Everyone helping everyone else. When they sell whatever they produce, they give me ten percent for use of my land. After that, if they want to purchase the plot they're on, we can negotiate a price, and they can start paying me an additional ten percent until they have it paid off. Then, I'll have a deed of sale drawn up, and they will own a small piece of property."

This was incredible.

He guided her over to Molly Ferguson. "We've built a house connected to a cow barn. I tried to convince her to have a separate enclosure for the livestock. She informed me that was foolish. I know when I've been bested, so I conceded defeat to her. Part of her pay for caring for the community cow is the connected cabin for her and her children."

Molly smiled and nodded.

Cordelia couldn't recall seeing the woman so happy before.

"At first, I was concerned the others might cause her trouble about the cow. Nothing to worry about. She has all the men in line. Don't you, Molly?"

"They are not so different from getting a two-year-old to cooperate." She laughed.

"Come this way." Lamar guided Cordelia away. He pointed to a teepee. "Running Bear, Little White Dove, and Little Bear have returned."

The trio stood outside their dwelling and gave Cordelia a nod.

Next, he showed her the Chinese brothers who were constructing a small house, as were the colored people and the ones from the Netherlands.

Cordelia eyed the large pile of lumber. "Is that where they get the wood for their houses?"

Lamar shook his head. "That is a project to be worked on over the winter as the weather permits." He walked her over to it. "This will be what makes this whole community function. We're building a saw mill. I've made arrangements with Nicole Keegan to harvest timber from her mountain. We'll cut it here and sell it. We hope to have this operational by the spring. The people in this camp will run it."

She never would have imagined being able to do so much for these people. Far beyond her dreams.

He pointed. "We're building a school over there. I've hired Miss Barwick to teach both children and adults to speak English. She'll also instruct the children on the regular school subjects."

Cordelia shifted her gaze from one structure to the next and next. "I can't believe you are doing all this. It's so wonderful. But why?"

"What is your main objection to marrying me?" His gentle smile warmed her.

"It's not that I don't want to."

"But the reason you said no?"

"God has called me to help people. I can't turn my back on that."

"You don't have to. I hope this proves to you, I won't prevent you from helping those in need. I look forward to laboring beside you in this endeavor."

Two are better than one; because they have a good reward for their labour.

Cordelia's eyes flooded with tears. "You did this for me?"

"Yes, for you but mostly for them. There are a lot of great people here. They just need a chance." He did understand.

Delight thyself also in the LORD; and he shall give thee the desires of thine heart.

Helping people was the desire of her heart, and so was Lamar. God had placed both desires within her heart and *now* had given her both.

She had been so blind and foolish. She didn't have to give up Lamar for the Lord's calling. Rather, He was giving her Lamar to partner in the calling.

Well, done, thou good and faithful servant.

"I'm thinking of naming this little hamlet Cordville or Cordeliaberg. What do you think?"

"I think you're amazing."

"Then you'll allow me to prove I'm worthy of you?"

"You have nothing to prove." She threw her arms around his neck and kissed him.

He wrapped his arms around her and returned her kiss. After several glorious moments, he pulled away. "Does this mean you'll reconsider my proposal?"

"I'll do better than that. I'll insist you marry me."

He kissed her again. When he stopped, the whole encampment was staring at them. He smiled. "She said yes!"

Everyone cheered.

When Cordelia had thought the Lord was asking her to choose by reminding her He was the Great I Am, in reality, He'd been telling her He was greater than any obstacle on earth. Even though impossible for her, He could do both. How could she have thought God was so limited? He was the Lord of infinite possibilities. *Forgive me, Lord. And I thank You more than I can convey.*

Twenty-Six

THREE AND A HALF MONTHS LATER, on the first day of the new year, Cordelia stood before the floor mirror in her Atwood Hotel room. The wedding gown of her dreams enveloped her. *Mademoiselle* Dumont had fashioned the gown just as she'd said she would, though it was more beautiful in person than the verbal description.

Mother and Father had attempted to persuade her to hold the ceremony at home in Connecticut, but she wanted to marry here, where she'd met Lamar. She had made a lot of fond memories in this place with him. Also, it would be easier to curtail expenditures in Kamola than back East.

Mademoiselle Dumont adjusted the train behind her. "You are a most beautiful bride."

"Thank you." Cordelia agreed, but not because of the dress. Lamar's love shining on her was reflecting as beauty.

Mother fitted the veil atop her head. "You are so lovely." Tears pooled in her eyes. "I can hardly believe this day has finally arrived."

"Don't you start crying or I might too." Cordelia didn't want to have red, puffy eyes, today of all days.

Father waited in the lobby and escorted Cordelia and Mother to the horse-drawn sleigh.

As she whisked along the street to the Stone Church, Cordelia gazed at the town she had come to love almost as much as the man she was about to marry. "I can picture him standing at the front of the church."

Father patted her hand. "He better be there, or he'll have to answer to me."

Cordelia smiled at Father's mock vibrato. She knew it covered his emotions of losing her. Mother had told her he was having a hard time letting Cordelia go, even after all his insisting. Cordelia had no doubt Lamar would be waiting for her. "He'll be there, Father. Don't you worry about that."

At the church, Father escorted Cordelia and Mother in through a side door.

Nan met them there. It had taken some convincing for her parents to have Nan be her maid of honor. "He's up front."

"He'd better be." Father's bluster was a little rough around the edges. "I'll seat your mother and return for you."

Mother kissed Cordelia on the cheek. "I'm so happy for you."

"I'm happy too. No, ecstatic. Is this much happiness really possible?"

With a nod, Mother patted her arm. "More than possible."

Father escorted Mother away.

Nan sighed deeply. "When I first met your Mr. Kesner, I suspected he was the one for you. There was something different about him."

Cordelia had sensed it too. She wished she hadn't resisted him so long. If only she had better understood what the Lord had been trying to tell her instead of wasting so much time. Fortunately, Lamar had been both persistent and patient.

Father returned, cueing Nan to lead the way to the sanctuary. She stood poised and ready. When the organ music played, and the doors opened, Nan took measured steps through the entryway and out of Cordelia's sight from where she waited off to the side.

Excitement bubbled up inside Cordelia. This was her heart's desire. It hardly seemed real, like a most wonderful dream one never wanted to wake from. But this *was* real, and she was wide awake. She couldn't wait to see him standing up front.

The music changed to the wedding march, signaling Cordelia's time was nigh. Taking Father's arm, she strolled into the doorway.

Everyone in attendance stood, watching her. All of her new friends as well as friends and relatives from back

East for both her and Lamar smiled at her.

At the other end of the aisle, Lamar smiled at her as well. A smile that not only encapsulated his love for her but reflected the Lord's love shining down on her.

Her breath caught, and her heart danced. He was who her heart had longed for all these years, and she hadn't even known it. She was going to be Mrs. Lamar Kesner. The urge to run to the front and throw herself into his arms tugged at her, quickening her steps. Marrying him was the perfect way to start the new year.

Father patted her hand on his arm. "Don't hurry. You'll be married soon enough. Allow me to have my daughter for a few more moments."

This venture had turned out quite the opposite of what she'd imagined. "Thank you for insisting upon coming to Kamola and meeting Lamar."

"It was only a matter of time before we found the right man, one worthy of you."

Lamar *was* the right man, chosen for her by the Lord.

After the ceremony and then the reception at the Atwood Hotel, Lamar assisted Cordelia into the hot air balloon basket.

He unfolded the bachelor quilt and wrapped it around her. "Grandmama's gift to us."

It was perfect.

Lamar blasted the heat a couple of times while Thomas and three others released the anchor ropes from their moorings. The balloon lifted up, up, and away.

She waved to the people below as they grew smaller.

Up and over the evergreen trees. The flight wouldn't be long in this cold. A short trip to the Kesner estate. They would wait until Spring to take their honeymoon trip.

Once out of view of prying eyes, Lamar hooked his arm around her waist. "Finally, I have you all to myself."

"Alone at last." She snuggled in closer then rose up on her tiptoes to press her lips to his. This is where she wanted to be, in his arms.

He tightened his hold on her, returning the kiss.

She never imagined she could be so happy.

Thank You, Lord, for giving me the desires of my heart.

Author Note

I knew in this fifth installment of The Quilting Circle series, *The Lady's Mission*, I needed to find the right woman for Lamar Kesner to fall in love with. The poor man has had several intriguing ladies within reach, but each of their hearts belonged to someone else. It was time for him to capture a special someone's heart.

I had two major problems. The first was to find an intelligent lady fitting for Lamar. I had no idea who that was, then in waltzed Cordelia Armstrong. Now that I had the girl, how could I connect this out-of-towner to Aunt Henny? This is the Quilting Circle series after all. I had read a tidbit about a group, in 1883, who constructed a "bachelor quilt". I thought what a great idea. This story was the perfect place to incorporate it.

My second issue was with Lamar himself. Though he took care of his grandmother's holdings, he needed something interesting to occupy his time, a hobby. So, I asked my critique partners (Hi Kathy and Suzanne!). They came up with the idea of a hot air balloon. I loved the concept. Then I thought, *Uh oh. That's going to take a lot of research. Did I have time to do it or even want to?* By then, it was already too late. Lamar had a balloon and he wasn't giving it up. I tried but didn't succeed in taking it from him. In doing my research, I learned that the big colorful part of the balloon is called the envelope. As I thought this might be confusing, I chose to simply refer to it as the balloon or the silk.

I enjoyed spending time in Kamola with Aunt Henny and the quilting circle ladies again. I love their friendship and how they stand by each other regardless of what one of them is going through. True friends are gifts from above.

I hope you enjoyed reading Cordelia and Lamar's story as much as I did writing it.

Happy Reading!
Mary
☺

If you enjoyed *The Lady's Mission*, or any of the Quilting Circle series books, I'd love it if you would consider posting a review on Amazon, Christianbook.com, Goodreads.com, BarnesandNoble.com, BookBub.com, or anywhere else books are sold or reviewed. Reviews are a tremendous help to authors! Thank you for anything you can do.

I'd love to connect with you. Readers can find me at:

Facebook: Mary Davis READERS Group –
www.facebook.com/groups/132969074007619/

Blog: marydavis1.blogspot.com

Subscribe to my Newsletter: marydavisbooks.us17.list-manage.com/subscribe?u=cbe8a2ec4ef27cfcf51813f02&id=82ad258f06

Amazon: www.amazon.com/Mary-Davis/e/B00JKRBJKE

Goodreads:
www.goodreads.com/author/show/8126829.Mary_Davis

BookBub:
www.bookbub.com/profile/mary-davis?list=author_books

Check out more of my books at:
https://books2read.com/marydavisbooks

Discussion Questions

1. What was your favorite quote/passage? Why did this stand out and how could you use it in your own life?

2. How well does the book's cover convey what the book is about? Do you think the back-cover copy did a good job of indicating what this book is about? If the book were being adapted into a movie, who would you want to see play Cordelia, Lamar, Grandmama, and Thomas?

3. In the 19th century, women didn't have the same freedoms we have today. Cordelia does her best to help others while abiding by the expectation on her. Can you relate to Cordelia wanting to do more than others expect of her?

4. Which character did you relate to the most, and what was it about them that you connected with? To what extent do they remind you of yourself or someone you know? Do you empathize with the characters? What are their hopes and dreams? What fears do they each harbor?

5. Describe the dynamics between Cordelia and her parents, Cordelia and her two friends Nan and Dutch, Lamar and his grandmother, and Lamar and Thomas. How do the characters change, grow, or evolve throughout the course of the story?

6. What are the major conflicts in the story? What events in the story stand out for you as memorable? What main ideas—themes—does the author explore? Are they relevant in your life?

7. Henny has married Saul. What adjustments have they both had to make so late in their lives? Which were harder and which were a little easier?

8. Did any parts of the book make you uncomfortable? If so, why did you feel that way? Did this lead to a new understanding or awareness of some aspect of your life you might not have thought about before? Has this novel changed you or broadened your perspective?

9. What do you think will be your lasting impression of the book and why? Did the issues that were raised touch or impact you in any way? Would you recommend it to a friend, and if so, why? Can you see yourself reading it again?

Made in the USA
Columbia, SC
28 September 2022

67743478R00164